GWEND

Coffin's Ghost

HarperCollins*Publishers*

HarperCollins*Publishers*
77–85 Fulham Palace Road,
Hammersmith, London W6 8JB

This paperback edition 2000
1 3 5 7 9 8 6 4 2

First published in Great Britain by
HarperCollins*Publishers* 1999

The HarperCollins website address is:
www.**fire**and**water**.com

Copyright © Gwendoline Butler 1999

Gwendoline Butler asserts the moral right to
be identified as the author of this work

ISBN 0 00 651361 1

Set in Meridien and Bodoni

Printed and bound in Great Britain by
Omnia Books Limited, Glasgow

I wish to record my thanks to Dr Barker, Dr Fink,
and John Kennedy Melling for the help given
me with this book.

AUTHOR'S NOTE

One evening in April 1988, I sat in Toynbee Hall in the East End of London, near to Docklands, listening to Doctor David Owen (now Lord Owen) give that year's Barnett Memorial Lecture. In it, he suggested the creation of a Second City of London, to be spun off from the first, to aid the economic and social regeneration of the Docklands.

The idea fascinated me and I have made use of it to create a world for detective John Coffin, to whom I gave the tricky task of keeping there the Queen's Peace.

A brief Calendar of the life and career of John Coffin, Chief Commander of the Second City of London Police.

John Coffin is a Londoner by birth, his father is unknown and his mother was a difficult lady of many careers and different lives who abandoned him in infancy to be looked after by a woman who may have been a relative of his father and who seems to have acted as his mother's dresser when she was on the stage. He kept in touch with this lady, whom he called Mother, lodged with her in his early career and looked after her until she died.

After serving briefly in the army, he joined the Metropolitan Police, soon transferring to the plain-clothes branch as a detective.

He became a sergeant and was very quickly promoted to inspector a year later. Ten years later, he was a superintendent and then chief superintendent.

There was a bad patch in his career about which he is reluctant to talk. His difficult family background has complicated his life and possibly accounts for an unhappy period when, as he admits, his career went down a black hole. His first marriage split apart at this time and his only child died.

From this dark period he was resurrected by a spell in a secret, dangerous undercover operation about which even now not much is known. But the esteem he won then was recognized when the Second City of London was being formed and he became Chief Commander of its Police Force. He has married again, an old love, Stella Pinero, who is herself a very successful actress. He has also discovered two siblings, a much younger sister and brother.

FROM THE DIARY OF SAMUEL PEPYS

May, 166-

On Wednesday last, I did go to Easter Hythe across the River Thames. I crossed the river in a waterman's boat from Rotherhythe with a joking waterman who challenged me to swim across if he dropped me over the side because the weight of me and my friend Mr Williams was like to sink his boat. We let him laugh and staid where we were.

We were met by Mr Williams's son. It was but a short walk – for walk we must – to the township of Easter Hythe which some say was first used by Viking sailors. Easter Hythe is a poor-looking place with low-built wooden houses and some stone-built hovels said to be of Viking origin.

In Easter Hythe we went to Drossers Market where were many stalls and great crowds. Young Mr Williams said here you might buy anything you wanted and most of it would be stolen and might be stolen back again before you got home with it.

From it leads Chopping Tree Lane and there I was shown the pit into which the bodies were dropped and which we had come to see.

For this was the Viking execution place, so it is told, where victims were sacrificed and criminals hanged.

Many skulls and other bones were found but young Mr Williams said that it was his belief it was nothing of the Vikings but more recent and more criminous. Mr Williams is a surgeon and sees many broken bones and it is his opinion that the bones in the pit are too new broken to be Viking.

The sense of evil in Chopping Tree Lane was mighty strong, creeping into Drossers Market, and Mr Williams said to me that the evil would be there for centuries.

We came back in poor spirits, although I bought a pretty bracelet for my wife and one, but not near so dear, for my maidservant Alice.

Editor's note: It is thought that Pepys's real motive for the visit to East Hythe with his friend Williams was that they had been told that it was home to some handsome and willing and pox-free young women whose embraces they could enjoy at a lower price than in the City of London.

1

'Who was it said that modern detective stories never have the murder of children in them?' John Coffin asked from his hospital bed. Then he answered himself: 'Graham Greene. And how wrong he was. Can't have read many.'

'Don't be so grumpy.' Stella Pinero had brought him in a selection of detective stories which lay scattered on the bed. She had also brought him in a local newspaper with her photograph and her description as 'the love of his life'. This irritated him too, although Stella, ever the realist, said what good publicity for both of them it was. 'Won't do anything for me,' he had grumbled, still grumpy.

'You'd be grumpy with a hole in your liver.'

It was healing nicely though, and someone had once told him that you could spare as much as half your liver.

He wondered who had told him that.

Not Graham Greene.

He turned over the books. Policemen don't read crime novels. They might write them but not read other people's. Except in training, which doesn't count.

'The Handbag,' he said aloud in a tone of deep scepticism. 'Doesn't sound like a crime novel. Simenon, perhaps. More like Oscar Wilde.'

He began to feel better. Nothing like a grumble. But he remembered The Handbag. It worried him for some reason. Stuck in his memory.

'I am going to have a wonderfully happy domestic time,' announced Stella Pinero, wife to John Coffin, with a wonderfully happy smile. She was a good actress.

3

In fact, she was more than a little depressed. She was well aware that she had almost lost her husband, and had gained the shocking knowledge that without him she would lose half herself.

Now this was something she had never believed possible. It was important now not to let him share this knowledge.

'I am going to stay home, and enjoy my unusual leisure.'

What she meant was that she had no stage performance at the moment, no television play contracted, and nothing on the radio: in short, she had no work. To cheer herself up and as a homecoming present for Coffin, she had had a large window put in to the ground floor of the strong-minded tower in which they lived. It lit up a very dark area which must be a good thing, even if some might count it a security risk. You need light, she told herself, to be happy and it has to be natural light, not the electric sort.

She was reluctant to count no work as a holiday. Anyway, with an expensive daughter whose career she was, to a certain extent, subsidizing, money was always useful. The daughter was the child of an earlier marriage, not Coffin's. The two were on friendly terms, and liked each other in a wary kind of way. They needed to get to know each other better, Stella understood this very well, but opportunity did not often come their way, since her child was a hopeful producer of films, having graduated from acting, and had little time to spare in her ambitious life. And Coffin always had MURDER. Stella put it in capital letters since it was spelt that way in her mind. Bright red, too, and occasionally flashing with lights.

It was early evening, on the very day Coffin, although forbidden to do so by the doctors, had gone back to work. A pile of letters, a pile of reports, nothing on the answerphone because his efficient secretary had dealt with those. E-mail was loaded but could be ignored.

One telephone call got through while Sheila was dealing with the printer which had stuck. He could hear her in the other room, swearing gently.

'Hello, Albie Touchey here.'

But he had recognized the voice.

'Glad you got out.'

It made it sound as if out of prison. Not remarkable since he was the governor of the Sisley Green Prison in the Second City.

'Always meant to, Albie.'

Touchey was a small, well-muscled figure, a tough terrier of a man. The unlikely friends had one thing in common: criminals.

Coffin and Co. sent them to prison and Touchey eventually shovelled them out.

But they had something else in common: they were both South Londoners and had, for a time, lived in the same street. They had not known each other in those days; Touchey had attended the local grammar school and Coffin had been a pupil at what he called Dotheboys Hall.

But the two had met at a civic dinner and become friends over the whisky and the port.

'That's what my lodgers always say. As if I fancied to keep them. I don't make favourites, you know. Move 'em on as soon as I can.'

'I know that.'

Albie was ready for a grumble. 'You have the easy side, all you have to do is catch 'em. I have to live with them.

'The average age of my lot is getting younger and younger. They'll be bringing their nappies with them soon.'

'They know you keep a well-run establishment,' said Coffin. Indeed, Touchey managed to run a humane and orderly prison at Sisley Green.

'Touch and go, touch and go.'

They chatted for a while.

'A friend of yours looked in on us while you were in hospital,' Albie said conversationally. 'Georgie Freedom.'

'No friend of mine.' Stella's, perhaps. 'Surprised you let him in. Or out.'

'Felt like keeping him there but he said, No, he was taking a tour because of a TV series he was planning.' In fact, Freedom had been inside for a bit while being questioned and was now out pending an appeal.

5

'Think of him as a toad,' said Coffin. 'We'll step on him and squeeze him in the end.'

They both knew secrets about each other, small things, nothing much, the sort of thing men say to each other as they drink. Women don't do this sort of confessing, they only pass on what they want known.

And the governor knew one big secret.

'Love to Stella,' said Albie, signing off. 'I'm going to ask her to put on a Christmas show for the lads.'

'I'm sure she will.'

'A great girl, you're lucky there.'

'I know it,' said Coffin.

He was sitting opposite her now in their tower sitting room, where the windows were wide open to catch what there was of moving air. There were windows on both sides, since this had once been a church tower in a church where symmetry was all, thus a smart breeze swept through the room.

There must be a window open on the staircase somewhere. That reminded him of a question.

'Who was the man just exiting with a vacuum cleaner when I came in? Was it our vacuum cleaner, by the way?'

'Oh, that was Arthur. No, his machine. He cleans for me now.'

'What happened to that nice girl? Gill, wasn't it? She took over after good old Mrs James retired.'

'Oh, she is having a baby. She only took the job because she wants to be an actress and she thought she would get nearer to me, and when that didn't happen she decided to have a baby instead.'

'Oh.' Coffin hoped the baby would be pleased to be the stand-in for a broom.

'Arthur and Dave, they have a house-cleaning firm.'

'Ah.' Coffin nodded. 'So Dave was the middle-aged chap in the van outside. I wondered who he was. Why is his face all dirty and dusty?'

'Hiding behind it,' said Stella lightly.

'A handsome chap when you get a look, with those grooves down the side of his nose. Compelling.'

Arthur and Dave had said much the same about their employer as they packed themselves and the brooms into the van marked 'House Men'.

'So that's the Chief Commander,' Dave had said. 'Not a bad-looking chap.'

'Yes, I could fancy him myself.' Arthur made no secret of his broad band of tastes. 'But no go – I know others who have tried.' He'd started the van and they had driven off.

'Where do they come from?' demanded Coffin.

'All checked with your security outfit,' said Stella. 'Genuine firm, no bombs. That pair are out-of-work actors, resting anyway, and probably hope I might put a part their way. Arthur has had one or two small parts and Dave's done some walk-ons.'

'Where do they live?' Security was tight round the Chief Commander's household.

'Arthur lives in a converted factory across the river in Greenwich with a gang of mates and Dave lives over a café called Stormy Weather.'

Coffin grunted: he knew of the Stormy Weather eating place, which was in a bad part of the town and had a reputation to equal it. It had started out as a simple eating place, then become a hamburger bar and now proclaimed it did the best steaks in town. What Coffin knew was that it smelt of frying fat, cigarette smoke with a hint of something darker but no one had ever caught Jim Billson, the proprietor (he probably didn't own it, he was reputed to have someone behind him) with any illegal substances. The woman who ran it was, according to Mimsie Marker, the fattest woman in the Second City, and the cook the most drunken. Coffin knew that every so often the Public Health crew, with a drugs man secretly with them, swept in and went over the place, but so far, it had been clean. Cleaner than expected.

'He hasn't been with Arthur too long . . . Arthur started it up with a mate who died.' She frowned. 'Cancer . . . it may have been AIDS-related,' she added reluctantly. 'Dave came in after that. They met in the theatre.'

Coffin grunted again.

'Anyway, it was too much for Gilly. This is a difficult house to clean. All staircase. Like a lighthouse.'

Coffin was hurt. He liked his house. 'You ought to have been brought up in a basement like I was.'

He was not showing it, since that would not have been tactful, but he was sympathizing with Stella in her workless state. The Stella Pinero Theatre Complex, in the body of the old St Luke's Church, which she had founded – and which now included a much smaller experimental theatre and a theatre workshop – was leased out to three companies. The main theatre housed a commercial production of *Guys and Dolls* which was proving very successful and would be occupying the theatre for another two months, through the summer, while the Theatre Workshop was being used by the University of Spinnergate for its Drama Department.

I told her that she ought to keep at least one of the theatres in her own hands, thought Coffin, studying his loved one's face, but she was pushed on by Letty who always had her eye on the money bags. And I think Letty was having a money crisis herself at the time, although that is not the sort of information Letty tells you. Laetitia Bingham was his own half-sister, banker and investment panjandrum. But panjandrums have their ups and downs and Letty had suffered with the collapse of the eastern Tiger economies. She was over it now, thank goodness, since an impoverished Letty did not bear thinking about. It was time the iron hand of Letty let one of the theatres go free so that Stella could work. It was her world, after all.

He looked with even more sympathy at his wife, before going back to his mother's papers. What a woman she had been, not one to stay in a scene, held down by children or husbands, always moving on. It was going to be a good book.

He ran his hand through his hair, mentally assessing (although he would never have admitted to this) whether his recent illness had made for a loss of hair. Felt as thick as ever, thank goodness. Nor was he going grey, or not what you could call grey, or not what he called grey; as a child he seemed to recall it had been what people called auburn, now it was dark with a hint of red in certain lights. Secretly he was pleased with his hair, colour and weight. Stella's hair changed with her mood and the part she was playing: at the moment it was fair, long and loose. Coffin, who knew her age, thought how well she carried it off.

Naturally, he allowed no hint of this to pass over to Stella.

The Second City Force, of which he was Head and Commander, was not in his mind for the moment, that too had had its ups and downs, but for the moment all was tranquil there.

Of course, experience had taught him that you never knew what was going on underneath the surface, and nothing could make the Second City a completely peaceful place. Just as well, or I'd be out of a job. He had been a police officer all his working life, except for a short period in the army, starting at the bottom and climbing up. No further to go, he said to himself, with a smile, unless he wanted to become one of HM's Inspectors of Constabulary.

Stella smiled back at him, not one of her professional smiles that meant she wasn't really seeing him at all, but a real smile that said I am glad you are here.

I don't know all about you, because we never do, you have your secrets and I am not going to dig for them, but I know I love you.

'Now I have a little time, I might arrange a dinner for us all. Even cook it . . . No, perhaps not.' Stella was not interested in cooking and always said that it ruined the hands. An actress could not have bad hands. She would take a table at Max's and perhaps Coffin's sister Letty who was so rich and so well, and so often married, would join them. She might put money in a film for her sister-in-law; film makers were always hungry, and rich people, for Letty was rich again, always wanted investments.

She looked across the room to where her husband sat, surrounded by papers and with his laptop on a small table by his side. At last, the long preparation of his mother's diary and his editing of her letters, more amusing than anyone had expected, was near publication. A young Edinburgh publisher, urged on by Coffin's half-brother, who was a Writer to the Signet and lived in Old Edinburgh, had offered a contract. The book was ready for the world.

'George and Robbie are coming in for a meal tonight,' Stella said, breaking into Coffin's concentration.

Eventually, he responded. 'Was that wise?'

'They're not too bad if you get them in a good mood. I quite like them really.' And they are powerful figures in my theatrical world. This she did not say aloud but it was understood by her husband who gave a cheerful grin in return.

'As long as it's business.'

The two men had moved into similar apartments in a renovated and restored warehouse in Spinnergate. The building now called The Argosy, was in Rickards Passage and had once housed imports from the East. It still smelt of spices, so George and Robbie claimed. Friends (or enemies, it was sometimes not easy to be sure which) for decades, they were also business associates who worked together in the theatre: George Freedom was the money man and Robbie Gilchrist was on the artistic side, choosing the plays, and then supervising the production. They had had a string of successes. Likewise failures. They had both married the same woman, she had left Gilchrist for Freedom. Coffin wondered about their relationship.

'Well, good luck to you. Shall I stay home and eat with you or clear off and eat at Max's?'

It would be the same style of food anyway as Stella had almost certainly ordered the meal from Max's since this was their local restaurant. Max always did his best for Stella, whom he admired.

'Oh stay, darling, and give me support. I want to try to launch a Festival of Spinnergate and if they will help it would be an enormous boost. I have already spoken to Robbie and he sounded keen.'

'If I won't be in the way.' He was aware that his presence, what he was and his position, made some people self-conscious, ill at ease in his company. 'I don't think they like me much.'

Stella shook her head. 'That's their professional look: No like, no trust. I think that's better than the pros who are all over you, all jovial and friendly, and you know it's all an act. At least with George and Robbie what you see is what you get.'

Coffin said he would probably enjoy it. 'Remind me which is which, I get them confused.'

This was not strictly true: he possessed a pretty good idea of George Freedom. They had met. He did not like him. Mutual.

Stella was ready. 'Freedom is the small, stout one, with a quiff of dark hair. Not a grey hair to be seen.'

'Dyed?'

'Probably. But well done. And Robbie is the tall thin one, bald as could be, but he doesn't seem to mind. He tried a wig once but said it was too hot and itched. That was when he was married to Mariette, it was to please her. Didn't work, she went off anyway.'

'He was lucky there,' said Coffin, who recalled Mariette vividly. Mariette you did not forget.

'Yes, I think so.'

Stella was silent for a moment, then she said: 'You heard about Georgie's problem?' But of course, he had.

Coffin said, Yes, he had heard.

She said hesitantly: 'It was when you were ill, so I wondered.'

'I heard about it, though. I wasn't ill, just an operation.' Did he say that aloud? Yes, he obviously did because she answered.

'Yes, just an operation.' They opened you up with a sharp knife, saw what the damage was, tidied up a bit of this and that, then closed you up again. A picnic. You enjoyed it.

The operation was made necessary by an attack, but she did not mention this: Coffin was touchy about it.

She was never ill herself. Performers never were. Provided she still had a voice, Stella knew she would crawl on to the stage and do her bit. Voice? Even when that went she would mime her part.

Slowly, she said: 'George knows he was lucky not to go to prison for much longer.'

Coffin said he had had a good lawyer.

'Not the end of it, of course. There's going to be an appeal. Damages, that sort of thing. You wouldn't think of him as violent, would you? Of course, he isn't really, he was just

11

unlucky, an accident, a terrible accident, a little push and . . .' Stella shrugged. 'She had a thin skull.'

Still has, Coffin pointed out, she wasn't dead, was she?

'No, not dead,' said Stella, 'but her mind – they call it brain damage . . .' She shrugged. 'Then there's his stepdaughter too. That's another problem, taken herself off. You know his second wife was Robbie's wife? Or one of them. So Robbie was her stepfather too and fond of her. It's complicated. I'm always surprised that Robbie and George still work together. Money, I suppose. Anyway, the stepdaughter took off about the time George got out from his spell in prison. The girl who was hurt was a friend of hers.'

'She might come back of her own accord, it can happen. Pretty kid, nice long fair hair.' Not clever, though. Simple.

'You do know all about it,' said Stella. Of course you do, you always do, whatever you pretend. Your job.

'Just heard about it, probably from Mimsie Marker, or someone, and saw a photograph somewhere.' He looked at Stella. 'Perhaps I'd better take myself out.'

'No, don't.' She knew, and she understood now that he too knew, that the 'problem' which had been mentioned was not what happened to the stepdaughter but what had gone before.

The other accident. Another girl who worked for him.

And the one before that. No official complaint there but all in the dossier.

Freedom was a man to whom accidents happened.

Stella looked at her legs. It was funny about flesh, some days bits of you looked saggy and tired, and other days, they looked good. Today her legs looked trim and neat. Might be the new tights she was wearing from the place in Bond Street. Cost the earth but worth it.

'I'll go and put something sleek and flashy on, that's what they like, those two.'

'I'll behave.' Coffin gave her a wary smile.

Coffin got back to his literary labours which he was enjoying. Nice to be free of crime for a bit. Not that the Second City was ever truly crime-free, any more than any other big city, only at the moment it appeared free from murder, rape, drugs and pornography. Someone's put the lid on it all for a bit, he told himself cheerfully.

And all the time, he had waiting for him on the doorstep of a battered women's refuge, four limbs: two legs and two arms.

George arrived first, but late (and he was usually punctual), to be received by Stella in her new Vivienne Westwood trouser suit of satin with a fringe. The soft golden colour became her, as she was well aware – she hoped George noticed, but he seemed abstracted. He accepted a strong whisky and was sipping it when Robbie turned up full of apologies for being late.

'My wife would talk to me on the phone.' He was divorced from wife number two (Mariette had been number three), but husband and wife kept in touch, more closely than he cared for at times. 'I thought she'd never get off the line. She's worried sick about her eldest daughter, Alice; my stepdaughter, but I'm fond of her.' He looked at George. 'His stepdaughter too, for that matter, we married the same woman. A beauty but a bitch. Alice is seventeen, not a kid, really. She's gone off with her boyfriend, that's my opinion.' He did not go into it because he did not quite believe it.

'It happens,' said Stella. 'Did it myself once.'

Coffin gave her a wry look. Wasn't with me, he thought.

'She was in your outfit, Stella, for a bit. In the stage manager's team.'

'I remember her, very pretty girl. Kind of innocent, really. She'll turn up.'

Robbie nodded. He hoped so. 'Her mother is worried, they had a quarrel before she left.'

'She's always been a trouble, that girl,' said George over his whisky. He had no children himself, although several times married. 'And you know it.'

'It's all money,' said Robbie gloomily. 'Always about money. Her mother says she spends too much, I say they both do. But the girl's not bright.'

'Money,' said George. 'Don't mention it. We all have our worries. How do you manage all this theatre complex, Stella?'

He really wanted to know. It was one of the reasons he

had accepted to come to dinner. Apart from the fact that he liked the grub and liked to look at Stella. More than look if he got the chance, but it didn't seem likely with her husband there.

Stella said she got support from the local university who used the small theatre for their Drama Department, and that the Second City Arts Council had been generous, but that it was a squeeze. 'We've been lucky, we've had a couple of good commercial successes which we have sent on to the West End, and in one case to New York. It all helps.'

Stella led them in to dinner. Max had sent an assistant to set out the table.

Coffin saw that Stella had laid out the best silver, chosen by and paid for by her out of film earnings. He picked up a fork and balanced it in his hand. He liked the stuff, good style, as you would expect from Stella, but not the sort of thing that a copper could afford. Like, yes; pay for, no.

The china was old Minton, apricot and gold. They did not have a complete set, never had had, bought it at an auction, but enough to use for a small dinner.

George turned one plate over to examine the back. 'About 1880, I'd say, the colours are right. Nice stuff.'

Stella was pleased. 'You are clever, George, they come from a house in Shropshire. Not a complete set, of course. Let me give you some wine. Claret or hock?'

The soup was vichyssoise and the toast that was served with it was crisp and hot. Cold soup, hot toast – Max's idea.

George took hock.

She doesn't know, thought Coffin, that it is possible that a few years ago he killed a woman.

And later yet another.

Something I know, and she doesn't. (Or does she?)

And all the time, he had waiting for him on the door-step of a battered women's refuge, four limbs: two legs and two arms.

The remains were wrapped in brown paper. There was no torso and no head.

'Delicious soup,' said George, crunching toast.

Stella took advantage of the good mood of both men to

14

start a delicate introduction to what she had in mind for them. They worked together as a team so regularly that when asked to dinner as a pair by someone like Stella Pinero they knew it was business.

An interesting story, Coffin thought, studying George's face. Did George guess that he knew? And did George care?

After all, it was only what the police, at the time, thought. Never got outside publicity. Oh, the deaths, yes, but not George's connection.

He was a bit of a comedian, Coffin decided, watching George with Stella.

Of course, it was all a soap on TV. Coffin had watched a lot of television in his private room after his operation, and enjoyed it more than he had told Stella. She had been in some of the shows.

Not the deadly, killing-off-the-ladies one, that George had produced and, some said, written.

Only TV, just a bit of script, but it told you something about a man.

When they left (rather later than Coffin cared for, that was the theatre for you), George Freedom suggested to Robbie that they walk home rather than go to the cab rank by the theatre.

'I'd like a stroll, take a look around.'

Gilchrist yawned, said he was tired, but why not. The air might wake him and he had work to do.

'I used to live round here once,' said Freedom. 'I was working on a local newspaper. That was before I decided there was more money to be made on television.'

'If you can do it.'

'But we can . . . Place has changed a bit. I had a grotty little flat over Drossers Lane Market. Let's go that way, it's on the way home.'

Of course, it was all changed now. Behind Drossers Lane was the new Pepys Estate, an area of small terraced houses with one block of flats. Central to it was Pepys Park, an attempt at urban prettification, although the spirit of Drossers Lane seemed to hang around it still and resisted prettiness.

Even the grass looked sad and the shrubs and small trees did not flourish. It was much loved, however, by the small gangs of roving boys that were also part of Drossers Lane, indeed of East Hythe itself. The police were always being called to Pepys Park.

'Changed now,' said Robbie Gilchrist.

'Don't suppose Drossers Lane has changed, still full of pushers and pimps and policemen looking for a catch,' said Freedom. 'You could eat well there, though, greasy spoons maybe, those cafés, but they turned out good grub for not much cash. Bet they still do.'

Freedom stepped forward confidently and Gilchrist saw he did indeed know the way. They stepped out together through the night, walking off Stella's good wine. Freedom stopped at the head of one dark road.

'Knew a girl who lived around here. Bit of a bitch but a real goer.'

He stared into the darkness.

'There it is, Barrow Street . . . Never liked the place.'

'You know it then?'

'Said so, didn't I? Once.' He turned away. 'We don't have to go down it. There's a better way home.'

Gilchrist yawned again. 'How's Mariette?'

Mariette was the moveable wife that they had had in common.

'Fine,' said Freedom. 'Don't see much of her these days.'

'Who's she with then?'

'You tell me.'

Gilchrist changed the subject. 'How did you think our host looked?'

'All right,' said Freedom, who never noticed anyone but himself. 'Lucky to have her.'

Chief Inspector Phoebe Astley said: 'He looks better, doesn't he? More himself.'

The two of them were standing in the car park of Police Headquarters after a long day, ending in a meeting of the officers dealing with the latest crime.

Murder, it looked like.

She admired the Chief Commander although he could be the devil to work with. She was talking to her immediate boss, Archie Young, whom she also admired, but differently. There was, she had to admit it, a strong sexual element in her feeling for John Coffin (sternly held in check these days, of course, but still there), but not so with the chief superintendent.

'Thinner,' said Archie Young. 'Thinner,' he said again, a shade enviously. He gave his own waistband a tug. He was losing his hair and putting on weight and envied the Chief Commander's apparent power to resist both processes. Didn't diet either, nor take much exercise. There was the dog, of course. Coffin did walk the dog.

No, you're not thinner, thought Phoebe. She was solidly, but attractively, built herself, and after a threat of a nasty illness a year or two ago, rather welcomed her solidity as a sign of health. She wore her usual working garb of a well-cut dark jacket with jeans. She admired the way Stella dressed, but clocked the price and did not seek to emulate her. 'Suits him.'

'He's never been ill before. Not that I remember.'

Coffin had been ill before, of course; Phoebe did not know everything.

'Doesn't like it talked about. Prefers to pretend it didn't happen.'

'I was really glad when he came back to life,' she said seriously. 'Resurrected.'

'It wasn't that bad.'

'I thought he was gone.' Then she laughed. 'Well, only for about a minute. But remember I was walking to the car with him when the chap dug the knife in. It was the Chief Commander or me, and the Chief saw to it that it wasn't me.'

'You got the man though.'

Phoebe nodded. 'Ten years inside. Wish I could have got the knife into him.'

Then she said: 'We haven't told the Chief about the legs and arms?'

'He's got to know. I am preparing a report which he will see in the ordinary way of things. Since he reads everything.'

And remembers it, he had a phenomenal memory. 'He will know.'

'On his doorstep too.'

'Not his present doorstep,' corrected Chief Superintendent Archie Young. 'He didn't live there at first, when he came to the Second City. St Luke's was just being converted and he was on his own. Her ladyship was working in the States.' He frowned. In fact, he was not sure what exactly had been the state of the marriage at that time. He had heard rumours. On and off. Happy enough now, though, it appeared.

Lovely woman, and talented, no doubt about that, but he personally always handled her with care.

'Miss Pinero wasn't there?'

'Not at the time, she always seemed to be on the move. She came and had a look round, of course, so I suppose she spent the odd night there but practically speaking, he lived alone in Moorbank House. It had been a doctor's house. Or was it a dentist's? Been both, I think. Called something else now.'

'So when he moved out, it became a women's refuge?'

'I think it was something in between.' Archie frowned. 'Yes. We used it for CID offices. We were all busy creating the Second City Police Force. Some of us came from the Met and others were local to the old Docklands.'

'And some were completely new to it like me.' Phoebe had come later from Birmingham. By the time she had arrived, the theatre complex was almost complete with only the smallest theatre waiting completion. The Coffins' home in the converted tower of the old church was lived in. Must have been expensive, she remembered thinking.

'You've been in touch with Stella, haven't you?' Archie Young put a question to which he knew the answer.

'Yes, sure, she was what you might call a character witness for George Freedom. I had to come at it sideways, as it were, not to make too clear what I was after. That I thought Freedom was a killer.' She was cagey, careful with what she said. Anyway, she thought he was the sort that got off. There were types like it.

Justice or not? She didn't know.

'Hit a girl on the head, didn't he?'

18

'Yes, his secretary, hit her with a log. He claimed it was an accident. But they had been quarrelling. He's out now.'

'What did you make of him?'

Phoebe shrugged. 'Wouldn't care to be shut up in a dark room with him.' But there were plenty of men you could say that of, although with some it might be a treat. She looked speculatively at the chief superintendent. No, probably not.

And Freedom had a history of violence behind him. Used to shoot, just for a hobby. But more of that later, Phoebe thought. She never liked men who used guns as a hobby, even though they only shot at paper targets. They had faces and bodies, those targets, and the thought was there, wasn't it? This reminded her of something else the Chief Commander was not going to like. 'I don't know if you've heard yet about the trouble at the Abbey Road Gun Club?'

He nodded. 'I have the report. No more.'

'Two of our men belong. Uniform. A PC and a sergeant, both from Cutts Street.' Cutts Street was a substation not far from Abbey Road which was near to the tube station. She would like to have said that both the constable, who was known as Loverboy, and the sergeant – Sergeant Will Grimm, known naturally as Death – were on her worry list, but she kept quiet. With Grimm she always wondered if she ought to wear a necklace of garlic. Attractive but horrible. Unluckily, it was something she went for.

'Got a puzzling side to it.'

'Certainly has. Bill Eager, who is the club sec, runs it, really, blames it on the flood they had. I've read his statement. Does seem to have done in all the security they should have had.'

'You'd better talk to him yourself. And the two men from Cutts Street. I want those guns back.'

'I'll see him again. I did go there at once, he was cleaning up the place, he had an outsider cleaning team in there.' She frowned. 'Perhaps that wasn't wise, but he's a careful chap, is Bill Eager.' She went on to another of her problems, keen to talk to him because she did not get many chances of easy talk with Archie Young. 'The Health people are going on about the sale of illegal beef . . . stuff from beasts

19

slaughtered as suspect of BSE. They think it's coming from the Second City.'

Archie Young nodded. 'We would get the blame.' He knew it was the sort of investigation that went on and on with everyone lying.

Phoebe came back to the packages containing severed limbs on the doorstep of the refuge. Not the kind of crime you would ever pin on George Freedom, she thought. If he packaged up a woman's limbs then they would probably be packed in Hermès bags.

There *was* a handbag, as it happened, round the corner, propped up against the wall of the house. Not Hermès, though. And the legs, otherwise bare, had painted toenails. A touching bit of vanity for such battered, bruised legs.

'It's sex, isn't it?' she said to Archie Young. 'A sexual crime. You don't chop a woman up like that without there being a sexual involvement.'

Archie Young nodded, and Phoebe came back to what worried her.

'Surely the fact he lived there for a bit will have been forgotten.'

'It got a bit of publicity at the time; the local news rag, the *Docklands Daily*, was still running and it had an article about the Chief Commander and the house.

Pictures. Coffin had obliged with reluctance but knowing that his new force in the new Second City needed all the help it could get. As he had done so lately: Coffin and his actress wife. 'The love of his life,' he had allegedly said not so long ago. All in the paper.

Wrapped in layers of brown paper, the limbs came in two parcels, legs in one, arms in another.

In blood, a message straggled: J.C. TO REMIND YOU, SIR.

And underneath, in pencil, not blood: *I send it back from me to you, although it was yours before.*

Archie Young was serious. 'We haven't spoken of it yet to the woman who runs the refuge. I don't know what she will make of it. I think she read what seemed to be the message but she is playing it cool. Her name is Mary Arden. And we may be getting it wrong. But I think we have to tell the Chief.'

'Oh sure,' said Phoebe. 'And won't he be pleased.'

She wondered a little bit what Stella Pinero would make of it. Still, no one really knew what went on in a marriage.

You are not suggesting, she said to herself, that the Chief Commander knew those limbs intimately in life?

She caught the chief super's eye and knew that he was suggesting exactly that to himself.

Two high-ranking police officers thinking the same thing.

The governor of Sisley Green Prison was thinking something even worse.

2

There was a police van outside the house in Barrow Street and several police cars parked along the road. Outside the big Victorian house there was an area taped off around the steps and the front door. A police constable stood on duty.

He looked bored and cold. A colleague who had been examining the ground around the house joined him.

'You knew one of the women here, didn't you, Ron?' he asked PC Ryman-Lawson, whose double-barrelled name, itself the subject of jokes, got reduced to Ron.

'Yeah. She worked here.' Henriette Duval. Long-legged, and very pretty. She had come over to learn and she had certainly learnt it. 'We went around for a bit. Then she dropped me. Said I was too young and she liked older men better.'

'Not usually that way.'

'I think she meant I didn't have enough money to spend on her.'

'Ah, that figures. A bit of a goer?'

Ryman-Lawson did not commit himself. 'Bloody cold here.'

'What's become of her?'

Ryman-Lawson shrugged; the rain was running down his collar. 'Gone back home, I expect.'

Barrow Street not being a place to ignore anything exciting was providing an audience even though it was raining and not warm. Barrow Street knew a good thing when it saw one and was making the press welcome also. There was lively expectation of a TV van. You might see your own face on the screen in your own living room.

'Always trouble there,' pointed out a sturdy woman as she

pushed her bike past on the way to work. 'Trouble House or my name's not Mona Jackson. Shouldn't be here in a respectable street. Police, we don't want them.'

She achieved a small triumph by running her bike over the toes of an approaching police constable, who leapt back. 'Watch it, missus.' He added something under his breath.

'Mrs Jackson to you, sonny,' and she passed on in splendour. 'And don't think I don't know you, Tad Blenkinsop, and I could report you for that language.'

Not everyone thought Barrow Street so respectable, and by his expression, he was one of them.

'I suppose we might be more popular if we were a nunnery,' said Mary Arden, warden of the Serena Seddon Refuge, a hint of a wail in her voice. Mary had a distinguished record with a degree in social studies from a famous college in the University of London, a period nursing in a hospital, and another time working as an assistant in a care centre. 'Although goodness knows, no community could be more off sex than we are here. Had too much of it.'

'Cheer up,' advised her fellow worker and assistant. Eve Jones was also a nurse and often needed in that capacity.

'I could call myself Mother Mary.' She was making some coffee. 'Have a cup? It's the real stuff, extravagant, I know, but I need it today.'

'I don't fancy being Sister Evelyn.'

'You've been called worse.'

'True. But being a nun means not just being off sex but also a vow of chastity. Don't see most of our lodgers taking that one.'

The police were already in the house, moving from room to room, trying to be tactful as they questioned the residents. Mary and Evelyn had already been interviewed. But they knew more would be coming their way.

Mary had handed over her records to be studied.

They were in Mary's small office and sitting room – they were too pressed for space for even the warden to know much privacy. Her comfort, too, was modestly allowed for, with one cupboard for clothes, and a divan bed. There were two bathrooms in the house and Mary took her turn with everyone else. 'At least it means I know if there is hot water and the bath is clean.'

Ready hot water, clean linen and a little, a very little, privacy, was the best she could do for her guests. It helped some more than others.

The residents helped to keep the house tidy and clean, but Mary employed a pair of contract cleaners once a week as well.

Her one luxury was a small flat of her own which she used when she had time off. She did not grudge herself this because she had to have somewhere to retire to if she ever reached that haven.

Evelyn did not live in, she was married, to a man who worked backstage in the St Luke's Theatre Complex, and she went home at night. A night assistant came in then to be on duty till morning. The Serena Seddon House was not one in which nights were necessarily peaceful. There was a telephone line straight through to the local police station in Pelly Row for emergency use.

Evelyn took two lumps of sugar to give her strength, while wishing that she still smoked. 'I suppose we shall have the police all over the place for days.'

She had been the first to find the bundles when she arrived for work that morning. 'As soon as I picked one up, I guessed what it was. It just felt dead and heavy. Thank God, I didn't do more than pick it up and put it down.' She went to the window to look out. 'Gone now.'

Mary pushed a tin towards her. 'Have a biscuit. Fortnum's best . . . it's all right, a present from my mother.' Her mother always chose the best she could afford. And this went for clothes and scents. Her mother thought she was mad to work where she did, while saying fondly that she admired her for it.

Mary chose a biscuit with nuts in it. 'I suppose the forensic lot will be in and looking us over. Depends what they find in the bundles.'

'Two legs, two arms. We know that.'

It was just guesswork, no one had told them, but Evelyn

was an experienced nurse. 'Didn't have to be human,' she said, 'but I guess they are. Right shape, right weight, right feel.' She shook her head. 'I think I felt a finger.'

'Phoebe Astley made it clear she thought it was one of our former lodgers, poor soul. I hope she was dead when it was done to her.'

'Mary.' Evelyn gave a shudder.

'You can't count on it, the men some of the women here attract. I'm not joking.'

'And I'm not laughing.'

'There was something written across the packets – did you read it?'

'Didn't you?'

Mary was silent. She answered after a pause. 'Yes.'

'Make anything of it?'

'No.' The best thing, the easiest thing to say. 'Some things you don't, do you?' Again the easy answer. 'Phoebe Astley will tell us something, perhaps. She's a decent sort. More coffee?'

Evelyn held her cup out. 'You ought to go in for mugs, they hold more. She a friend?'

'We belong to the same club.'

Evelyn waited, and eventually asked, 'Which club is that?' She did not have a club herself, not being clubbable. I suppose I have a husband instead, she told herself.

'The University Club in Lomas Street. Not the same university, she was Birmingham, and I was St Andrews, but the same club.'

'I always knew you were more of an intellectual than I am. I knew it when I heard your mother crying about your hair.'

'No, she didn't.' Mary shook her unshorn locks indignantly.

'Yes, she did. Implored you to go to her hairdresser.'

'So I would if I could afford it.'

Evelyn smiled. She knew all the signs of comfortable private income when she saw it.

'Anyway, you know yourself that it wouldn't do to look too . . . well . . . too groomed here.'

Evelyn laughed. 'Have a go, they might enjoy it. Don't be patronizing.'

Mary looked shocked. 'Do you think so?'

There were bangs and sounds of screaming from above.

'Oh, screw it.' Mary jumped to her feet. 'Come on. You too, in case there is bleeding.'

Side by side, they ran up the stairs in the direction of the shouting. On the stairs they passed a young WPC who gave them a questioning look. 'Leave this to us,' said Mary as she passed. 'Our job, we cope.'

As she sped on, she muttered:

'Whenever I hear two of our residents going on at each other like this, I think that maybe they were not the only ones in the marriage to get battered. Not an acceptable PC view, I know.'

The noise was coming from the communal sitting room on the first floor.

'Miriam, Miriam,' said Mary as she pushed open the door. 'At it again.'

A small, sturdy figure, a round face with short, cropped hair, swung round. Miriam Beetham; she called herself Mrs Beetham but no marriage ceremony had taken place with Tommy Beetham and the title was purely honorary.

The room showed signs of battle with a chair overturned and a sofa shoved at an angle against the wall. A small child was sitting on the sofa, looking interested rather than frightened. Billy Beetham recognized Mary.

'How do you know it's me?'

'I recognize your voice. And you, Ally.'

Ally was tall, thin, but capable of swift physical action if required. Learned behaviour, Mary thought sadly.

The two women had been friends and enemies since schooldays, the relationship not improved by the fact that Ally was indeed Mrs Beetham, although she called herself Ally Carver. Husbands and lovers had shuttled between the two since they first took up sex. It was bad luck that had brought them into the refuge at the same time.

Or had they fixed it between them? With this pair, you never knew.

Evelyn was examining Ally's nose. 'Not broken. It'll stop bleeding soon.' She produced a wad of tissues which she held to the nose. 'And keep quiet.'

'What's it all about?' demanded Mary. 'No, don't tell me. Come to the office later. I wish we had a vow of silence in this place.'

The battle was over, showing every sign of starting again. 'Her fault,' muttered Ally through the tissues. 'And you can't say we'll have the police in, 'cause we got them already. And they will know about whose fault it is . . . they know.'

'She said my Billy was simple.' The rejoinder came from Miriam in a loud voice. 'So I hit her. Do it again.'

'He is simple.'

Looks sharp enough to me, thought Mary, ageless too, six coming on sixty and the devil kissed him. Now what do I mean by that, she asked. I mean he's wicked through and through. Shouldn't think like that, should you? Children can't be wicked.

But she knew they could be.

'Tidy up the room,' she said. 'And get Billy to help you. And calm down. Have a cup of tea.'

There was always tea and milk left ready in the sitting room.

'It's because of what was left on the doorstep,' called Miriam after them. 'We're all upset.'

The child Billy gave a cry, something between a wail and a hiccup of laughter.

I think he likes bits of bodies, Mary thought. But no, he can't know anything about it. We haven't said: Keep quiet, the police told us.

On the stairs, she said to Evelyn, 'What is wicked?'

Over another cup of coffee, Evelyn said she thought it was a matter of feeling. You felt something or someone was wicked.

'Even a child? I shouldn't have been so sharp with those two. Not professional. Gentle does it.'

'You mean Billy, I suppose?' said Evelyn, crunching a biscuit. 'The wicked bit?'

'Yeah.'

'He's a mite young to get the full judgement, but he's coming on nicely.'

'They all know about the parcels of limbs on the steps. When they asked, I said I had no idea. But they know. They know there wouldn't be all that police activity for just a dead dog.'

'Probably making guesses who it is.'

'Oh God, yes.' Good accurate guesses too. On such a subject they would be well-informed.

'Phoebe Astley will know how to handle it, she'll assess what they say, work out if there is anything in it.'

'They'll say plenty.' Mary continued to be gloomy. 'Make it up if they have to.'

'Phoebe . . .' began Evelyn.

'Yes, she'll know how to weave her way through it. If she does it herself. You know how it goes.' They were not without experience in police visits. 'Uniformed branch first, then CID, it'll be women because of what we are, and then, if it's important, we shall get the top brass. Or toppish. Remember how it was when Jodie Spinner hid the stuff her husband had stolen in her bedroom?'

Evelyn nodded. That had brought Chief Inspector Astley in sharpish.

'She'll check on the really interesting stuff . . . if any.'

'I wouldn't mind asking her a few questions myself.'

The interesting thing was that Phoebe Astley had been round here so speedily that morning, even before the first SOCO team had finished photographing the front steps. Off again now.

She had not had much to say, even to Mary. Police business, her expression said.

Evelyn said: 'Do you think it could be Henriette?'

'The dead woman? Etta? Oh no, she went home to France.'

'We've never heard from her. No one has.'

Henriette Duval had worked with Mary and Evelyn in the Serena Seddon for about eighteen months to earn her keep while doing an English language course at the University of the Second City. Then she had said her farewells and gone home to Versailles.

'Oh, but that's not so surprising.'

'She said she would keep in touch. We liked her, everyone did, and she was marvellous at cleaning the kitchen, a real eye for dirt.'

'People always say they will keep in touch; they hardly ever do. Doesn't make her a candidate for being chopped up.'

Evelyn was quiet for a minute, then she said: 'Thought I saw her in Drossers Lane Market. Tried to catch up with her but she disappeared.'

Mary shrugged. 'A mistake, the girl just looked like Etta.'

'Not many like Etta . . . red hair, tall and thin, skirts up to her thigh. No, I thought it was Etta.' She added: 'With a man, of course.'

'Well . . . Etta . . .' said Mary. 'If it was Etta . . .'

'She would be with a man.'

'Still doesn't make her a candidate for killing.'

'You know the sort she went with: either villains or police-men. Both the type that might kill and cut up a girl.'

Mary wondered what Phoebe Astley would make of this comment, then realized she would raise an eyebrow and laugh, half accepting the judgement. It was true, the police did deal in violence.

Some truth in what Evelyn said then; violence was part of their life for the police. For some of them, not necessarily the worse, just the more vulnerable, perhaps because of some-thing inside, it rubbed off on them.

'Just because you saw Etta alive in Drossers Lane Market doesn't mean she's going to turn up dead on our doorstep.'

Evelyn looked unconvinced.

'You can't even be sure it was her.'

Evelyn looked even more unconvinced, and Mary remem-bered that you could never argue Evelyn out of anything: she just got more stubborn.

'Have another cup of coffee,' she said instead.

'Swimming in it already.' But Evelyn held out her cup. 'Should I say anything about it when I am interviewed. I suppose we *are* being interviewed?'

Mary nodded. 'Bound to be. Especially you, you found the bundles.'

'I've already told them about that.'

The police noises about the house were becoming quieter; Mary sensed that they would be leaving. And others coming.

'We've all answered a few questions. It's just a beginning. We will have to go through it again, and perhaps again.'

'Even if we don't know anything?'

'They have to be convinced of that.'

'You seem to know a lot about it.'

Yes, thought Mary. I once went to bed with a policeman. In fact, quite often. It lasted about six months. I learnt a lot.

I learnt that you could lie to him, and get away with it, or thought you had, but somehow in the end, and sometimes not too much later, you found the truth came out.

Not that I ever had much to lie about, she added to herself. If I did it at all it was in self-protection because otherwise I would have gone up in smoke.

A uniformed sergeant appeared at the door. 'Just off, Miss Arden. Anyway for the moment, but there is a constable on the door and the forensic team would like to come in, if that's all right?'

Mary nodded assent.

'Try saying no,' growled Evelyn as he left.

'You go home. If you are wanted, I'll telephone you. Don't go out to eat a quick curry with Peter though, just in case.'

Evelyn swung her shoulder bag on. 'Wouldn't dream of it. Peter doesn't eat curry. But I'd like to get back. Miss Pinero has two new contacts who might be putting together a show: Freedom and Gilchrist, sound like a stand-up comedy team, don't they? And they have this driver and handyman who aids and assists. All means business, which as you know has not been brisk lately. But you can always trust Miss Pinero to bring it in, I say.' Having said this, at the door, she turned. 'Look after yourself, and do ring me if there is anything I can do.'

'Miriam and Ally will be quiet now, they like each other, you only quarrel like that with friends. I'm on their side, or I wouldn't be here. But they don't like to feel I am kind of a social doctor treating a disease, so in a way they feel better when I lose my temper. It puts us on a level.' She added: 'You have to be a bit tough sometimes, of course.'

'Yes, sure,' said Evelyn. With a wave, she was gone.

After the front door banged behind Evelyn, and she heard her speaking to the constable outside, Mary tidied up the coffee pot and cups, then went up the stairs to see Miriam and Ally.

She passed one of the other occupants on the way up. 'Everything all right, Fanny?'

'Fine, Mary. I'm just off to get my prescription from Dr Meener. The police girl said it was all right.'

'You do that then.'

Fanny nodded towards the sitting room door. 'They all right, then?'

'I think so.'

'Do they know who it is outside? Whose bits, I mean?'

Mary said, No, not as far as she knew.

'I just wondered . . .' Then Fanny stopped. Mary waited. 'Just wondered if it was that foreign girl who helped here for a bit.'

Mary said in a careful way: 'I think she went home.'

'Only I saw her around in Poland Street.'

Poland Street was close, very close to Drossers Lane Market. In fact, Drossers Lane Market was virtually in Poland Street.

'The other day . . . She did put it about a bit.'

'You'd better tell the police when they ask questions. If you think it's important.'

'Might be, mightn't it?' and Fanny took herself down the stairs and out the front door.

Mary made her way to the communal sitting room where Ally and Miriam were sitting companionably side by side, smoking and watching TV. The boy, watching too, no longer looked evil, but just like any unsettled child who had seen too much of life for his age.

Someone, Miriam probably, had made the room tidy, picking up the knocked-over furniture and restoring the cushions to the sofa. Someone else, again probably Miriam, had made a pot of tea and yet another person, and this time probably the boy, had managed to get a bag of chips which they were now passing from hand to hand in a peaceful and friendly fashion.

They had been joined by one of the new arrivals, Betty, who had come in last night and was still nervous. She seemed to have been welcomed into the group and was certainly getting tea and a sympathetic chip.

'You shouldn't be eating chips, Miriam,' Mary reminded her. 'You know what the doctor said.'

No one bothered to answer this comment, although Betty looked even more nervous.

And who could blame her, Mary thought. What a welcome to the Serena.

The chip bag was waved in her direction, and absently she took one. The vinegar and salt were harsh and strong but somehow it was tasty. The programme they were watching didn't look bad either.

At this point, Billy slipped off the sofa and, ignoring his mother's request to sit still and stop being a regular nuisance, went to the window.

'There's men out there in white suits like ghosts,' he announced loudly.

'Scientists, forensic ones,' growled his mother. 'Seen on the telly.'

Mary went to the window to look. Three men in hooded white cotton outfits were on their knees.

'What are they doing round the side of the house?' demanded Billy acutely. 'The bits were found on the steps.'

Mary had been wondering this herself. 'They have to study the ground all around.'

A sudden burst of laughter from the sofa drew the boy back to the television screen, muttering that it was a waste of time out there.

Mary, who had been thinking this herself, moved away from the window and towards the door.

As she touched the handle, Miriam said, over her shoulder and not looking at Mary, not taking her eyes off the television screen: 'They found a handbag there, round the side of the house.'

Mary swung round, walked over and deliberately planted

her body between them and the television screen. Impolite, pushy, irritating, but essential, as experience had taught her.

'Where'd you get that from?'

Miriam gave a little nod of her head sideways. 'Betty told me.'

Mary looked at Betty, who shifted her shoulders uneasily – alarm came promptly to her.

I must be gentle, Mary reacted at once, I am not always gentle enough here.

No, perhaps gentleness isn't right. What is needed is to give to each what they need, and that is harder, because you have to be intelligent and responsive.

Words, she said to herself sadly, you use too many words, girl. 'Where did you learn that, Betty?'

Betty looked down and fidgeted again. 'The copper told me,' she whispered.

'The one on duty outside?' said Mary doubtfully. It didn't sound likely.

'I was at school with him,' Betty whispered. 'We lived next door. My brother was his best mate.'

'Right . . .' Mary hesitated, wondering whether to say anything. 'Perhaps he didn't mean you to tell anyone else.'

Betty was silent. 'Only told Miriam. She asked.'

'Don't worry,' said Miriam, again without turning her head. 'You can trust us: we won't tell our stories to the newspapers or TV. Unless they pay us.'

'Ha, ha.' A mirthless comment from Mary as she left the room; she never found it easy to know when Miriam was joking. No doubt Miriam could have said the same of her. We don't understand each other, that's the truth of it, she thought, giving Miriam a last look: an enigma wrapped up in a thick cosy cover of flesh, and inside not cosy at all.

That helped explain the boy. And probably why she was here in the refuge.

From the policeman to Betty, from Betty to Miriam, and from Miriam to me, this was the channel of communication.

Mary walked down the stairs wishing she could talk to Phoebe Astley. Phoebe always gave a straight answer to a question. If asked if the dead woman was Etta, Henriette Duval, who had worked in the refuge, she would answer Yes or No.

If she could. Answers did not always come easy.

And if asked further if it was possible her killer could be a member of the Second City Force, Phoebe would answer that too. But with circumspection.

Mary paused on the stairs to look out of the window. She ran her finger down the glass. Outside it was beginning to rain, the rain would come through this window.

The Serena Seddon House needed money spent on it, money it did not have. It was as comfortable and welcoming as it could be made inside, and that was what counted. Outside in Barrow Street it aimed for anonymity with no blue plaque displaying the name and just a discreet Number 5 on the door. And you had to come up to the door to see that.

The partners of the battered women had been known to come looking for them so being unnoticed counted. Even so, the house was known in the area and not loved.

Number 5 had been built at the end of the last century, it had celebrated its centenary, but it was showing its age. And who could blame it, Mary thought, since it had been a private home, home to a doctor who had been a police surgeon, and afterwards a dentist's surgery, afterwards rented as home to the new Chief Commander of the Second City, one John Coffin, and then left empty for a clutch of years.

Now it was a home for the fearful and the dispossessed. Interestingly, in the time of its first occupant, the doctor, it had got the reputation of being the home of Jack the Ripper: Dr Death.

Mary Arden walked down the stairs. There was a WPC sitting on an upright chair in the hall.

'You all right? Would you like a more comfortable chair?' If there is one, Mary thought, even as she asked the question.

'No, thank you, Miss Arden. This one does me.'

'Is it true that a handbag was found outside the house?'

'I haven't heard, Miss Arden.'

And wouldn't say.

Mary opened the front door to breathe in the cold, damp

air. Phoebe Astley, who had been talking to the forensic team, swung round to look at her.

'Hello, you advance guard, or doing the questioning yourself?'

'Just checking.' Phoebe came into the hall, sniffing the air. 'I always wonder how you manage to keep this place smelling so fresh when . . .'

'You mean when we don't wash enough here.'

'No, I didn't mean that and you know it. I mean you have a very mixed and floating population here, and yet it never seems institutional.'

She does mean it doesn't smell. Mary grinned.

'I work on it, it's meant to be pleasant. We all like a hot bath or shower and there's always hot water. And I provide lavender bath soap . . . they don't have to use it, they may prefer their own, but it's there.'

Phoebe looked trim and brisk, her dress sense had tightened up; she carried a neat black notebook, the successful detective officer.

I admire you, Phoebe, Mary said to herself. But what would you say, if I said: I could read what was written on the two terrible bundles and I saw the initials J.C.?

What would you make of that, Phoebe?

Not the signature of the sender, you would say at once, but a suggestion of the recipient?

All she said was: 'I suppose you want to talk to everyone here?'

'Not me in person, but a couple of WDCs will be in.'

'Don't upset them, please. All the women have been through a lot. They need to be treated with care.'

'That's why I am sending women officers. They have been carefully chosen.'

'Good.'

'Just whether they heard or saw anything in the night or early morning. You too will be asked, Mary.'

'I saw nothing,' said Mary quickly. 'Heard nothing. I don't think anyone here will be able to help you. It can't be anything to do with current residents.'

Phoebe nodded but did not commit herself.

'And the bag?'

'May have nothing to do with the remains of the body.' Phoebe was still being cautious.

Suddenly, Mary said: 'I know what was written across the bundle. I did go out to look when Evelyn came running in. I couldn't make it out.'

Phoebe allowed herself a shrug. Who can, it said.

'I send it back from me to you, although it was yours before . . . Sounds like a quotation.'

'We're working on it.'

'And J.C.? What does that mean?'

Phoebe did not answer. Not even a shrug this time.

'Some of the girls here think the body or what there is of it might be from Etta . . . she worked here for a bit. I thought she'd gone home, but it seems she's been seen around the district . . . She had some risky friends, the sort that might use violence.' Mary let the next words drop out slowly, as if she had just thought of them: 'And she went about a bit with a few local coppers.'

Phoebe could have said that she had heard this, but she did not. Never divulge information unnecessarily was a dictum she had been taught. Especially in a case like this. 'We'll work it out,' said Phoebe patiently. 'Trust us.'

But trust, as she knew, was always in short supply in the Second City.

And she wasn't too sure how much she had of it herself. She nodded to PC Ryman-Lawson as she left, acknowledging that he was wet and cold.

3

Because Coffin had once lived in the house in Barrow Street (which was attracting intense if discreet media attention), he was being kept informed of the investigation as it went on. Reports of all important crimes in the Second City always went to him as a matter of course, but this was different. Archie Young had decided he must see and hear of everything.

The message scrawled on the two bundles was being kept quiet although rumours went around the watchers.

Coffin knew of them, had seen a photograph of the bundles, although not the bundles themselves. He knew what was written there, and understood why Archie Young and Phoebe Astley were keeping an eye on the investigation.

Keeping an eye on him too, he thought with some irritation.

The initials J.C., taken in conjunction with the fact he had once lived in the house was giving them pause for thought.

And they were probably thinking also, quietly to themselves: And what about the woman?

The House in Barrow Street – he thought of it as The House that belonged in a sensitive part of his memory when he had lived there alone. Alone, new to the Second City, wondering if he was going to regret leaving the Met, a time when Stella was in New York and the marriage was rocky. Or seemed to be so.

I love you, Stella, he thought, but you can be difficult.

This is the point where you laugh, he said to himself, because probably she says the same about you. Bound to. It was always mutual, that sort of complaint, wasn't it?

He went to the window to look out. He had returned to work, against his doctor's advice, earlier than that luminary thought wise. He had a deputy and an assistant, but work was piling up and he wanted to get on with it himself. He did not find it easy to delegate.

Outside it was raining; the Second City did not look at its best when the sky was grey and heavy with rain.

He returned to his desk where a tray of coffee had been put ready for him by his secretary with a look of sympathy. The way he felt at the moment he did not want sympathy, it irritated him.

A kind woman but too full of sympathy. What the pot of coffee and biscuits said was: You were stabbed by that maniac, he wanted attention and attacking you was his way of getting it. You nearly died.

It was the second knife wound he had suffered. This time it had got to his liver.

I must watch out for knives, he thought. I seem to attract them, and some in the back too.

He drank some coffee. His first secretary in the Second City had been one of his mistakes: efficient, but hostile, wanting him to know that he was a newcomer, an intruder, here.

There were other mistakes, but she was his first, and at the time, all subsumed in his feeling that his coming here at all was one big mistake.

He had been promoted beyond his powers. The feeling niggled away inside him, taking away all pleasure at his new position – well, nearly all, he had to admit, some pleasure remained, he couldn't help that. It was marvellous to have power, to feel the lad from the London Docklands but south of the river was now part of the Establishment. Albeit one with more than a dash of the revolutionary in him. But he had already realized that you needed this in the Second City, which was never going to be docile. The population of the Second City had lived through wars and depressions, been bombed, and was now rebuilt, had seen old industries fade away and been replaced by bankers and journalists, had seen the great River Thames lose trade but become more beautiful;

38

he was moving into a city of change and he was part of the change.

But in this changing city, where he had to make his mark, he had enemies. Within the police team were men well-entrenched who had worked their way up and resented the arrival of the newcomer.

Flashy, playing to the media, talks too much, thinks too much, not one of us. These were the comments flung about, some made a hit, as some always will, and hurt.

Not one of us, was the criticism shouted the loudest.

At the same time, he was coping with the mountain of reports, letters and memos that a new position inevitably entailed. He was learning faces, sorting out friends and enemies.

And Stella, ah, Stella, was not with him. She was working in New York. He had missed her. At first, settling into the new job it had not been too bad, but Stella had stayed away. What was more, she had proclaimed that she was not coming back to live in that terrible house in Barrow Street. It smelt wrong to her.

She had already bought the St Luke's Church with plans to start the theatre there, and even then the tower was being converted into her home. She would come back when it was ready to live in. Oh yes, when work permitted, she would fly over to see him, but he would have to rent a flat or take a room in a hotel. Barrow Street did not suit her.

It was the difficult side of Stella which he knew existed, he had met it before, and never known how to handle it.

And then he wondered, could not help wondering, who Stella had in New York. Was she unfaithful?

Suspicion was an evil plant, he had admitted to himself, but it was growing inside him vigorously at that time. A fine flower with a bad scent.

He had been feeling particularly depressed and irritable when Anna arrived to interview him.

In those early days he was still doing interviews for the press and the television programmes to get the Second City Police known and respected.

Or that was the idea put to him by the PR people.

This was when Anna came on the scene. At first it felt like an invasion. A one-woman invasion.

Anna Michael was young, handsome rather than beautiful, and dressed in a casual way in jeans and a thick sweater. She couldn't have been more different from Stella.

Anna was tactful and admiring in the way she questioned him, so that to his surprise, Coffin found himself responding.

This interview took place in an office in the old Second City Police HQ, since then rebuilt. She talked about where he was now living in Barrow Street.

'When I was a kid we used to think that Jack the Ripper had lived there. We'd frighten ourselves talking about it.'

'You come from round here?' He was surprised, she seemed, somehow, international, conceived in an airport, born on a runway.

'Oh yes, sure. My father was a docker . . . in the days when there were dockers.' She laughed. 'He's still alive, screwed a lot of money out of his employers as redundancy and took himself off to Scotland.'

'Is he a Scot?'

She nodded. 'Remotely. Great-grandfather. I'm Carmichael, really, but I trimmed the name down, better for a journalist to have a short name . . . takes up too much space otherwise. Not Anna either, but Joanna. I didn't care for the initials J.C., they were too holy.' She went on: 'There was a famous murder in Barrow Street in the sixties . . . the Triangle Murder, it was called.'

'I've heard of it.'

'Of course. They got two killers, didn't they? But there was one they never got. Dead anyway by now, I suppose.'

'Probably.' And to his surprise he heard himself asking her for a drink at the house in Barrow Street.

She accepted at once.

He drank some coffee, which was good and hot, and considered lacing it with whisky or brandy, but rebuffed the idea without much trouble, although in his younger, wilder days, before becoming the Chief Commander of the Second City Force, he would certainly have done so.

He had probably topped up his coffee on the day Anna came to do her interview.

By the time that interview came out, he and Anna had become – he hesitated to use the word lovers because he didn't think love came into it, because he knew he had remained in love with Stella, but love or lust while it lasted, whatever it was between them was powerful.

Love, lust, technical terms for a jumble of emotions. Behind his emotion was anger and disappointment with his new position and irritation with Stella. He wanted something to soothe away the frustration.

Anger can be a powerful impulse to sex. For men, anyway. Different for women, perhaps. Better not dwell on that thought.

He would like to think there was no anger on Anna's side, ambition, yes, he now thought cynically. But I admired Anna, he thought. She had force and energy.

She had brought a copy of *Notable British Trials*, containing the Triangle Murder in Barrow Street. The Triangle was the name of the seedy nightclub-cum-gambling-parlour-cum-brothel that existed there in the mid nineteen fifties and sixties. (Certainly three angles to that place, Coffin had thought, as he read.) A couple of CID men were sitting there drinking when a masked man shouting abuse and waving a shotgun, with his two pals, burst in and aimed at the proprietor, Alby Hilter, who fell down with a bullet in his chest. He died later.

The masked man turned out to be an ex-copper with a grievance whom the CID men were obliged to identify and bear witness against.

It's different now, he thought, things were like that in the outfit then, which was probably one of the reasons I was brought in to the area, and I have cleared it all out. Although there might be one or two rattling nests I haven't got to yet.

He remembered that he had thought of those few weeks as a pleasant interlude, helping him through a bad time, and he had been grateful to Anna and those regular meetings in Barrow Street.

A nice easy relationship, not meaning too much to either party. No guilt involved, later he might tell Stella all about it and she would be humane and understanding. 'My dear,' she would say, 'life is like a war, you are entitled to your comfort.'

Stella, in fact, would never talk like that, her dialogue, honed through years of the best playwrights, was sharper.

Or more likely, he thought, taking another drink of coffee, she would have given me a swift blow and stalked out of the room. Not forever, his behaviour would not have rated that high in the range of life's misdemeanours, she would have been back.

Anyway, he hadn't told her. Or not yet. He trusted that the initials J.C. and the terrible offering on the steps of the house in Barrow Street were not a preview of what was to come.

He remembered the last time he had seen Anna.

She had called at the house in Barrow Street, spontaneously, unasked, when he was working. He had gone down to open the door himself, there was no one else, he had no servants. The house was kept clean by a commercial firm with whom he had not much contact.

An image of that last time came sweeping back from beneath the careful stones he had buried it under. Not a memory to keep on display.

She swayed through the door; she had long legs, and skirts were minimal that year, and tight as well.

Tucked under her arm, she had something long and thin, wrapped in silk. A very pretty pink and blue printed silk, Italian silk for sure.

'What have you got there?'

Without a word, Anna slowly unwrapped the silk. Inside was a whip.

'I thought policemen liked a touch of violence.'

Coffin was silent. Then he said – he remembered the words so clearly – 'That's been your experience, has it?'

She just smiled.

Coldly, he said: 'I don't think it would be an aphrodisiac for me. I doubt if it would bring me to the desired consummation.'

Anna looked at him for a long minute, with no expression on her face. Then, in a soft, gentle voice, she said:

'Pompous git.'

She swung round and made her exit, wrapping up the whip as she went.

'You're not worth a flick,' she threw over her shoulder as she closed the door behind her.

They never met again. He made cautious enquiries about her and knew that she had left her post on the local paper . . . or been sacked, stories varied, and disappeared. She might be around still, if so he did not know where. Just as well.

She couldn't come walking out of the past without her legs, he thought dryly.

He took another drink of coffee, which was still hot, so he could not have been far away in another world, another time, for long. Then he opened the file that Phoebe Astley had handed him and studied the medical report on the limbs found in Barrow Street.

You should go to your grave with all your limbs attached, he thought. But many didn't.

Sex: Female
Colour: White
Age: Between 25 yrs and 45 yrs

A bit of guesswork there, he thought.

Height: 5' 8"
Weight: Nine stone
Shoe size: 7
Hair on legs and arms: Light brown to ginger
Fingernails: bitten

A tall thin woman, probably a redhead, and large feet.

Anna had been tall but not thin; still, women changed, lost weight. A woman heading to the sort of death this woman had had, yes, she might well have lost weight.

She hadn't bitten her nails, nor dyed her hair, but who could tell what time and trouble did for you.

Identifying marks: 1. Scars on left wrist, possibly the result of
                        a suicide attempt
                     2. Damaged bone on left ankle
                     3. Scarring on the right leg
Blood Group: O

He hadn't known what blood group Anna was, but O was about the most common.

Drugs in blood: Desmethyl-Diazepam traces were found which
                 is a drug breakdown product from several
                 tranquillizers such as Cloraazepate (found in
                 Tramene) or Chlordiazpaxide (found in Librium
                 and Tropium) and Diazepam (found in Valium)

Anna might have been on drugs even then. These were all sedative-type drugs. Some of the details matched with Anna, but without the face, how could you be sure?

Neither of them had made any attempt to keep in touch. Coffin knew danger when he saw it and he had seen it then in Anna.

It was possible that the remains left on the steps in Barrow Street were those of Anna.

One of the three telephones on his desk rang, this was what he called his private line and was the only one which Stella used. She was careful, scrupulous even, about breaking into his working life.

Stella wasted no time. 'Darling . . .'

That meant business, it was the theatrical darling, meaning nothing, except here I come and I have a request to make.

'Yes?' Coffin was cautious.

'Robbie's very worried about his daughter. His stepdaughter, really, but he loves her and she took his name.'

'I gathered that last night.' Was it last night? No, it was a bit longer ago than that. He had been so deep in the past, that the present was hard to hold on to.

'Yes, but more worried . . . She's missing, really missing, not just playing. She hasn't got a very high IQ. Learning

44

difficulties, they call it, don't they? She's lovely to look at, by the way, a beautiful girl, but a simple soul. I had her working in the theatre, in the wardrobe and so on, that side of things, she did well enough while they kept it simple. Then she went off without a word. She's an innocent and he thinks she's in real trouble.'

'He can tell, can he?'

'He thinks so. He'd like your advice.'

'Well,' began Coffin.

'He's important to me.' She didn't say darling again, but it was there in her voice. 'And the limbs found on the house in Barrow Street . . . well, he's wondering if they could be his stepdaughter, Alice. That's her name . . . her mother married George Freedom next . . . not with him now.'

What a lot, Coffin thought. 'Where does the girl live and how long has she been missing?'

'She lives in a room her mother found for her in the Second City. She works three times a week. I gave her the job here. She is seventeen, and innocent.' Stella hesitated. 'That's one reason for worry, she may not be able to protect herself.'

'Stella, that unlucky woman was older and more battered than the young Gilchrist girl. It cannot be her.' Not if she was young and lovely.

'But, if there's a killer out there –'

He interrupted her.

'What is it you want?'

'Could you meet us for a drink in Max's, about six? We might eat there afterwards if you feel like it.' Max and his restaurant was the favoured eating place for those working in St Luke's Theatre Complex who could afford his prices, which had risen sharply in the last year. Max also ran the various bars and eating places in the three theatres.

Coffin, whose income had not risen as sharply as Max's prices, was thinking about it, when Stella said: 'My dinner.'

Stella, although out of work, was temporarily rich: the theatres were doing well, while a TV series she had done was endowing her with money for repeats from North America, Germany, Australia and from what Stella called the Monkey Islands. She used to complain that her TV series travelled much more than she did. A false complaint, since Stella hated to travel except in the greatest luxury.

'If I am going to be an expense item, I accept.'

'You are all right, are you, love?' This time the affection was genuine. 'You sound a bit strained.'

'Just the first days back at work.' And digging myself up. I may have a confession to make to you, Stella. 'And a rather tricky murder.'

A set of limbs, anyway, we have to assume the body and the murder.

'Don't, love,' said Stella solemnly. 'You are too important to worry about the odd murder.'

He laughed. He never felt important.

'You're uneasy, though, I can tell, and that means you are involving yourself. Take my advice: work out what is bugging you, find it, and then leave it. You don't need it.'

She put the telephone down gently.

'I need the face,' Coffin said aloud. 'Where is the head?'

Phoebe Astley was thinking this too. 'We had better find the head and quickly. If it's not in a freezer or such, it will be deteriorating rapidly. Wasn't there a killer who boiled the heads to keep them what he called "nice".'

She was having a conference with Chief Superintendent Young, if you could call their conversation such: she was tacitly seeking support and advice from this so much more senior figure. They were meeting in his office, which was tidy and very neat, with a potted plant, small and tidy too, on his desk. She thought his wife had provided the dark blue primula. Her own office was not tidy.

'That was Dennis Nilsen,' said Archie Young. 'I believe he did cook bits of bodies, but I don't know about heads. I should think the hair might make a difficulty there.'

Phoebe, who had dropped her observation in to see how Archie reacted (she knew that immensely experienced and tough as he was, he still had his squeamish side), had to admit that he had capped her.

'How are we going to give her a name? Fingerprints?'

'I don't think so. Not unless she has a record and even

then . . .' He said no more. No need. The computer might go through all the fingerprints of all the females with criminal convictions, but even that would take time. Could be done, no doubt.

'No,' he said. 'We need her doctor. With all those drugs inside her, she was on someone's list. We just have to send out a letter to all GPs in the locality of Barrow Street and hope one of them holds up his hand.'

'Yes,' Phoebe sighed. 'We've already started on that, of course. Tony Davley is in charge of that operation.'

Sergeant Antonia Davley was an up-and-coming young officer whom Phoebe liked. She had accepted the task of checking on all local doctors and hospital clinics without pleasure, but determined to do her best. She had sent a circular letter out. She was assisted by one detective constable who kept pointing out how hopeless it was.

'And any of the women who have stayed in the Serena Seddon House who have the initials J.C. Or anything like it: J.G., I.C., or even just a J or just a C.'

'You're joking there, I suppose.'

'Not a joke in me . . . and going back before it was the Serena Seddon Refuge House,' Archie Young went on.

'Agreed,' said Phoebe sadly.

She brightened a bit. 'She was a great drinker, Lady Serena, did you know that? A real toper.'

'How do you know?'

'My mother knew her, their paths crossed during the war. Both at Bletchley. Didn't drink there, of course, but she did when she got out. Relief from tension, I suppose. It's why she left her money to found a refuge. She saw she could go that way. Never married herself, but got beaten up once or twice.'

'I never know when you are inventing things,' said an exasperated Archie Young.

Phoebe left his office laughing. On the way out she rubbed the leaves of the primula between her fingers and discovered that it was plastic. That settled the question: Adelaide Young was not the sort of woman to buy plastic flowers: Archie had bought it for himself.

And that in itself raised an interesting question about the sort of man who would buy a plastic flower.

She looked back at him almost with sympathy. Come on, Archie, life is real, not plastic.

But as she ran up the stairs to her office (only the very top brass like Archie had their office lower down) she reflected that if anyone knew the world wasn't plastic it was Archie Young. Think of the cases he had tackled: the Sacker murders, a whole troop of dead children; the arsonist of Perill Lane, and the woman who . . . No, bury the memory of that one, she killed herself in the end, God help her, if there was a God.

The telephone was ringing in her room, she considered ignoring it, but decided against it. Experience had taught her that messages always get through if they bring bad news and only the good-news ones get lost on the way.

Hard to be sure which the call was, she thought as she heard John Coffin's voice.

'Phoebe, I want you to come to dinner tonight.'

'Thank you, sir.' She liked him, always had done; she liked Stella, but it was a working relationship, an odd drink but no dinner invitations.

'I have a missing-girl problem wished on me. Daughter of a friend of Stella. I can't do anything myself, but you come and hear and see if you think there is anything in it. Then hand it on.'

'Can you tell me any details now, sir.'

'Daughter of a man called Robbie Gilchrist.'

'Oh yes. I met him in connection with the Georgie Freedom case. I had to ask him a few questions.' Didn't like him but preferred him to Freedom who struck me as violent when he fancied to be. And he had made a snarling reference to the Chief Commander. 'Did you ever get across Freedom? I don't think he loves you, sir.'

Coffin searched his memory. 'Sure he doesn't, now you mention it. I tried to get him for trading in drugs. Didn't stick though. I'd forgotten.'

'Right, sir.' Watch your back, she felt like saying.

'The girl's name is Alice,' went on Coffin. 'He's divorced

from her mother but kept in touch. More or less. That's about all I know at the moment.'

'Age or anything?'

'Only seventeen.' But her stepfather had seemed vague, not the type of man to be sure about his daughter's age.

'Get me a report on Gilchrist and Freedom. Don't leave him out. Check, as tactfully and quietly as you can, where they both were over the last forty-eight hours and the period before . . .' For some of it, they had been at dinner with him, but never mind that.

'Yes, sir.'

'I don't like their attitude, jointly or singly, to a missing seventeen-year-old.'

Not likely to have provided the legs and arms on the doorstep of the Serena Seddon Refuge, then.

But certainly responsible for the edginess in the Chief Commander's voice. He was worried about missing women and who could blame him?

He knew that when he lived in the house in Barrow Street he had had a brief affair with a woman journalist.

And knowing his fellow members of the Second City Force, he also knew that they knew about Anna Michael.

Even as Phoebe was talking to him, a message was building itself up on the screen in front of her.

The handbag found near to the package of limbs held a bloodstained photograph of John Coffin in an inner pocket. It had been cut from a newspaper, as yet unidentified, and was several years old. It was ragged and torn as if it had been about a bit, and only two-thirds of the Chief Commander's face was there, but he was easily recognizable.

He's not going to like that, thought Phoebe.

4

Coffin did not like it, but he was not one to run away in the face of trouble. On the second day back at work and after some thought, word having got around to him about exactly what had rested on the doorstep of Serena Seddon House, he had insisted that Phoebe Astley and Archie Young give him the complete record of what they had. The word complete carried an emphasis. He suspected that there was more than the first file had shown him.

And there was: a photograph of a smiling man with blood on his face. Not his own blood.

Blood from who knew whom?

The chief superintendent was occupied with checking the arrangements for a visit from the Russian Head of State. 'Asked to see a Dickensian relic, some old workhouse or other that was knocked down when the motorway went through,' he had muttered to Phoebe. 'You go to see the Chief on your own and let me get on with this.'

'You could take him to see the section house where I stayed for a night when I first came down from Birmingham, that was Victorian enough.'

'I think they built that into the motorway . . . there's something that looks very like it under exit two, only I think it's a public lavatory now. No, you get off and handle the Chief carefully. I bet he's twitchy about this. I would be.'

Phoebe sighed. It was the morning shift and she was as well-groomed as usual. She wore very little make-up, but in the morning she applied a bright-red lipstick; as the day went on, it wore off. She was tall with a crop of dark hair which she kept well-cut. Amazed as she shot up to nearly six feet in her teens, she had then decided that the only career for her would be in the police. Or is this what she said?

'Do you think he is fit enough to come back?'

'Probably not. But that wouldn't stop him. I've worked with him long enough to know that much.' He added thoughtfully: 'He knows how to make a good entrance, and, if he had to, he'd know how to make a good exit.'

'I don't like the sound of that.'

'Just go off, Inspector Astley.'

So Phoebe had made the chief superintendent's excuses and arrived with the folder of reports herself. She did so without comment. He could work out what they thought for himself.

He raised his head from the file of papers to look Phoebe in the face. She had dined with them last night to meet Gilchrist and listen to his tale of woe.

'Before we talk over the limbs on the step in Barrow Street, let's clear the ground of extras.'

Phoebe nodded.

'There's this missing girl, Alice Gilchrist. What do you make of it? You've heard what Gilchrist had to say, let him talk to you. As you saw, there is this worry that the limbs might be hers. We both had to spend some hours yesterday evening listening to him tell all about it. We both know that is rubbish: the dead woman, whosoever, is not a girl called Alice.'

Phoebe shrugged. 'Alice is in her late teens. Pretty, although a bit retarded, yet lively, if the picture her dad showed us is anything to go by. She's gone off with a boyfriend, that is my guess.'

'Seventeen,' said Coffin thoughtfully. 'About the right age, I suppose, to cut and run. Felt like doing it myself.' In a way, he had actually done it, but he had not had much of a home to run from, and his mother had gone first.

Phoebe nodded without speaking. In her experience, missing adolescents either came home or got in touch with their parents in the end. The days when they came home with a crying bundle in their arms were gone, but they might come back with a drug habit to be serviced. She had no illusions.

'Yes, not one for you,' said Coffin. Missing babies and

children were looked for and usually found, but if all the adolescents who took themselves off were searched for, then the police forces of the whole kingdom would have time for little else. 'But add her name to the register, and I will explain to Gilchrist.'

'The wine was good,' said Phoebe. 'Did you think that he cared one way or another? It sounded as though the pressure was coming from the mother.'

'He's a selfish bastard.'

It had been a good meal which Phoebe had enjoyed, somewhat to her surprise. Stella was a skilful hostess, choosing food and wine which pleased her guests while bearing in mind that one guest was worried. Or claimed to be.

To her surprise, considering he was a humped, complaining figure, seated across the table from her and swigging the wine like water, she had liked Robbie Gilchrist.

Meeting Stella's eyes, Phoebe recognized that she too felt the strong sexual charge emanating from Robbie Gilchrist. Without doubt, the Chief Commander picked up all these vibes too. His face was expressionless, a faint smile occasionally crossing his lips.

He was running over in his mind the report on both Robbie and George Freedom.

Because of the shortage of men and money, the report was short: on the night in question both men had been at a club in the Second City called Empire. It was on the site of a long bombed and gone (but fondly remembered) old cinema. It was respectable enough on the surface and doubtful underneath. Sex is its game, said the report.

Both men *could* have come and gone, picking up chopped-off limbs, and depositing them. *Could*. It was hard to be sure.

No one was in the position to say that they had done.

Coffin eyed Gilchrist with some cynicism and possibly suspicion. 'Like it to be you, chum, but is it?'

'Glad you enjoyed the wine,' he said.

Was there a faint note of irony there? Phoebe had drunk deep and merrily last night, which Coffin had certainly noticed. I wasn't drunk, though, she said fiercely to herself.

He went on: 'There may be a case to be investigated there, I don't know yet, but in any case, it won't be for you. I had a word last night with Gilchrist and he is going to use a private investigator.'

'Which one?'

In the Second City there were several outfits, some respectable and others not.

'He had used Fraber and Shrewsbury for his divorce and will use them again.'

Phoebe knew Geoff Fraber from her Birmingham days, he had been a good copper and a hard-working if not a clever detective.

'He could do worse – Geoff Fraber will peg away at it and get somewhere if anyone can. Depends if the girl wants to be found, some do and some don't. She may not be one of the easy ones.' Phoebe ran over the details of what the father had said. 'Did it strike you that there might be an element of self-hurt here? All those accidents, the slashed arm, the cut artery, that they might have been self-inflicted?'

'It did cross my mind.'

'In that case, she needs help because she might move on to suicide. Self-damage is often a substitute for suicide.'

Coffin took a pace up and down the room. The dog, who was with him that morning, looked up in alarm. 'I daresay Gilchrist has thought of this, he's not a fool. But it is not our problem. We have plenty of others.' He patted the file on his desk.

'There is something I have to say, possibly contribute to this other bloody business.'

Phoebe gave him a sympathetic smile and decided that silence was the best option.

'You know that I lived in that house once . . . it was very different from what it is now. I had a few sticks of furniture in it, not much, because St Luke's Tower was already being made ready for us, and Stella was busy with the first theatre . . . she's done well since that beginning.'

'Very well,' agreed Phoebe. She fed him the next line in the script. 'It must have been a difficult time for you, though, sir.'

'Lonely. I'd come from the other side of the Thames, didn't really know anyone here, and Stella was away a lot setting up the business side.' He smiled. 'I nearly went back home. Only I didn't have a home. Living in that house in Barrow Street did not promote home-making.'

'It does well now as the Serena Seddon Refuge. The warden, Mary, does a good job.' Phoebe tried for the bland, neutral answer.

'And now my name seems to be associated with the place once more.'

'Only guesswork, sir.'

'And my face,' said Coffin grimly. 'On a newspaper cutting in an empty handbag.'

'I didn't think it meant much, sir.' A lie, she had wondered, debated, and thought, Yes, it must mean something.

'Nevertheless, it was there in the file, you wanted me to see it. With blood on it.'

Phoebe protested. 'We thought you ought to see it.'

'And who's we?' He knew the answer to that one: all the bloody Second City Force. Grinning all over their faces and avid for the next instalment of the soap.

'No one's laughing, sir,' said Phoebe with dignity. And some truth: a lot of interest, some look in the eye that might be a laugh if it ever got out, but no more.

'Who is in charge of the case?'

'I am in overall charge. With Inspector Brownlow and Sergeant Davley. It's all in there.' She nodded towards the file.

– I am going to have to tell her this before I tell Stella, Coffin told himself, and it's the wrong way round. But here I can give her a strictly edited version, knowing she will read between the lines with that tact the police are noted for.

But Stella will want the whole thing spelt out. She won't need it done because she is very good at jumping to the right conclusions, but she will give herself the pleasure of watching me as I spell it all out.

'When I was living there in Barrow Street, I was interviewed by a young journalist on the local paper. Anna Michael. I liked her. We became friends. She came to the house once or twice. I took her out to dinner. Max wasn't open then. Before his day.'

I hate apologizing, he told himself, especially to Stella. I hate admitting that I was in the wrong.

Usually with Stella, I have managed to avoid it. Been grouchy, shifty and shuffled away.

I am not proud of this.

Perhaps he was overdoing the wallowing in guilt bit, but it seemed right to feel churlish.

Phoebe Astley was still staring at him. 'You said something but I didn't hear, sir.'

'I think I was talking to myself.' A sudden pain on the site of the old injury made him draw in his breath.

Phoebe saw it. 'Are you all right, sir?'

'Yes, just memory of where the knife went in. Pain's like that. Gets you when you don't expect it.'

'You went a bit white . . .' She stood up. 'Can I get you something? A drink?'

'Nothing. Sit down. I want to tell you something.'

Phoebe sat down obediently.

'The young journalist.' The one who took my fancy, he said to himself. 'Anna Michael was not her name, just her writing name. She was Joanna Carmichael. J.C.'

Phoebe stood up again. Whereas just now the Chief Commander had gone white, now a blotchy red was creeping up his face. 'I don't think you are well, sir. You shouldn't have come to work today.'

Coffin ignored her. 'Did you hear what I said? J.C., her initials. Her real initials. Joanna Carmichael. I think the limbs may be hers.'

'I suppose it's possible, sir.' Privately, she thought the Chief Commander was having a kind of fantasy fit.

'I want to see the limbs.'

DCI Astley was not the only one who thought the Chief Commander had come back to his office too soon.

Stella Pinero was even more anxious. She was worried about him, worried about their relationship. She had never seen him quite so troubled as he was now over what she called crossly, 'Bloody Barrow Street.'

She knew the Serena Seddon Refuge to which she had donated money. When it was setting up, the St Luke's Theatre Company had given a special performance of Michael Frayn's *Noises Off* (always a crowd-puller) to help raise money. Stella herself had performed in it.

On this occasion she had met Mary Arden and thought her pretty and gentle, possibly too gentle for the disturbed and distressed women she would have to live with. Not to mention the husbands who would certainly be both disturbing and probably violent.

I'd be better at it, she had thought. I mean, when you have coped with a cast of performers all rampantly enjoying one form of sex or another (she was thinking of the cast of *Major Barbara* which she had just produced . . . It was surprising how sexy Shaw was when you came up against him), then you can cope with almost everything.

Mary Arden's assistant she knew better because Evelyn's husband worked in the theatre, a nice brawny lad with curly hair. A bit younger than his wife, Stella assessed.

He had found an opportunity to talk to her about the limbs deposited on the Serena Seddon Refuge. His wife was upset, he said, and all the present residents were, as he put it 'on the twitch'.

'Must be a woman with some connection with the house, you see, Miss Pinero, and that makes them nervous. For themselves, each and every one having a close experience of violence. Her now, one of us next, that's how they reason. And I've had the kid, Alice Gilchrist, she used that name, working for me. A nice girl, if simple, she's off. It's worrying. You can understand it.'

Stella agreed that you could, but put in the proviso that the police would be watching the house and protecting the women in it.

'The warden thinks the limbs belong to a girl who used to live there . . . Helped run the place, I think, not a battered wife. French girl, Henriette. Etta, they called her. Supposed to have gone back home, but did she?'

'Has she told the police?'

Peter was vague, he didn't know, might have mentioned it.

'Why does Miss Arden think it's this girl Etta?'

'She hasn't heard from her and she believes she would have done. Or ought to have done. But someone else was saying that she'd seen Etta around the town, and with a rough crowd.'

Stella gave the firm advice that either Miss Arden or his wife ought to tell all this to the police if they were really worried.

She walked away, thinking that gossip must be all over the town. A juicy case.

Some houses attracted violence, she thought. Wasn't there a local story that Jack the Ripper had lived there? It wasn't a place she had liked during the short time it had been the Chief Commander's living quarters.

She had kept out of it as much as she could do, leaving him alone there. Looking back, he must have been lonely.

She tidied up her office in the theatre, taking some work back with her to the tower so that she could let in Arthur and Dave, and then stay while they did their two-hour stint. Stella felt she did not yet know them well enough to hand over the keys and tell them how the security worked.

They were just arriving as she got to the door so they all went in together. Stella worked in the sitting room while they cleaned upstairs, then, when they were ready to dust and polish the sitting room, she moved up to her bedroom.

She could hear them talking as they worked, it seemed to be Dave doing most of the talking. As she came down to the kitchen to get a drink of water, she met him polishing the taps.

He looked at her with a smile. He seemed to wear a light layer of dust over his face and his hair, greying him down like a statue that had been kept in the attic.

A good-looking man underneath it all, with those interesting grooves on his face.

'You don't remember me, Miss Pinero.'

She did remember him, memories can go and then come back.

'I was with you when you were just setting up the theatre . . . I was only a general kind of dogsbody, not surprising you don't remember me. I hoped I might get a foothold on the acting side. I played young middle age then, but it didn't work out.'

'I'm sorry.'

'I get by. Do a bit of TV as it comes along. Play older types now, *The Bill* and *Corrie* and the odd documentary. If they want a real street figure or an old market man, they call on me.'

'Or a dustman,' Stella thought. 'What about your colleague?'

'Arthur? Oh, he has his ups and downs like all of us. Went up for a part, good one too, in a radio soap . . . he does a beautiful kid's voice, you should hear his baby crying . . . lost it, though, because he wouldn't do a baby screaming . . . said he daren't, it might ruin his voice.'

Stella wasn't sure if she believed Dave. Behind the dust, it was possible there was a laugh.

Arthur appeared at the door. 'Finished the kitchen, Dave?' He didn't wait for an answer but started to check his cleaning equipment – part Stella's, part they brought with them. 'Let's be off then. Morning, Miss Pinero.'

It was his beautiful voice that had persuaded Stella to hire the cleaning team, although their prices were high.

'Look after your voice,' she called as they prepared to depart. He gave her a surprised look. 'I'm working on it, Miss Pinero, trying to deepen the tones, get more richness.' He smiled. 'Covent Garden, here I come.'

Soon she heard them leaving, dustman and hopeful opera singer, climbing into the van, with Dave still talking and Arthur listening. He was wearing a hat now, a dark felt with a big brim.

'Did you tell her about the new murder?'

Dave shook his head. 'No.'

'Why not?'

'She doesn't collect murders. Nor do we. Besides, you don't know the woman was dead.'

'I bet she was,' said Arthur. 'She dropped like a stone.

58

Dead gone, sure of it. You couldn't see. I was in the van. You weren't. Where the hell were you? That was a long shit!'

'And what were *you* doing? Didn't let the police know.'

'I was parked illegally,' said Arthur. 'Besides, the man in the PO Telephone van rushed to do it. Not my business.'

Arthur took his hands off the wheel to adjust the hat in the car mirror and wave to Stella. There was no doubt, she thought, that a touch of madness helped in the entertainment world.

Perhaps that was what was the matter with her and Coffin: they were not mad enough.

But no, she knew that wasn't the trouble, there was an unease between them at the moment which she couldn't account for.

Not my fault, she thought.

'Do you want to go alone, sir, or shall I come with you?' asked Phoebe Astley.

'I'm not a child, this isn't a trip to the park,' said Coffin irritably.

The chief inspector took this for a kind of backhanded permission, which suited her as she intended to go with the Chief Commander anyway. He was the boss figure and entitled to look in at whatever he chose, but it was her case too. In the end, she would be responsible for what happened or didn't happen. She admired and respected Coffin, but she had her own career to consider.

The limbs were in the care, if you could call it that, of the Pathology Department of the Second City University Hospital.

'Slung in a refrigerator and waiting for Dennis Garden to give tongue,' as Archie Young had said sardonically. He was no friend of Professor Garden. Socially and intellectually, they lived in different worlds. Archie did not admire the carefully chosen blue and pink shirts from Jermyn Street with matching ties, nor the equally carefully chosen band of young men with whom he consorted. The professor's technical skills he respected.

But the new laboratories for which Garden had fought

several successful wars in favour of dead persons getting the best, Archie Young, no mean fender-off of cutbacks, did admire. The Second City Police Forensic Unit was first class, Coffin had seen to that, and it maintained a small pathology group, but for anything major then it called on the University Hospital and Dennis Garden.

'Been in here, sir, since it was rebuilt?' asked Phoebe as she led the way into the gleaming, sterile, antiseptic new laboratories.

Coffin had to admit that he had not. 'Was invited to the grand opening but I couldn't go. Stella went and said that there was more champagne than seemed decent in the presence of so many dead.'

Phoebe had been there herself – one of our best customers, Garden had said – and had heard Stella Pinero say something on the lines Coffin reported, and had heard Garden say: 'Not all dead, I have a few bits and pieces of people who are just dying.' You couldn't best Garden, Phoebe had thought.

The great man was not to be seen, having been drawn away to an important committee in London, but his assistant Dr Driver was on hand.

He was talking to a tall, pretty woman who held herself very straight.

'That's Mary Arden,' said Phoebe Astley. 'Now why is she here?'

'Pretty obvious. To see the limbs. To identify them. Did you ask her to come?'

Phoebe shook her head. 'Certainly not. She wouldn't be on her own, I'd have sent someone with her. I was thinking of getting her in, but Davley was off on something else.' Which had seemed more urgent.

'What's Sergeant Davley doing?'

'Checking the local doctors . . . as far as we can without a name, but the owner of the limbs must have been on someone's list.'

'Is there any chance Mary Arden could make an identification?'

Phoebe shrugged. 'Who knows? She was worried that the

limbs belonged to a girl who worked in the house. Etta, she called her. But those legs belonged to no girl.'

Coffin was watching Mary Arden, who was shaking the doctor's hand and turning towards the door. 'She's leaving. Better talk to her.'

'She's seen us,' said Phoebe. 'And doesn't want to talk. I'll get her though.'

This she did, walking towards Mary Arden with the question on her lips.

'It wasn't Etta, was it?'

'He wouldn't let me see the legs and arms. Just showed me a photograph.'

'That was good enough, wasn't it?'

'I don't know . . . the real flesh . . .' She shook her head. 'One might get a different impression . . . Colour, feeling.' Mary Arden seemed genuinely anxious.

Phoebe reassured her. 'Can't be Etta, wrong age.' Even as she said it, she thought, this girl Etta might just fit the younger age estimate, girls do get into trouble, disappear, or worse, but she persevered: 'Wrong life history from what one can tell. I think it's brave of you to want to see those limbs. You are really worried, aren't you?'

'They were left on the doorstep of the house I live in and run as a refuge for women who are sheltering with me from violence. Of course I am worried, I am worried about Etta. She left, she has never been in touch with me as she promised and she has been seen around the town.'

'I'd get off home if I were you.'

'Home? The Serena Seddon Refuge? Do you know what it is like now? My poor residents whom I am supposed to be helping are worried because of what turned up on the doorstep. Each and every one thinks they will be next.'

Her eyes flicked across to where Coffin stood talking to the young doctor.

'Who's that with you?'

Phoebe did not answer.

'Another policeman? He's got the look.' Mary began to move away. 'Who is he? I fancy I have seen him before.'

Again Phoebe did not answer.

'Or are you arresting him? Could be, he has that drawn look about the eyes. Rather attractive.'

Still no answer, and Phoebe could see that Coffin, although still talking politely to the doctor, was growing restive.

'Oh, you're right,' said Mary Arden. 'I did have a very strong vodka and tonic – that's the chosen tipple in the Serena establishment – before leaving home . . . to strengthen me to look at the legs but much good it did me . . . I will go home.' She was gone, with a brave wave of the hand.

'What was all that about?' Coffin asked as Phoebe came back.

Do you say to your boss: She thinks you look haggard but attractive? Also a likely criminal. Phoebe thought not.

'She wanted to view the limbs, she was shown a photograph which failed to click with her.'

'That was a long talk about nothing.'

Can he lip read? Phoebe asked herself. 'She's upset.'

The young doctor had disappeared through one of the shining glass and chrome doors. The old pathology rooms had been dark brown with dim unpolished floors. Coffin, an occasional visitor, had thought it suitable for death, polite and quiet, but the new atmosphere was bright and brash and highly sterile, which he had to admit, the old place probably had not been, although it had always smelt strongly of disinfectants which yet failed to mask other deeper, darker, more intimidating smells.

All gone now, there were even pictures on the walls of the corridor down which Phoebe was leading him. Although to be fair to Professor Garden, they were photographs of interesting autopsies and specially selected corpses, with here and there a greatly enlarged mordant eye or a scrap of malignant tissue.

Lessons in mortality all the way along, thought Coffin. A learning experience every step of the corridor with a desiccated adult body placed next to a tiny, mummified foetus. Even just a hint of Garden's sense of humour.

Once out of the corridor, through the anteroom and into the working area, the atmosphere changed.

Here inside was all clinical with almost an industrial feel to the tables, with running water draining down into large chrome apertures, and wall cabinets with their freezing drawers.

Coffin nodded to the white-coated pathologist standing by the cabinets.

A figure clad from head to foot in white, booted in white and wearing gloves, came up to him. He was carrying a neat camera.

'DC Rodders, sir. I'm here on orders from the chief super to get some photographs.'

Why? thought Coffin with irritation. Archie Young could be a nuisance sometimes. Photographs, photographs.

The irritation came out. 'Why the hell are you gowned up like that?'

'Against infection, sir,' said a pained voice behind the masking.

'She didn't die of AIDS, you fool.'

DC Rodders may have blushed behind his screens but he said nothing, and muttering that he had the photographs, he retreated. Walking backwards.

As if I was the Queen or the Pope, thought a still irritated Coffin.

He turned to the pathologist, patiently waiting for him.

The young pathologist – and he was very young, since Professor Garden always employed the youngest graduates as being on a low salary scale and also likely to move on, he liked a turnover of young men – this particular one being very left wing, did not approve of the police. He had nothing personal against DCI Astley and the Chief Commander, except that the latter had a very successful wife and was therefore too rich. (On which point Coffin, who had the usual quota of overdraft and mortgage debts since his church tower home, while charming to live in, had been expensive both to convert and run, could have enlightened him.)

A drawer was pulled out.

Inside, as if nesting, were two legs.

No one spoke as Coffin walked over to take a closer look. He bent over the drawer, not touching the limbs, but studying them intently.

He could see there was a damaged bone on the left ankle,

63

from which radiated a scar, deep and red, running up the calf.

The right leg was also scarred with what looked like the pucker remains of a burn.

He nodded.

'Turn them, please.'

The backs of the legs were smooth and unscarred. 'No one kicked her there, anyway.'

'She didn't shave her legs,' said Phoebe.

'Yes, I noticed that. Light brown to ginger, the hairs.'

The bones of the legs were fine and slender; whoever she was, she had good legs. He felt a sense of grief as he looked down on them.

'May I see the arms, please?'

The arms were stretched out with the hands reaching for each other, a grasp they were destined never to make.

Hands can tell you more about a person than legs and feet. Hands are the tools which dragged men up the trees and out of them, making a world. Not a perfect world by any means but better than crawling in the mud round the dinosaurs' feet.

The hands of this woman had worked hard, breaking the nails, and leaving many scars of cuts on the fingers.

What had she been, he asked himself, a cook, a butcher?

On the arms were signs of injections. So she had been on drugs.

'On them for years,' said the knowledgeable Phoebe.

'Yes, sure.'

'Signs in the blood too. We knew about that so no surprise.'

Coffin found himself wanting to reach out to the right hand to see if he remembered the touch.

But you didn't do that sort of thing because, apart from anything else, it was frozen. Cold, heavy and hard.

He nodded to the pathologist. 'Thank you. I've seen all I need.'

As they walked towards the car, he said: 'No identification. I need to see the head.

'Phoebe: I want you to find out what happened to Anna

Michael; try the local paper first. Do you know anyone there?'

'I know the editor, but he hasn't been there long.'

'See what you can do.'

Phoebe said she would do her best.

– And perhaps I will come back with that head that is worrying you, and it will still be on its neck and shoulders, not dead at all, but a big success and editing a mag or paper somewhere, or else on TV.

It was so like a man, she thought, to believe that any rejected woman must end up dead.

5

Coffin wanted the head, as did several other people, including Phoebe Astley, the pathologist, and the funerian (no burial without the head) and he was soon to discover that, with a celebrated writer, heads do talk.

If you can hear the voice.

The word went round the investigating unit like a chant: He wants the head.

But, Coffin wonders, if they find the head, will it come complete with the trunk?

For obvious reasons, he flinched from a view of that trunk. He reassured himself with the conviction that those legs could not be those of the young Anna he had known so briefly. The initials J.C. were a joke, or a coincidence. Nothing to do with him or any past relationship.

But what about the bloodstained picture of himself – himself, and no other?

Curse it, he thought. Thank goodness, as far as he knew, Stella was not aware of all this.

But there was an alarming gentleness and sympathy in her manner to him lately which he had put down to wifely affection after the stabbing he had suffered. But now he wondered. And at the back of her eyes there was a hint of something he liked even less: amusement. And with Stella being such a good actress, if there was anything in her eyes to be read, then she meant you to see it.

He was not something to laugh at, was he?

He was not a proud man, he said to himself in the looking glass as he shaved that morning, but he had the natural sensitivity of any male to being laughed at by his wife.

By anyone really, but especially by her.

He gave a slight shiver – feeling the cold since the op, he told himself. But no, distantly, quietly, he could hear the ancient, archaic gods laughing at him from beyond the river and above the clouds.

Perhaps he ought to learn to laugh at himself.

Phoebe Astley was tired and tense, she had more than one case that she was nursing, and the affair of the legs and arms came to be like a film which she was watching and yet taking part.

She seemed outside it and yet of it.

Chief Inspector Phoebe Astley would like the trunk and the head to be found so that the case could be wound up, but she fears neither will be found. Ever.

Either would do, she says to herself.

Meanwhile, she had used her friendship with the editor of the *Second City Chronicle* to ask him if he could find a trace of Anna Michael, once a journalist on his paper. It's thought she went to work on a London paper, possibly the *Independent*.

In spite of his protests that he was a new chap here and did she know what he had on his desk, Phoebe called in a few of the favours she had done him (most notably in where and how he parked his motorbike), and he agreed to try. First reminding her when, taken as her guest to the annual Second City Police Ball, he had held her back when she had wanted to rush to the Chief Commander to offer to go to bed with him. And shepherded her, drunk as a lady, back to her car and driven her 'ome . . . He was a professional cockney.

Some hours later, he called back to say, Yes, Anna had gone to a London paper, thought to be the *Independent*, had worked there for over a year, and then left.

It was thought she had come back to the Second City. 'Over to you, love,' was his message to Phoebe, received with a grinding of teeth.

On the streets, as many officers as could be spared were searching open ground, empty buildings, old factories and warehouses (not so many of these, most have suffered conversion into smart apartments), along the railway embankment.

Nothing had been found relating to the limbs deposited on the house in Barrow Street, although one or two items had surfaced which related to earlier crimes. Such as the old mailbag, a relic of a PO robbery, and a cache of silver, small stuff but pretty, in a tin box in a dustbin down by the docks, a theft from somewhere. An antique shop, maybe, was the suggestion and Henry Hemmings, their antiques expert, was being consulted.

We just need a tip-off, thinks DCI Astley. A hint, just a something, to get us going.

Better give Tony Davley a prod, time she came up with something.

Before doing so, however, she telephoned the Chief Commander to tell him what she had learnt of Anna Michael's career.

'I think she did come back,' said Coffin. 'Thanks for finding out.'

No result had come from the questioning of the residents of the Serena Seddon Refuge House. All had been asked but not one of them had any useful ideas other than those handed around already. Mary had come back to report that she did not, could not, believe the limbs to be those of Henriette, known as Etta. One by one the women relaxed and settled down to their usual occupations. In some cases, of course, this meant a quarrel over the cards as they played whist – a particularly cutthroat version of the game with their own rules. Not much money changed hands because no one had much, but the feeling was intense. Miriam Beetham and Ally Carver could be relied upon to row, but they had met their equal in a new arrival, Mrs Ellen Newbattle, who was not badly named.

'She's a cow, that woman,' said Ally with admiration. 'What a tongue on her.'

'She'll be gone soon, she's not a stayer, you can tell.'

'Not like us, eh? We know the ropes.'

'Aye, and where to pull on them.'

It was a shifting population in which Miriam and Ally were the old residents. There was a housing association, part of the Serena Seddon establishment, which owned properties into which residents could move. If they so chose – some houses were less popular than others.

'We're a full house now,' said Ally. She had turned down the offer of a flat in Bellhanger Road as 'slummy', and was waiting for one to come in Cheeseborough Place which was more upmarket.

'Joan Benson upstairs is going,' said Miriam, who was always first with the news, because she listened to all telephone calls and read everyone's letters. 'She's going to Bellhanger, the one you turned down.'

'She's welcome. They say they've got rats the size of rabbits there.'

One family was on the point of being rehoused and another was arranging to go to stay with Grandma.

'And I hope Grandma will be pleased,' was Evelyn's comment to Mary, even as she set up the travel arrangements, 'because they are a difficult bunch. D'you know, Mrs Addington asked me if they could travel first class because of the cat.'

'I didn't know they had a cat.'

'It's been living with the old neighbours . . . I bet it would prefer to stay there. I pity Grandma, if the cat's as fertile as Mrs Addington.'

Mary agreed absently and said that it wouldn't last long but was worth a try. She is busy catching up with business, checking the bank accounts, paying bills, and then working in the kitchen.

'You know the police went over the house for drugs while they were here.'

A police call on the Serena Seddon House was not unusual. Things just happened; vandals breaking windows or pouring paint down the basement, the lost and drunk trying to break in, the man from Glasgow who thought it was a brothel and would not be turned away; the police took their chance and had a quick look round. After all, some of the residents were old acquaintances with interesting pasts.

'They usually do.'

'Pretended it was just a routine check-up, but I knew.'

'As long as they didn't find anything.'

'We've been lucky,' said Mary. 'The worst trouble was when Serena herself was warden, she really fell for that girl who was on heroin.'

'On anything that went,' said Evelyn. Both women had worked in the hostel with Serena. In the end, Serena had been losing her grip. 'She was dead attractive, that girl, Phyllis something, poor Serena couldn't resist her. She was lucky when Phyllis moved on. She's still around and not so lovely. Drossers Market is where she hangs out.'

Drossers Market was the real, dirty centre of drugs, prostitution and violence in the Second City. Coffin was trying to clear it up. But it was also lively, and attractive to many, which made the task harder. Nor was he quite sure of some of his own officers. One or two names were in the frame and being watched. DC Radley, from the Met, and PC Ryman-Lawson of the uniformed lot. Nothing proved, and there might be others.

Mary shrugged her acceptance; Serena's sexual tastes were well known to her. But she wouldn't dwell on the past, she knows that in her office, the answer machine is flashing its little red light. Mary hates attending to the answerphone since it always means more work.

Let it wait.

'She was standing up and suddenly she dropped like a stone.'

'Dead,' said the gravelly voice.

'Dead in the middle of the car park on Vestey Road and no one there.'

'Who said?' asked a sceptical Tony Davley. She was supposed to be following what leads she had on the limbs affair – precious few, as it happened, and she shouldn't be dealing with this business, but she had been unlucky enough to be around in the office when the message about the killing came in so she got it.

She had come in early to clear up some notes left over from last night, she had been standing there drinking a mug of lukewarm coffee as breakfast and mulling over some of her own writing which she could not read, when the phone went and her immediate boss, Sergeant Jimmy Silver, took the message, nodded at her and said, You might as well take this one as you are here.

That was how life went: you got the jobs by standing around and being there. It was taken for granted that you not only could but would work on two investigations at once and not get them muddled.

But she had to admit that this one was not without interest. In short, she did not realize that what she had got was a snip.

'I said' – the voice was firm, putting a firm underlining beneath the *I* – 'I telephoned for the ambulance and the police.'

He repeated the story. There was a van there which drove away fast, and there was a Post Office van which stayed. This was his van.

He was a short and sturdy figure with a crop of dark curly hair. Bright blue eyes behind spectacles took in DS Davley and flicked round to the scene behind her where the body of a woman lay on the ground.

The police surgeon had arrived and certified her dead, and the pathologist was this moment making a careful, preliminary investigation before taking the body off to his laboratory for a closer investigation.

It was murder and not suicide, that was clear.

'So there was someone there: the other van, the one that drove away fast, and your van.'

'Now don't you start griping at me, miss. I waited there till the ambulance came, but she was dead. I knew she was. And I knew she was shot.'

'How did you know?'

'I heard the noise and I saw the blood on the side of her face.'

'And you didn't see who shot her?'

'No, sorry.'

'What about the van that drove off?'

'Wasn't from the van. I had my eye on it because it shouldn't have been here. I am allowed to bring my van in

71

because it is PO business, but otherwise private vehicles only.'

'Well, thank you, Mr . . .' She hesitated.

'Terry Jones.'

'You'll have to come into the station to make a statement, Mr Jones.'

'It'll have to be when I've finished work, I'm all behind now.'

DS Davley longed to say: It'll be when we want you, sir, but she restrained herself and said nothing. She longed to have been able to snap out the sort of sharp remark that DCI Astley excelled in, but she was still too junior (and ambitious, the two went together) to allow this to herself. So she contented herself with a nod and the suggestion that it was always best to get things over, wasn't it?

By which she meant, You are bloody coming with me, chum, if I have to drag you there.

In the event, a stand-in driver (complaining bitterly that he was off duty and needed the rest) arrived to take over Terry Jones's duties for the day, thus allowing Jones to come into the central police station and give his statement.

She despatched them in a police car herself. All the while he was insisting that he had not seen who fired the shot. Nor did he know what the woman was doing in the car park, but he thought the fairest assumption was that she was taking a short cut across it from Victoria Street to the tube station to get a train.

He muttered that he could be no possible help.

'Don't be long,' he grumbled.

'You've got the day off.'

'It's my day,' he shouted after her.

Can't deny that, she thought.

Tony Davley took the statement herself, having handed over the scene in the car park to the SOCO team and the forensic scientist. A gun expert was on the spot to work out the angle of fire, using the latest laser equipment, and hence the most likely place from which the shot had come.

On one side of the car park was a patch of roughish ground, and on the other a low block of flats due for demolition, while the back of a row of shops formed the third side. The fourth side was huts and sheds belonging to various associations like the Scouts and the Sea Cadets and the Bottle Banks.

'Check the flats,' Davley had said as she left. It seemed likely that the shot had come from there.

She had waited till the woman's body had been photographed, and then taken off to the pathologist's department.

Murder had its rituals and rites which had to be observed.

Even though it was still early there was a crowd by that time watching and listening. One of the crowd was Mimsie Marker who sold newspapers from her stall hard by the tube station. She had abandoned her stall to take a look. The body was hidden beneath a white sheet, but as it was lifted to be taken away, the corpse's feet peeped out.

She went back to her stall where she sold a copy of that day's London *Times* to Robbie Gilchrist on his way to an important meeting in London, passing on to him the news of the dead girl in the car park.

'Quite young, poor kid.' She didn't really know this, it was a guess. Not everyone listened to Mimsie, since she was a well-known gossip, but they were well advised to because she was right.

Robbie did listen, and then worried all the way to London that this dead girl was his lost stepdaughter. She might well be her, he said to himself.

Terry Jones did not change his statement when Davley eventually got back to him.

'I was sitting at the wheel, checking what I had to do, as I always do, I like to get things right. I saw the woman, wearing a bright red coat. She was crossing diagonally towards the tube station.' He paused.

'And then?'

Terry put his head on one side. 'I can't say I heard the shot, shut in the van as I was; I may have heard something, perhaps even been aware of the passage of the bullet, because I looked up and saw the woman. One minute she was standing. Next she dropped to the ground. Like a stone. You're dead, I thought. And I wasn't wrong, was I?'

'No.' This chirpy fellow irritated Tony Davley and she would like to have told him he was wrong, but this comfort was denied her. 'So you didn't see where the shot came from?'

'No, I've said so, haven't I?'

'Not from the white van that drove away so fast?'

'No, couldn't have. Because if it had come from the van then the wound would have been on the left temple, and it wasn't. The hole and the blood were on the right side of the face. I was there, remember.'

'On the right temple,' repeated Tony.

'Yes, and it wasn't me that shot her. There are security cameras in that car park and if you look you will see a picture of me in the van and getting out and running across to her.'

There were security cameras but they were not working, an economy measure on the part of the owners of the car park, who thought a threat was as good as an actual picture.

'No,' said Terry Jones. 'That shot came from the block of flats. Empty, they are, we all know that. Someone got in and fired at her from there. Hit her. On the right side of the head.'

There was an exit wound on the other side, though, much larger than the entry wound, commented Tony Davley silently, but he would not know that, not having touched the body. There usually was in a head wound, so both pathologist and forensic expert had agreed, unless the bullet was deflected by bone and coming in at an angle.

Not so in this case.

'A nice clean shot,' the forensic man had said, half admiringly.

The ground and the bushes beyond were now being searched for the bullet. The soft, blancmange-like tissue of the brain often deflected the bullet more than the hard bone of the skull. This might be the case now.

She ran Terry Jones through everything once again, but he did not change his story.

A first forensic test of his van had been made already, which showed nothing that pointed to the shot having come from him.

Reluctantly, Tony told him that after his statement had been typed, he could read it and then sign it. Then he could go.

Still grumbling, he was offered, and took, a cup of tea. No biscuit, he noted that and gave a black mark.

He said goodbye to DS Davley without regret. The two of them were not sorry to part, he did not like what he called lady policemen and Davley wanted to hand this business over and get back to the Barrow Street affair. Chief Inspector Astley was a good boss and easy to work for, but she was also one of those who thought you could produce results on two cases at the same time and just as fast. Perhaps *she* could, Tony knew she could not. Accordingly, she wanted to get back to what was her priority.

She had no idea of the gold about to drop into her hands.

By the time he got to London, Robbie was so disturbed and worried that he went to a telephone booth on Charing Cross Station. For a moment, he was undecided whom to telephone. His estranged wife or the police?

Coffin, the Chief Commander, Stella Pinero's husband. That was the man.

He caught the Chief Commander at his desk, checking letters and reports.

'Coffin? Robbie Gilchrist here.'

'What is it?'

'You know about the dead woman in the car park?'

'I do,' said Coffin thoughtfully. 'Just about.'

'Is her identity known yet?'

'I think not. Not as far as I know.' His report had mentioned a handbag but no identification in it.

'I'm worried it's Alice.'

Coffin looked at what he had in front of him. 'She was a young woman between twenty and twenty-five years. Long curly hair. Blue eyes.'

Robbie groaned. 'Could be, could be.'

Coffin hesitated. 'Where are you speaking from?' He could hear noises, voices, people moving around, an announcer proclaiming something difficult to pick up.

'Charing Cross Station.'

'You could come back and see for yourself.'

'You mean identify her?'

'Don't jump in. If it is her.'

'I will come back.'

'You can cross Barrow Street off your worries: that victim was a much older woman.'

'Thank you,' said Gilchrist. He hesitated, then made one more call, this time to his former wife. 'Liz, it is possible, just possible, that Alice has been killed . . .' He listened to her outburst of shock and anger. Liz was always articulate. 'No, of course I'm not sure, but I must check.' Then wearily: 'No, George Freedom is not my closest friend, I have known him a long while and we work together. If you want to know, I don't trust him. And you were the one who married him and that was how he met Alice.' He eats young girls, and she was ripe for him. 'And I am going off to see who this poor dead bitch is.'

He just caught the train back to the Second City.

Mary Arden stopped her work in time for a cup of coffee with Evelyn in the mid-morning.

She pulled a face. 'Better hear my messages before I enjoy my coffee.' She switched on the answerphone.

The first message was from the plumber with an estimate for repair to the washing machine. And yes, he was afraid the price was high but someone had put football boots in the washer and that did the damage.

Mary groaned and took the next message, which was from her mother, recommending a good hairdresser's just off Bond Street and why not have a tint, dear, like I do?

There was a bit more about how important it was to 'look good', as Mother put it, and to keep her weight down because you really needed a waist this summer, the bust wasn't so important any more.

'I laugh,' said Mary to Evelyn. 'I really do laugh. If I didn't I might cry. I can get my hair cut in the Second City, this is not Timbuktu.'

Those two messages had come in the course of the morning, and so had the next message.

'Mary . . .'

Mary jumped and gave Evelyn a surprised look.

'Hey, Mary . . . I am sorry I did not get in touch when I got home. Well, the reason is I never got home. Love can take you like that and with me it was swift and strong. I knew you wouldn't approve, not that you would have said anything, but I would have felt it, anyway. Somehow I wanted to hide, take myself and this delicious feeling into a secret face. It didn't stay that way, I haven't been too lucky. Two lovers and both turn out bad. But you don't like policemen, do you?'

Mary protested aloud. 'I don't dislike policemen. I never said that. Only some of them.'

'But I am off home back to France. To tell you the truth, I think I will be safer there. I have seen and heard something I was not meant to have seen – I might be in bad trouble here. Bad company, bad trouble. And I have heard I am supposed to be dead. But I am alive and planning to stay that way. Etta.'

By the time that Mary Arden heard those words, Etta was lying dead in the car park by the tube station.

Some time later, DS Davley found a passport and a mobile telephone in the jacket the victim had worn. There was also a number.

She telephoned and got Mary Arden, whose voice she knew at once.

She identified herself. 'Miss Arden, do you know someone called Henriette Duval?'

'Yes, I've just been speaking to her.'

'You have?' Tony was surprised.

'Well, that is, I had a message on my answerphone.'

'When was this?'

'It was left on it this morning, but I was late in hearing it.'

'I see. Is Duval a red-haired young woman, about five foot seven, with blue eyes?' Well, they had been blue, one eye at least was shattered and bloody.

She did not have to ask much more.

'I am afraid your friend is dead.'

And Mimsie Marker was thinking to herself: My goodness, I know those shoes.

So she knew the dead person. And she said quietly that she was not surprised, she was one of those girls who does get into trouble.

6

'At least this one hasn't got my name on,' said Coffin with gloomy satisfaction. He was speaking to his two trusted allies (only did one trust anyone in this game?), Phoebe Astley and Archie Young.

It was late morning, and the room, his inner office, was full of a reluctant sunshine, with the rain clouds still hanging in the sky. Earlier Stella had sent round two bowls of sweet-smelling flowers, carnations and roses, to give him pleasure when back at work.

Say it with flowers, that was Stella.

An ignoble thought, he told himself. Then with a wry smile: Not my season for being noble.

'But Barrow Street again.'

Although there was no identification in the handbag on the victim in the car park, a passport as well as an airline ticket had been found tucked inside her jacket.

Henriette Duval, and an address in Versailles.

With a telephone number scribbled in pencil on a piece of paper.

When the police, in the shape of DS Davley, rang that number, Mary Arden answered. Both parties recognized each other's voice. Tony Davley had not enjoyed the conversation. Handing over the death sentence is never agreeable.

'And the Serena Seddon Refuge again,' continued Coffin, without pleasure. 'We do seem to get too much of it, and how are they taking it?'

'Mary Arden is calm but frozen, and the rest . . .' Phoebe gave a shrug. 'Wild hysteria. Quite enjoyed, I think. Especially when the TV van plus camera arrived. The boy Billy is a natural performer, they say. He's loving it all. Evelyn is the only normal one, but she escapes to home and husband Peter and dog Humphrey.'

'Peter Jones? I think I know him. He works in the theatre, sir,' said Archie Young, thinking it was time he reminded them of his existence. 'Haven't met the dog.'

'I know him. Dog too,' said Coffin. 'Nice man, bit lame in one leg.' He drank some coffee and studied the other two who were sitting there, drinking his coffee, which he had offered them on politically correct grounds, because the whole force was having a low-drinking, no-smoking, keep-fit drive.

Politically correct rubbish, he thought, just meanness on my part, and got out the bottle of Famous Grouse.

'Add it to the coffee.'

'Oh, thanks.' Archie Young accepted cheerfully. 'Seems hard on good whisky.' But he took a good swig.

Phoebe Astley said nothing, but smiled and took the same, her usual technique learnt from an Empress of Austria who had wept but taken what was on offer. Half a kingdom, in her case.

The pair of them looked cheerful and unembarrassed, their only worries professional.

– Join the embarrassed majority, he wanted to say. Surely you have something you are not proud of? But what had they to be embarrassed about? Archie Young lived a straight-forward family life, while Phoebe, unmarried, did what she liked and kept quiet about it.

'I'd like to talk to Mary Arden myself,' said Coffin. 'She may know more than she is telling.'

He had a transcript of the answerphone message in front of him. 'I don't like this reference to the police. Does she know who is meant?'

'She says not.'

Coffin considered. 'Worth pushing her a bit.' He turned to Phoebe Astley. 'What do you know? Any views?'

'Young Ronnie Rvman-Lawson was one of them,' said Phoebe, with some reluctance since he was a protégé of hers. 'But there may have been others.'

'What's known about Ryman-Lawson?'

'He's a graduate, came in after a good degree. London University.'

Coffin looked at her with a raised eyebrow. 'You knew him?'

'I gave a talk at his college, King's, it was, on the modern policing. He came up and spoke to me, he seemed intelligent. I thought he'd do better with us than with the Met.'

'And has he?'

'He's earned himself a bit of a reputation as a roughish customer,' she admitted reluctantly. 'I think he just wants to show a graduate can be as tough as any other. He may have overdone it a bit.'

'Anything else?' Coffin pressed her.

Damn you, she thought. Can you read my mind? Even more reluctantly: 'He's been a bit broad-minded about some of his friends.'

Archie Young shifted in his seat, but did not speak. Leave it to Phoebe. She knew as much as he did about Ryman-Lawson and possibly just a touch more.

'How broad-minded?'

'Got a bit friendly with Mack Mercer and Tolly Lightgate. I believe he got to know their women too.' Put it tactfully, she told herself. It was going to sting however she told it. 'We have a case against Mercer for drugs, intimidation of witnesses. There might be a murder charge . . .'

'Why didn't I know about this?'

Why not, indeed.

'You were ill at the time, sir.' Phoebe was now glad of her whisky in the coffee and took a quick swig. She had known all this had to come out, but it was quicker than she had expected. Damn Coffin.

'Ryman-Lawson explained, admitted it was unwise, took some leave and came back to work. Knowing that he had put his promotion on hold. No one is suggesting he knew anything about the murder.'

Coffin felt sympathy for Phoebe but not the young man. He had been in and out of trouble often enough himself not to be a judge. Knowing Phoebe, he felt sure that Ryman-Lawson might or might not be handsome, but he was sure to be intelligent and easy-mannered.

Archie Young felt it was time to speak. He drained his coffee cup, letting the whisky sting his oesophagus and appreciating its impact on his brain chemistry.

'We have two deaths to deal with here. One, the shooting of Henriette Duval, is certainly murder and it seems very likely that the unlucky woman whose limbs were found in Barrow Street was also murdered. When we find the torso we should be able to establish whether this is so. Both deaths have one thing in common: Barrow Street and the Serena Seddon Refuge.'

He waited for the Chief Commander to speak.

'I don't like coincidence in a murder case. Somewhere in this there is a connection. It's for us to find it.'

Archie Young chanced it: 'The connection is the Serena Seddon Refuge.' He had learnt that it never harmed you to state the obvious. You could then pause and wait for someone to fall in any hole there was. A lot of his success had been based on this principle.

Coffin worked in a different way; he fell into holes but climbed out of them.

He felt he was in a big hole just at the moment from which he would dig himself out by telling Stella about Anna. Being Stella she would gracefully, gently, forgive him.

Or she would slap his face, pack her clothes and move out. Taking the dog with her.

You couldn't tell which.

'We have to think about the so-far unnamed owner of the limbs: dead, where and why and by whom. Why cut off the limbs?'

'Sex,' said Phoebe at once. 'It's a sexual killing.'

'Yes. I think you are right. Then there is Henriette Duval, Etta . . .'

'It looks as though the shot came from the block of empty flats bordering the car park. It's being searched.'

'Be lucky if they find the gun.' This was Coffin, in whose experience gun killers usually held on to the weapon, ditching it later. 'Or the shell or a bullet.'

'Unlikely . . . he or she will have taken it with him or her.'

'No woman fired that shot,' said Archie.

'Don't you be sexist.' Phoebe shook her head at him. 'Women can shoot. I'm a pretty good shot.'

'Are you putting yourself forward? There was a mention of the police in the telephone call from Etta.'

'That's a joke, I hope, Archie,' said Phoebe savagely.

Coffin intervened. 'Of course it is. Come on, Archie, say you are sorry.'

'Sorry. I apologize.' He blamed the whisky. 'Silly, not even funny. Of course, women can be good shots, very good. I am not good myself.' He was being modest. He could shoot well.

Phoebe accepted the apology.

'Then there is Alice, stepdaughter of Robbie Gilchrist.'

'She'll turn up,' said Phoebe.

'Yes, I think so, but let's carry her name forward.'

Since she is the daughter of a friend of your wife's we will do so, thought Phoebe. Also we are getting together quite a little file on Freedom and Gilchrist. Pretty free and easy in the sexual interests . . . Anything but horse, one officer had joked, and only that is out on account of height.

'It might be a group,' she admitted. 'Perhaps all three are part of a group. Alice, Gilchrist and Freedom.'

'What makes them a group?'

'Something they are, something they know, someone they know,' ventured Phoebe.

'Work on that. Try to find out what they have in common.'

'Apart from Barrow Street?'

Coffin was silent. As far as he was aware, he had never known Henriette Duval, Etta, but she might have known him. 'Yes, apart from Barrow Street.'

'What about Robbie Gilchrist, did they all know him?'

'Try and find out.'

'He knows George Freedom,' said Phoebe suddenly. 'Friends. It bonds them.'

Coffin nodded at Phoebe Astley. 'It's for you, Phoebe.'

Phoebe took a deep breath. 'I don't think I am the one to handle it on account of Ryman-Lawson.'

'I think it's why: you will know where to pinch him.'

Oh, lovely, Phoebe thought. She felt she knew what was going to come next.

It came.

'And you won't be on your own. I shall be there.'

'We're going to have to knock on a lot of doors,' said Phoebe gloomily. She liked nice, straightforward cases, perplexing and difficult in their own way, but with nothing personal about them. This case was highly personal.

'Agreed. Take whosoever you want, first clearing with Archie, of course.'

Archie Young nodded his head. So he had been noticed. It was nice to know he was really there and not floating in outer space. He sneezed twice, carnations always did that to him.

Tony Davley got the news when she returned to the office which she shared with four other young detectives of mixed sex, very mixed in one case, but all powerfully ambitious. They watched each other like cats watching a mouse.

Phoebe Astley put her head round the door. 'You there, Davley? I want you in my office. Come now.' She disappeared.

Tony stood up and gathered herself and what she needed together; this was promotion material. She knew it.

'Or you might go straight down the drain,' said Bob Pierce, the most mixed up and the nicest one there. He was gloomy today, the man he loved (at the moment) was being difficult and even in this liberated Second City the affair had to be conducted with caution. I could go for the Chief Commander, he told himself, especially now he looks a bit haggard. I always love a face with lines.

'I won't go down. But bless you for thinking of it, Bob.' Tony patted him on the shoulder as she left. He was a character she liked. He was a kind of innocent in his way and how he would hate her for saying that.

Coffin thought about Stella and the flowers and decided

to go home early. And then he would face confession to Stella.

In the end, it wasn't so early because his chief secretary, Gillian, came in with the crisis news.

'Fire down below,' she announced cheerfully.

'And where is that?'

'Where it usually is: in the money bags. Accounts say every unit is overspent.'

'Money, money, money,' said Coffin sadly. It would have been savagely if he could have mustered the energy. Suddenly he could. 'Damn the lot of them. From the Home Secretary downwards.'

She planted a file, stuffed full of important papers, with estimates, figures and calculations. Forms to fill in, forms that had been filled in and some that looked as if the dog had had a go at them.

'Some of the chaps aren't so good at doing their figures.'

'It'll be Christmas in the Workhouse,' said Coffin, going back to his sad voice.

'No, it won't. It can be sorted. You can do it.'

She and the accountancy unit had been trying since before he was stabbed to get him to deal with what they could see was brewing, but Coffin, usually so meticulous and efficient, had not given it much attention.

Now they had him.

'Let Mr Giles come in and go over the figures with you. He's great with figures, he makes them do what he wants.'

All Bert Giles said when he came into the office was: 'All it needs is a few cuts here and there.'

'Like cutting throats,' said Coffin.

Giles ignored this. 'I've made a few suggestions.'

This is the real business, life as lived, thought Coffin. Solving crimes, keeping the peace, that's the fancy stuff.

He sighed and got down to it.

'They won't really notice,' said Giles as he departed, all comfortably tidied up.

'Don't you believe it.'

So he was late back home and Stella was not there.

So not confession night tonight.

He stood for a moment on the threshold of his home. Always enjoyed that moment; when the peace and gentle dignity of where he lived spread itself around him.

He hung up his coat, and patted Gus the dog who had followed him silently up the stairs. The answerphone in the sitting room on the desk he shared with Stella informed him there was a message, but he decided to have something to eat first.

He made himself a sandwich with some smoked salmon that Stella was no doubt saving for some other function, which seemed to take the taste away. Then he sat working till Gus put the dog's case for walkies very forcibly upon which they went out together to walk in the little garden, once part of the churchyard and still having an immemorial feeling.

When he got back Stella was there, finishing up the smoked salmon. She was eating it with toast, lemon, and a glass of white wine. A tacit rebuke to his sandwich.

'Glad you found the smoked S. I left it for you.'

She wanted to talk, not to him, at him. He didn't mind this since it meant she was in a vibrant, cheerful mood.

'Did you like the flowers?'

'I did.' They made Archie sneeze, but better not say that. 'They are lovely.'

'It's so tricky with flowers, isn't it? You don't want to be like a funeral. Go for smell, I thought, that's why I chose roses and carnations.' She frowned. 'Although I am never quite sure about carnations. Pinks, yes; carnations . . . a little vulgar?'

'Never.'

'Oh, good,' She finished her smoked salmon, wiping her fingers delicately on a white linen napkin.

'That's a nice bit of dialogue you wrote there.'

It was a game Stella played, making life a scene in a play. Rarely a cross noisy one, rather a sophisticated one of easy manners. Occasionally she was Lady Macbeth, sometimes Clytemnestra, and sometimes, but only for her husband's good, another Portia. Generally speaking, she preferred to be a well-dressed lady in what used to be called a drawing-room comedy with a nice line in witty dialogue. All keeping the hand in, she used to say, you never know what parts I might be called upon to play.

Coffin knew that he was forever and unalterably the same.

Stella laughed. 'I thought so too. Come on, now, cheer up. Life does go on, you know.'

'Now that's another play altogether.'

Stella said: 'I've been asked to put on a fashion show in the theatre to celebrate the millennium. I think I'll do it, after all, the Dome is only just down the road.'

'Near enough, I suppose. Can't they do it?'

'Full up. It'll be good publicity.'

'Where will it go?'

'In the main foyer and through the corridors. Viewers will walk through it.

'Young British fashion designers, new names. Perhaps a few French and Italian if I can get them . . . Letty says she will help me there . . . She'll get the clothes somehow. She says she'll use witchcraft . . . Did she tell you she was a witch?'

'No, but I believe my mother is.'

His mother's career and continued vitality, her various lives, yes it could only be witchcraft.

'Does that mean you are a warlock?' asked Stella.

'No,' Coffin said solemnly. 'It does not descend in the male line.'

'I'm sorry.'

'Let me know when the model girls roll in. I'll enjoy that part.'

'Not real models, of course. Wire frames, I think, very minimal. I'll do the commentary.'

'Have you got the time?'

'Oh, I won't be there myself. Not in person. I will be on tape.'

No models, no Stella, almost a non-fashion show. 'I suppose the clothes will be there?'

Suddenly, Stella stopped talking about clothes.

'So it wasn't Robbie's stepdaughter who was shot dead?'

'Oh, you know that, do you?'

'Of course, he rang me. He asked my advice . . . if you'd help and so on. He's worried about the girl all the same. Still worried.'

'Was all this on the phone?'

'No, I had a drink with him and Georgie Freedom later . . . business.' She paused. 'Robbie confided in me that his wife thought Alice might have gone off with Georgie. Nonsense, of course.'

'Has anyone asked him?'

'Robbie did. Georgie just laughed. Said he didn't find girls that age attractive. That might be true or might not be – I'd call George's taste fairly catholic. He does have a pull in the theatre and that might attract Alice.'

'You don't seem to trust your friends too much.'

'Freedom and Gilchrist are business, that's all. And I don't like Freedom too much. You know that.'

'Let's hope the girl turns up.'

He knew that Phoebe, and probably Archie Young too, would like to get Freedom for something. He was on their list of most desirable catches.

'Robbie saw the limbs . . . not Alice, a much older woman. A whore, I think. The legs give it away.'

'That's hard.'

'It's what Robbie said, the way he described them. It's likely, though, isn't it?'

'I can't say.' Or didn't want to. If this was Anna, then she had gone a long way down hill. The hellish thing was it might be true.

'The legs and arms must mean something . . .'

'A thoroughly unpleasing killer,' said Coffin.

'But until you get the head and torso you don't know how she died. Or why.'

'The informed opinion is a sexual crime.'

'Well, that yes, but there must be something else. Why the steps of the house in Barrow Street?'

She stood up. 'I'll go and make some coffee.'

He opened his mouth to start telling her about Anna all those years ago when he was living in Barrow Street, then he looked in her eyes.

– She knows, she knows everything, she probably knows who did the killing.

There was a pause. 'Wait,' he said.

She did so, hand on the door, poised, waiting. Certainly a pose from some drama, possibly a Hitchcock thriller this time. 'Well?'

'The house looks nice and clean,' he said weakly.

'Yes, Arthur and Co. have been in. Is that it?'

'Yes, for the moment. Shall I carry the coffee.'

Stella gave him an assessing look. 'No, you sit there and go on thinking. It's what you do best.'

And that was certainly a joke at his expense.

While he was waiting for Stella he took the message waiting for him. He recognized Albert Touchey's voice.

'Hi there, you evasive chap. I need to talk to you. Get in touch, will you?'

There was a pause during which he could hear Albie breathing. Then:

'If I don't hear, I might drop in later this evening after I have called on my ma; she lives round the corner from St Luke's in Despenser Street.'

7

Stella came back into the room with the tray of coffee. She said cheerfully: 'One thing I did learn all those years when I was on tour, was how to make a decent cup of coffee.' She put the tray down and then she looked at him. 'What was the message about?'

'Albert Touchey . . . might drop in later. Wants to talk about something.'

'Oh yes, he's after me putting on the show in the prison for Christmas . . . I'll do it for him and his ma, she's such a love.'

She handed over the coffee. 'Well?'

'Can't keep anything from you.'

'You wouldn't want to, would you?'

Coffin thought about it. 'Sometimes.'

Stella smiled.

'I love you.'

'You should have said that first.'

But she wasn't going to let him off. She wanted the story even if she knew it.

'When we moved here, and I was settling into the job.'

'Moaning a good deal.'

'Did I?' He hadn't showed it, surely. He was quite hurt.

'And kicking the door down.'

'But you were in the States.'

'The noise travelled,' she said dryly.

'I thought I didn't show it.' He drank some coffee which was hot and strong, so perhaps Stella had learnt how to make coffee on tour as well as how to manage an audience and learn different lines every week for not much money.

'She was a young journalist. She was called Anna Michael, but she told me her real name was Joanna Carmichael, the other was her working name for the paper. I don't know if this was true, never been sure how much truth she told . . . I suppose I was flattered.'

'Of course you were,' said Stella with some amusement, and, he feared, not much sympathy. Not to be expected, no doubt, she had had troubles of her own at the time and probably managed them better than he had managed his. What had it been about? – Do you know, he said to himself, I didn't really listen to her, so full of myself.

'She was attractive,' he said defensively.

'So?'

'So what do you know? What have you heard?' And from where?

'Oh, you know what the theatre is like . . . word gets round. And after all, she was a journalist.'

So you knew that all the time, Coffin thought.

'She talked herself. Of course she did. What a fool I was not to think of it.'

Stella nodded.

'I ended it. Why? Two reasons: I realized what a fool I was being, and how much you meant to me. A third reason, our tastes were dissimilar. Mastigophily, Philip Larkin called it to Amis,' he added gloomily. 'I didn't go for it.'

Then Stella said: 'I had a little adventure myself in New York.'

'Confession time, eh?' He finished his coffee. 'Don't tell me too much about it.'

Stella, who had never intended to, moved on:

'So you think it is Anna who has been killed? Why not start looking for her? She may turn up lively and living in Manchester.'

'I did start some enquiries . . .' He shook his head. 'No trace.' He had not tried very hard on what seemed the good principle of out of sight, out of mind. But Anna seemed to be one of those characters who won't stay out of mind.

Stella looked serious. 'I hope it wasn't her, because if so she had gone right down and down.'

'And you wouldn't like me to be a part of that.'

I didn't do this the right way, he thought. I should have handled it lightly, found some jokes, made Stella laugh.

'I don't think I would blame you . . . or not very much . . . what was that thing you said she went in for?'

'Mastigophily . . . Larkin claimed it was a taste for being whipped . . . or whipping someone or both. I don't think he thought it a good idea for himself.'

Stella said gravely: 'I can think of better ways to get pleasure.'

Coffin said huskily: 'Darling Stella.' The gods had been kind, he had got it right after all.

'By chance,' said Stella, 'I have a bottle of champagne in my bag. I left it at the bottom of the stairs. It ought to go in the fridge . . .'

He stood, it was good to be moving. 'Which bag is it?'

'The big white one with two handles, the Vuitton.'

'Wait a minute.' Stella came up to him and took his hands in hers. She ran her fingers gently up and down his, softly stroking them. She said nothing.

He ran down the stairs, followed by the dog, who, for some reason, was growling quietly.

As Coffin came near the front door, he heard the noises. First a voice, a muffled shout. Then another voice, another man, screaming in anger.

The heavy front door to St Luke's was always difficult to open, it took time to work the keys. Even then the heavy old door, as old as the tower and warped and stiff with age, stuck. The security light, heat sensitive, was out again, damn it. So the images on the CCTV screen were blurred.

As he pulled he was listening.

He knew enough about fights to pick out the sounds: one body struggling with another. Gasps as blows struck home. A thud as one body fell.

Followed by the sound of more blows, or they might be kicks.

All the noises were scrambled together, hard to sort out even to his experienced ear.

Then silence.

Stella was behind him on the stairs. She called out to him just as he got the door open: 'What is it?'

'Stay there.' It was a command.

'Come back, you fool. You've been stabbed once already.'

Twice, said Coffin's internal voice, which spoke whether he wanted it to or not.

Gus was already through the door and barking loudly. Then he too went quiet, sniffing at a figure lying on the paving stones around the tower. He raised his head and howled. Gus did not like blood.

Nor did he like what he saw. A man was drawing away, walking backwards, eyes on the body on the ground. The man's face and eyes seemed veiled. Gus liked to see a human animal's face, not unknowable. Also he picked up a smell that he seemed to know.

Over his shoulder Coffin called to Stella: 'Call Security, tell them to get an ambulance.'

A security guard was coming round the corner of the building from the direction of the theatre complex. Coffin shouted at him to go after the masked man.

'Get after him.'

There was something familiar about the covered man, but he couldn't pin it down.

The figure on the ground started to pull itself up, and stood there, rocking, swaying.

'Careful, Albie,' said Coffin, moving forward quickly to his friend.

Albie raised his head, the blood running down his face, he seemed neither to see nor hear. Then he slumped and slid to the ground again. This time face down.

Coffin was kneeling by the man on the ground, turning his face towards him, when the bullet hit.

It was not going to be a love scene after all.

'You bloody fool,' said Stella fondly. 'You might have been killed.'

'Not a fool, it's my job.' He ran his hand through Gus's fur. 'Anyway, Gus was nearer death than me. He deflected the bullet by leaping around and barking.'

'Yes, brave boy . . . Did they catch the man?'

'No, the silly buggers let him get away.' Irritably, he added: 'We really ought to have higher-grade security men here.'

'We do the best we can, the theatre is always hard up . . . I suppose the theatre is bound to attract louts and vandals.'

'That was no lout,' said Coffin grimly.

Stella studied his face, but decided to approach what she wanted to know in another way. 'How is Albie?'

'Still unconscious. I'll go to the hospital later.'

'I'll come with you.'

'Thank you.' He reached out his hand to take hers. 'Bless you. Not quite the way I wanted the day to end.'

'Hasn't ended yet.

'I suppose this chap, whoever he was, was after you?'

Coffin hung on to her hand. 'I don't know, Stella. Too early to know.'

Archie Young on the telephone had said laconically: 'Plenty after you, sir. Any names to suggest?' No answer there, and none expected.

Outside, forensics were searching for the bullet which had passed through Gus's fur, hit Albie at an angle, then passed on.

It was a shame that Gus could not speak. He had been slightly singed by the bullet and would have said something sulphuric.

'But by God, I'll find out.'

The hospital ward, intensive care, was busy and cluttered with equipment: plugged into patients, hanging over patients, draining into patients, draining out.

It couldn't be called noisy, but peaceful it was not. But of course, they didn't want to encourage the residents to die. Privacy comes expensive, but a few beds had screens around them.

Behind them they had left their tower home with increased security and a guard on the door, with Gus happily asleep on their bed.

The bed, thought Stella, who had a sense of joy inside her

in spite of the worry over Albie. Bed and lovemaking do truly help. I am glad it happened.

The very shock and sadness of what had happened had wiped out everything except pleasure in being alive and with each other. Nothing else managed such a feat.

Out of pain, joy.

Of course, in the morning, all the pain for Albie came back, but between the two of them there was a kind of peace.

'About what I was saying last night,' began Coffin as he poured some coffee.

'Forget it,' she had said.

Stella now touched her husband's arm. 'Is Albie behind one of those' – she sought for a word – 'sort of shelters?'

'No, you only get one of those if you're really on the edge . . .' He nodded towards the end of the ward by a window. 'That's Albie, I can see his face.'

The shape of it, he meant, and that was a guess because the features were masked in bandages which seemed, at this distance, to be yellowish rather than blankly white. Soaked in something, perhaps.

A uniformed police constable sat on guard a tactful distance away. He stood up when he saw the Chief Commander.

'I shouldn't have brought these.' Stella indicated the bunch of roses she held.

'No, he might come round and see them.'

A pretty young nurse came up to them. She had soft brown eyes in a golden face.

'I've come to see Mr Touchey,' said Coffin.

'I know.' She had a nice smile too. 'Chief Commander Coffin, isn't it?'

Coffin nodded.

'And Miss Pinero?'

Stella said, 'I think the roses were a mistake.'

'No . . . he can smell them. The sense of smell is very sensitive even in a state of deep unconsciousness.' She was leading them forward. 'At least I think so . . .'

'How is he?'

'You will have to ask the doctor,' she said tactfully. 'But he is stable.'

That dread word, Coffin thought, the preamble to a gentle sliding away.

She was drawing up a chair. 'You'll need one more. I'll get one. If you want to see Mr Fairlie . . . he'll be along soon. And Mr Touchey might be able to listen to you . . . I wouldn't be surprised.' She held out her hand: 'Let me take those, Miss Pinero, I'll get them put in water.' As she went off she said: 'My sister is one of yours, Chief Commander: Sergeant Carmel Edwards, Ditton Street.'

Stella rolled her eyes at Coffin. 'She wouldn't make a bad detective herself. Do you know her sister?'

'Know the name.'

He could see a tall, thin, tired-looking man wearing a pale-blue shirt with no tie approaching. Mr Fairlie, I presume? You had to be a distinguished surgeon to look so tired and dress so casual. What had happened to the consultant from the past in a long white coat, cold and a controlled expression? Gone with the snows of yesteryear.

Gone too the remoteness from the nursing staff. Mr Fairlie put his arm round his pretty, dark nurse, told her to hurry back with the flowers, because he would need her help.

A consultant needing help from a nurse? Depends on the nature of the help, Coffin thought cynically.

Stella seemed to pick up his thoughts because she frowned, a particularly effective theatrical frown that she had perfected in *The Importance of Being Earnest*. ('I started out as Gwendoline,' said Stella, 'now I am her Ladyship.')

Mr Fairlie took Coffin's hand, murmured something polite. Coffin flinched at his grip, which was at once neat and powerful.

'Mr Touchey . . . Albie . . . well, we both know him, don't we?' and he gave Coffin a gentle smile. Clever fellow, was Stella's thought. 'Albie Touchey is a well-known local figure. As you are yourself, Chief Commander.' Was there a hint of a bow? 'He is still deeply unconscious.'

'He is going to come round?'

Mr Fairlie did not answer Coffin directly. 'We are investigating the head injury . . . a scan . . . the neurologist is going to investigate.'

'Do you mean open up?'

'I mustn't say what Dr Paston thinks of doing, but he will certainly want to do an X-ray or two . . . Then he may decide to operate.'

By now they were at the bedside and the nurse had returned with the flowers. She still wore her pleasant smile which she donated to everyone, not forgetting the young police constable who dared not, in Coffin's presence, allow himself to smile back.

Coffin watched as Fairlie made a swift check of Albie, who showed no signs of consciousness. His lips moved, his eyelids fluttered, once he opened them wide to stare forward but without comprehension.

And then, for a second, before the eyelids went down, there was just a flash of the old Albie. The blue eyes had that hint of amusement with which they usually regarded Coffin.

Coffin stepped forward. 'Albie, old thing . . . Coffin here.' But Albie had gone again. But at least he had been there, was still there, even if locked up.

Mr Fairlie shook his head. 'He may have heard you, probably did, but don't expect an answer just yet.'

'He's an important man.'

'I know.'

'The attack on him was meant for me.'

'He may have something to tell you on that when he comes round,' said Fairlie in a soothing voice.

'I wish it was me there.'

Stella, selfishly – I'll put the show on at Christmas whatever happens – did not. She held on to her husband's arm.

At this point, cautiously but interestingly sure of herself, the nurse said: 'Sorry to interrupt, sir, but Mr Touchey's brother is outside and wants to see him.'

Coffin said suddenly: 'He hasn't got a brother. No one, he's alone.'

'A journalist,' said the knowledgeable Stella.

'Stay here.' And Coffin walked towards the door of the ward. He stepped into the corridor.

A couple of nurses walking together, talking. A male nurse

pushing a wheelchair, empty. A man with a trolley piled with what looked like bedpans.

Further down the corridor, in an alcove, protected from the light from the window, was a tall thin man with a big black hat that seemed too big for him.

Coffin moved forward. 'Hi, there!' But the man was faster, he turned, and ran down the corridor and out of the swing doors.

Coffin pulled out his mobile phone. Thank God for this, he thought.

Not that they'd get the man with all the description he had been able to give them. He had a fleeting vision of his force arresting all the men in the Second City unlucky enough to be wearing black hats. Or any hats, for that matter.

Back at the bedside he said to the man on duty: 'Stay with Mr Touchey all the time.' He could feel medical protests rising up at this but he put out his hand, brushing them aside. 'And if he says anything, anything at all, let me know at once.'

Coffin drove Stella back to the theatre where she had a meeting with Georgie Freedom and Robbie Gilchrist.

'Don't let them beat you up,' he advised Stella as she got out of the car.

'I don't know what you mean by that.'

Neither did he, except a vague warning. 'I don't know either, but they both look hungry men to me.'

'I'll bear it in mind.'

He then drove on to his headquarters where an incident room had been set up to deal with the Barrow Street body. Or the bits of it.

Presumably by now, another incident room was dealing with the attack on Albert Touchey.

Over the years since he had arrived, Coffin had managed to get sufficient high-class equipment – computers, telephones, faxes and printers – to make for heightened efficiency. He remembered the primitive conditions which had prevailed when he had been a young detective and contrasted it with what he saw now.

But the past would not be put down. It had a voice, his own voice: we did good work, though, in the old days; it's hard work, intelligence and cooperation that counts.

He stood for a moment outside the glass swing door through which he could see Phoebe Astley talking to a slim young woman whose face he knew and about whom Phoebe had been talking. DS Tony Davley, an up-and-coming officer, one to watch, a future star. Cheltenham Ladies' College and Cambridge, father a judge. Or was it the mother who was the High Court judge?

Yes, truly one to keep an eye on for more than one reason, she was remarkably handsome in a well-bred English way, which, as it often did, had that hint of something warmer underneath.

In one corner of the room, a woman detective was tapping information into a computer. In another a young man, jacket off, was talking into a telephone and making notes. A door in the opposite wall swung open at intervals to let in messengers whose function seemed to be to deposit papers on a central table.

It was near this table that Phoebe and Tony stood, arms akimbo.

Phoebe seemed to be doing most of the talking.

'So, it's not two cases but one.'

'I always did think that, didn't you?'

'Two shootings so close together? Yes, it looked as though there was a connection . . . May not be two cases into one, though.'

'Is there a difference?'

Phoebe left this question of semantics. 'Think a bit deeper.'

'I see what you are getting at, and the thought did come to me. Maybe not two into one but three into one. It's all one case with one killer.' She paused. 'I'm still trying to think it out.'

'It's like a bit of knitting, you think it's a muddle, all tangled up, then you see what you've got is in fact the pattern.'

'I don't think I've quite got the pattern yet,' said Tony humbly.

She had seen the Chief Commander push through the door and humbleness seemed a wise precaution.

Phoebe went forward. 'How is Mr Touchey, sir?'

Coffin did not ask how she knew where he had been because he was aware that all his movements were known.

'Not good.'

'He's going to come through, isn't he, sir?'

'Yes, I believe so. The doctors say so as much as they allow themselves to say anything. I wish he could talk, but he can't as yet . . . he's not in this world at the moment. But we need something.'

Phoebe Astley looked at Tony. 'We've got something. You may be surprised. I don't know. I wasn't altogether. Puzzled, yes . . .'

'Come on, out with it . . . It's the bullet, isn't it?'

'You've guessed.'

'Not difficult, couldn't be anything else. Not at this stage of the game . . . It's the same gun that killed Henriette Duval.'

She leaned forward. 'He was after you, sir.'

'Do you think so?'

'It has to be so. Outside where you live . . . he thought it was you.'

It echoed in his brain: it's you he's after.

Well, plenty of people had been after him in the past. Maybe one would catch up with him.

Albie may say something. If the poor sod ever speaks again.

Stella was enjoying her meeting with George Freedom and Robbie Gilchrist this morning, she had the feeling that money was in the air. Or flowing into her pocket.

– Keep 'em talking, her moneywise sister-in-law, Letty Bingham (Laetitia had had several surnames but had chosen to stay with this one) always said. You get more money out of a man when he thinks he is being clever.

Stella poured out coffee and added whisky with a lavish hand and laughed happily at all Freedom's jokes.

You didn't have to give much of a laugh when Georgie cracked his jokes, but something he expected: it was his due.

'Bad about Albie,' volunteered Robbie. 'Is he going to be all right?'

Is he going to live? he meant. Not will he be able to walk, speak, think. To Stella all those seemed doubtful.

'I hope so,' she said. 'Have to hope. He asked me if I would put on a show at the prison at Christmas. I'll do it come what may.'

'One of three: the limbs in Barrow Street –' began Robbie.

'No, no,' said Freedom. 'Can't be connected. Who says so?'

Robbie went on: 'The shooting dead of the girl in the car park and now Albie. The way the girl was killed, that makes him a good shot.'

'Not such a good shot,' protested Freedom. 'He missed Albie.'

'Oh yes, I forgot you knew about shooting. Belong to a club, don't you?'

Freedom picked up his coffee cup and held it out to Stella. 'Drop more, please, ma'am . . . I don't shoot seriously.'

'Not any more?'

'What do you mean?'

'Haven't I seen a silver cup and platter in your library?'

Stella gave a pleading look at Robbie while offering him some more whisky.

'All right. Joke over. You are an ex-gunman . . . Mind you, George, wouldn't this make a good film . . . no, correct me, a good TV three-parter. Limbs first and end first part with the shot girl, second part find the attack on Albie, third part find the rest of the body and solution.'

'Sounds easy,' said Stella.

Robbie grinned. 'As I am writing it, it is easy. Not for your husband, I daresay.'

'No. Never is. He's hoping Albie may remember something. Say something when he comes round.'

'I know how he feels,' said Robbie with feeling. 'I wish my missing stepdaughter would get on the blower and tell us where she is.'

'She will when she wants,' said George Freedom. 'You fuss. Kids these days like their freedom.'

'OK, OK.' It was Robbie's turn to look to Stella for help.

Stella moved the conversation deftly on to what she wanted for the theatre. As she did so she had the uneasy thought that in all the anxiety about Albie there was something she had forgotten to do.

Or wasn't someone going to remind her about something?

Dave, sitting in the car and feeling cold, said: 'It's your fault. You were supposed to remind her.'

There they were outside the St Luke's Tower, home to Coffin and Stella. It was cleaning day, an extra built in because Stella thought the windows needed cleaning.

'No, it was you.'

Dave smiled. 'I must be getting old.'

'Not you, me old mate, ageless, you are.'

'OK, so I forgot to tell the lady to be there to let us in. Why can't we have keys?'

'Security, security.'

'On which point, the security guard is giving us a dirty look.' Dave started the car. 'Let's go and have a cuppa at the café and you can telephone and ask Miss Pinero to come round. And before you say anything, you can phone because she likes you better and you are the boss. I just work for you, I'm the hired help.'

They sat drinking coffee in the plain white mugs which the Stormy Weather café produced. The large woman who ran the place mopped at the sweat on her face – she was busy frying sausage and chips for a table of workmen across the way. She was over-fat, what had once been a handsome, if not pretty, face embedded in too much flesh. She wore her hair puffed up round her face. She worked politely and with efficiency but she did not meet your eye readily.

Arthur found her intimidating but Dave seemed fond of her. Of course, she was his landlady and he had already guessed from what he knew of Dave that he was usually behind with his rent.

'Flo seems to be doing everything,' said Arthur, finishing his coffee. 'What's happened to that greasy cook that was here?' He had only caught a glimpse of the lady but had not cared for what he saw: unhealthy somehow, not what you wanted close to food.

'Around somewhere,' said Dave. 'But I don't ask Flo.'

'You keep on good terms with that one,' Arthur said as he got up.

'Sure I do.'

'Thought she was called Jo.'

'Only on Mondays,' said Dave placidly. 'Today's Wednesday.'

'Ha ha,' said Arthur, going to the phone.

Dave waited, finishing his coffee while Arthur telephoned. Doesn't know he's born, that lad, he thought.

Arthur came back. 'She says to drive round, she'll give us the keys and we can get in and she will arrive as soon as she gets the present talking over. Dunno what she means by that, but off we go.'

'You go. I'll finish my coffee first and wait here.'

'I don't know why I let you get away with things.'

'Because I'm a magician,' said Dave, still placid.

Arthur went off and was soon back.

He threw the keys on the table so that Dave could pick them up.

'She didn't sound cross, although she'd had the right to be . . .' Arthur frowned. 'I don't want to lose this job, it's a good one, and apart from that, she hires actors.'

'I knew she would hand over the keys,' said Dave placidly. 'Worth the gamble.'

Arthur led the way to the car. 'Well then, let's go and have this party.'

When they got there, Dave leapt out. 'Get the cleaner out. I'll make a start.'

Arthur took a look behind him into the back of the van. 'The mess you've made in there, I'll have to dig it out. What were you doing, burying it?'

'Just looking for something.'

Dave was already getting the front door open.

Arthur yelled out. 'Be careful, don't set off the burglar alarm.'

He saw Dave hesitate at the door, take a step inside, then

draw back. He shouted: 'Sounds like it's already sounding . . .'

Arthur couldn't hear anything, so with a shrug and a curse, he went to try to extricate the cleaner. If Dave had buried it on purpose he couldn't have done a better job.

He was dragging it free when he heard a shot. 'Dave? Dave, you all right?'

Silence.

He found himself running towards the tower. He was trying to run fast, but it seemed to him he was going slowly, slowly. As in a nightmare.

'Dave, Dave?' Breathless, he paused on the threshold of the tower. He heard a voice calling him from up the staircase. So the man was alive, anyway.

Straight ahead he could see the big window which Stella had created, from where he stood it looked as though a great pane of glass was broken.

Dave came running down the stairs. 'I was looking for him but I think he got out through the window.'

'Someone smashed it, did a good job.' Arthur had come into the hall and was surveying the window with incredulous eyes. 'How did he do it?'

Dave pushed him. 'I don't know, do I? Probably had a hammer on him. Or used the gun . . . Come on, I'm going after him.'

Muttering something about the police, Arthur was also saying to himself: Who's he? Did you see him? 'I'll look inside.'

But suddenly there was the police presence. A young constable had stopped Dave. 'What's all this, sir?'

'If you were protecting the tower you haven't done a very good job,' said an angry Dave. 'A man broke in. Did you see him? Did he go past you?' Dave was spluttering.

'Calm down, sir.'

'We've lost him now,' said Dave, slapping his side with anger. 'The tower broken into, me shot at, and the man away because you were slacking.'

PC Vallent was about to defend himself strongly on the grounds that he had been round the other side of the tower, patrolling as requested, nay ordered, by his sergeant, but he decided that attack (except with a sergeant) was better than defence. 'Are you sure you saw a man, sir?'

Dave opened his mouth in fury when Arthur shouted: 'Come, come quick, there's something wrong inside here.'

Nasty wrong.

8

On the first rising step of the staircase lay something small.

It was the head of a cat. A black and white cat.

Underneath it was a sheet of paper with letters cut out of a newspaper.

SO YOU WANTED A HEAD?

Coffin, summoned from his office, swore under his breath. 'Does anyone know whose cat it was?'

Phoebe Astley shook her head. 'A stray, I expect. Plenty of them around in the Second City.'

She stepped back to let the photographer continue taking the picture of the poor little head.

She turned to Stella who had arrived to collect her keys in time for the drama. 'Not your cat, anyway.'

'We haven't got one at the moment.' Stella looked sick. 'What a terrible, loathsome thing to do. Poor little creature.'

'I hope it was dead when the head was cut off.'

Stella moved away. 'I don't suppose you do a postmortem on a poor old mongrel cat. No, of course not. Why did I ask?' She was getting rid of her pain with a dose of anger.

'I expect we could get a vet to take a look,' said Phoebe doubtfully.

'I'll pay the bill.'

Coffin came up to Stella, put his arm round her. 'It was a lousy thing to do. Thank goodness you had the dog with you.'

'I can't even get into my own home,' wailed Stella.

'No, the forensic and scene-of-the-crime people must go

over it all.' He looked towards the van where Arthur and Dave were sitting, uncomfortable but forbidden to leave until they had made a first statement with the promise of another to come to be signed later. 'They will clean up for you afterwards. You go off to Max's, order lunch and I will join you when I can.'

'You will come?' He was famed for making a promise to arrive and then failing to turn up. Police business was tricky and unpredictable was his excuse.

'Sure. Have you got the dog with you?'

Stella nodded. 'Not actually with me. I left him behind in my office, but he will be safe.'

'I am thinking of you, not him,' said Coffin. 'He's not a bad protector.'

Of course, he had to see this second attack on his house as a clear threat.

'He's got teeth,' agreed Stella dolefully. 'I suppose he would defend me.' He had in the past. She kissed her husband on the cheek in a neutral kind of way and went to her car, passing Dave and Arthur on the way.

'You can come and clean up after this.'

'Sure. We will be there,' said Arthur.

'I'm glad you didn't get hurt, Dave.'

'Oh, no question of it, Miss Pinero.' Dave nodded his head sagely. 'Not after me, I don't think . . . he made off as soon as he saw me.'

After me or my husband, thought Stella. And all part of this horrible sequence of events starting in Barrow Street.

'Are we stuck here, Miss Pinero?' asked Arthur; he was the paymaster. 'We have another job to go to.'

'You'll be told when you can go, when the forensics and the photography are done,' said Stella. 'Not too long, I shouldn't think.' She gave them a sympathetic wave as she drove off.

'What's all this forensic stuff they do?' asked Arthur.

'Oh, body traces and suchlike in the house. Fingerprints. They will want mine, I daresay, as I went in.'

'Did you touch anything?'

'Can't remember. Must have done. It's all a bit of a daze now. I told them that.'

'Wonder how he got in?'

'Oh, through that broken window,' said Dave with confidence.

This was not the story that the Chief Commander was hearing.

'He got out that way, yes, possibly,' the forensic man was saying, supported by mutterings from the scene-of-the-crime officer. 'But not in . . . you can see from the way the glass was shattered. Done from the inside.'

'Thought so myself,' agreed Coffin. 'That glass was meant to be shatter-proof.'

'Nothing is ever what it's supposed to be,' said the man from forensics. 'And I ought to know . . .'

'How was the window broken?'

Forensics put his head on one side and adjusted his spectacles. 'At a guess, I'd say with that bronze bust of Miss Pinero which is on the shelf behind you.'

Coffin looked behind him. There was the beautiful portrait bust of his wife done about two years ago, by Henry Mister. She looked happy and young.

'I've had a first look, but there are marks on it where it smashed into the glass . . . don't worry, it isn't damaged.'

Coffin thought about it. 'So . . . he, if it was he and not a woman, got in with a key . . . He didn't know how to deal with the alarm system, so that went off, but he got in.'

He left a head and used a head.

The head of Stella Pinero.

And he had a key.

In Max's, Stella was sitting drinking a dry white wine and talking to Robbie Gilchrist. Max was hovering, trying to persuade them to choose what they wanted to eat.

Coffin walked in, not too pleased to see Gilchrist there. In his mind, Gilchrist, although less questionable than George Freedom, was not a man he cared to see near his wife.

Business, she would say, nothing personal. They are willing to invest and I want their money. But what did they want, he wondered? Too many pretty young girls, and lads (because to his mind Freedom was up for anything) came into the St Luke's Theatre Complex.

'Freedom not here?' Coffin asked as he sat down.

'No.' Gilchrist gave Coffin his charming smile, a smile which never reached his eyes. 'He's gone to London . . . We don't call here London, you know.'

Max bustled up, eager to talk, to pour a drink, to help Coffin choose his lunch.

'Bit later, Max. Not sure if I will be able to stay to eat.'

Max looked disappointed. 'You should eat, sir, feed the brain.' He shook his head. 'Miss Pinero, can I suggest a light omelette as you are not hungry?'

Stella agreed and Gilchrist announced that he was hungry and would have a steak, pretty rare. 'Ashamed to say I like blood,' he confided to Stella.

Stella paled but was gallant. 'We were talking about money.'

'Oh?' Coffin motioned to Max, after all, he would eat. He began to feel he was going to need food. 'Whose money?'

'Spoken like a husband.'

I'm going to be even more like one in a moment, a husband who is a copper, a husband who is a copper from whom a relevant fact has been kept.

He leaned forward.

'Stella, tell me, have you recently lost your handbag?'

Stella gave him the look which he had learnt to recognize meant she was considering telling him a lie. Or at least wrapping up the truth.

After a pause long enough for Coffin to order steak and for Robbie to suggest with false tact that maybe he should leave them alone to sort it out, she settled for wrapping it up.

'Mislaid it. I mislaid it.'

'And where did you mislay it?'

Another pause.

'In the public library in Cater Street . . . I was getting some books on the French Revolution. Might be doing a play . . . No, not *A Tale of Two Cities* . . . A woman, one of those who takes up the space of two, jogged my arm and I dropped the books. I think that's how I came to forget my handbag.'

'And?' he probed.

'I came out with an armful of books, went straight into my office in the theatre and did not notice I had left my bag behind.'

'And how long before you noticed?'

'It might have been a couple of hours. Or a bit longer.'

Say four hours, Coffin doubled it quietly. 'And then?'

'Then I went back, and retrieved it. A nice man had found it in the reading room there and handed it in to the librarian,' said Stella triumphantly.

I always knew a handbag was going to come into it somewhere, he told himself.

'Thank you. Forgive me while I make a call.'

He went into the lobby where it was quieter and called Phoebe Astley. 'Phoebe, send someone, or go yourself, to the library in Cater Street and find someone who can tell you who it was handed in Stella's handbag. Which,' he said, with measured irritation, 'she left there.'

'Right,' said Phoebe. 'I know the librarian in Cater Street, I use the place myself. You want the name of the man who handed in Stella's bag – it had the keys to your house in it.'

'He may be our killer.

'Any news on the head, the other head?'

'No, sir. Still looking.'

'It's out there somewhere. That bugger wants us to go on looking, he's taunting us.'

'Does he want us to find it, though?' asked Phoebe.

'Yes.' Coffin was decided. 'He wants us to find it.'

One more query for Phoebe, who felt she was fielding all unwelcome oddments that worried the Chief Commander.

'I've been talking to Gilchrist ... he didn't mention the daughter, worried but not worried enough. Too cool altogether. Do you have anything?'

'No, sir. As far as I know, the girl is still untraced. Do you want me to push?'

'Leave it for the moment.' He wasn't himself sure why he was worrying over the girl. 'Get on with the other thing.'

Phoebe skipped lunch and made her way to the library where

her friend would be on duty. She bought a sandwich at the deli round the corner from her office and sat in the park just opposite while she ate.

She was not deliberately going slow on her errand. But I am deliberating, she thought. Trying to make some sense of what has been going on.

She ran it over in her mind, making a mental list, giving little ticks when she felt she had got something right.

From where she sat, her mouth full of tuna salad and dark-brown bread, she could see a low line of buildings beyond the trees. This had once been a brewery, Daker's Ale, and made Mr Harry Daker a rich man. But a couple of centuries had passed since his apotheosis and the buildings had afterwards become a warehouse for cottons from India, and then a poorhouse and now was a listed building housing a museum of local trades and manufacturers.

Phoebe knew all this because she had gone round the museum with her friend Monica, a passionate student of the history of the district. One of her topics, subject of a book she was planning, was the making of fine china in a factory near the docks and that this factory had produced a teapot, particularly popular at the time, known as the Deacon's pot, after the maker Mr Deacon. Round and fat-bellied, Monica had explained, as Mr Deacon was himself.

It hadn't meant much to Phoebe at the time, other than a pleasant trip with a friend, and yet there was something about this place, the Second City, that got into your mind.

She brushed the crumbs from her skirt and walked on, reciting a kind of litany in her head.

The limbs of an unknown woman, still no head and trunk discovered.

A young woman shot dead in a car park near to the station. She is identified as Henriette Duval, and she seems to have some dangerous knowledge that caused her to run away.

She hadn't got far.

And then the attack on Albert Touchey. How was Touchey? Holding his own, whatever that meant. He too seemed to have some information. He was willing to pass it on, unlike Etta who had hung on to hers and preferred to run.

Much good had it done her, poor girl.

And now the head of a cat on the staircase of St Luke's Tower. Actually inside his own home.

Oh yes, and another shot fired.

She walked on to the library; she could have driven but it was always difficult to park and she had found herself wanting to be in the air. You could hardly call it fresh air here in the Docklands, and while it no longer stank of stale drains and burning coal and the smell of the tin works that had once been here, yet it was still heavy with diesel and petrol.

She reflected that through the centuries the inhabitants of the old Docklands must have been heavy smokers ever since the first tobacco came across the seas. Indeed, Tobacco Dock was just up the river. The smell of tobacco still seemed to float in the air.

Monica was busy when Phoebe pushed through the swing doors. She was the senior librarian in this busy library. She saw Phoebe and gave a little wave of her hand before turning back to deal with a reader with a query. Or complaint. From where Phoebe stood it sounded like a complaint. Something about waiting over a month for a special book.

'Miss Pinero's handbag? Oh, we got that back for her, someone dropped it in, said it had been found, and I telephoned her. What's wrong?'

'Nothing wrong,' said the cautious Phoebe. 'I expect she just wants to say thank you.'

'She did that at the time.'

'To the person who found it?'

'Oh.' Monica started to tidy up a file of papers; she was busy. 'I'll ask around.'

Phoebe reached out to put her fingers gently but firmly round Monica's right wrist. 'Now, please.'

Monica remembered what her friend was: a policewoman. You could call her other things, like a Keeper of the Peace, a Law Preserver, but what she really was, to Monica's mind, was a chaser of criminals.

'This is serious business then?'

Phoebe just increased the pressure on her wrist.

'OK, I think it was Lizzie Chatham who took it in.' She looked around. 'You're lucky, she's just going to lunch.'

Across the room, Lizzie was just hitching her shoulder bag over her arm and preparing to depart. She had a date to meet her young man for a sandwich then off to house hunt; they were looking for a flat to share.

'Catch her before she goes,' ordered Phoebe.

'She's entitled,' protested Monica, who did not like being ordered around, even by a friend. Come to think of it, less by a friend.

If Lizzie had seen them coming her way she might have escaped but she was busy dabbing a little of her new scent on her wrists: Escape, it was called.

They bore down upon her. 'Liz,' said Monica. 'You took Miss Pinero's handbag from the person who found it, didn't you? Know who it was?'

Liz gave a brisk answer before making her move to the door. 'It was Mr Copley, dear old Copley. He said someone handed it to him.'

'Oh, it would be Copley, wouldn't it?' Monica turned to Phoebe. 'You're in luck again. You won't have far to go.'

'Local, is he?'

'Nearer than that. He's always here. Don't think he has much of a home, or much to do in it. Where is he, Liz?'

'In the reading room,' said Liz, already on the move. 'Or it might be the audio book listening room.'

'Good, just want a word with him. Checking. Get him to tell me who gave it to him.'

Name and description, Phoebe thought. Be a start. Enough to tell the Chief Commander.

'Might not do you much good,' said Liz, making her escape at last.

Phoebe understood what she meant when Monica took her to the reading room and pointed out Mr Copley.

He was certainly studying a newspaper. But with difficulty. Oldish, tall with grey hair and neatly dressed, he was wearing the darkest and thickest spectacles she had ever seen. More, one lens was covered with a patch.

'Can't see much,' said Monica helpfully. 'He does try though. The magnifying glass helps.'

Mr Copley smiled when questioned and said that he had indeed been given the bag to hand in, he had just been going up to the desk to talk to one of the nice young girls there when this chap had tapped him on the shoulder, said he'd picked this bag up in the hallway and would he drop it in.

He screwed up his eyes. 'Didn't get a good look. Taller than me, the light wasn't good, never is in here.'

Monica looked around her brightly lit library and gave a shrug.

'Thank you,' said Phoebe. 'Think you'd know him again if you saw him?'

'If he came close,' responded Mr Copley. 'Real close. And the light was good. I'd enjoy to do it.'

Phoebe accepted his good will. 'Thank you.'

'And he had a lovely voice. I'd know that.'

'So what we have,' Phoebe began when she got back to the incident room, where Tony Davley was taking a call. 'Yes,' she was saying. 'What I expected really. Seemed likely. Thanks for the quick work. Yes, quite right, you do have to be quick with this one.'

She turned from the phone to Chief Inspector Astley. She did not speak first, with chief inspectors you waited to see what they had to say.

'What we've got,' went on Phoebe, 'is that the bloody bag was on the loose for about two hours, plenty of time to get keys copied, when it was returned by a man with a nice voice, who might or might not be the killer, to the almost blind Copley.'

'Who couldn't shoot anyone.'

Phoebe agreed not. 'No, he certainly couldn't. Even have difficulty shooting himself,' she said savagely. 'So what are you leading up to?'

'That was a call from forensics. They wanted you but you weren't there, so I took the call. A bullet which was found outside the tower matches the one found earlier which hit Mr Touchey and which matched the one that killed Etta Duval.'

*   *   *

John Coffin received the news with interest but equanimity. For once he was in a very, very strong position with his wife: she was apologetic about the loss of her bag. Should have told him, but hadn't. That was worth an apology and he had got one, with the hint of a more loving one that evening. He was content to rest on that promise.

'The locks are being replaced,' he told Phoebe, who knew it. 'And the head of that poor beast removed. I hope it gets a decent burial with the rest of it if that ever turns up.'

Yet another torso to look for, he reflected. One easier buried.

'I'm going to talk to the gun outfit. See where that leads.'

He was proud of the Second City's Police Gun Range. He had set it up himself.

'And Phoebe, go back to Copley and see what you can get on the voice of the man who gave him the bag. He may be almost blind but he seems to have sharp hearing.'

'Yes, sir. I thought of that myself . . . he's a careful, sensible man.'

'Don't do it yourself. Send someone you trust.'

'I shall send DS Tony Davley. She's good.'

'Yes, I've noticed her.'

Oh, have you? Trust you to notice an attractive woman. I think she's spoken for.

Then she felt ashamed of herself. She knew how deeply the Chief Commander loved Stella Pinero: she had learnt the hard way. By observation.

'She's clever, hard-working, doesn't miss much.'

'Use her.'

The Police Gun Range was in a converted warehouse by the river, not far from the tube station where Mimsie Marker sold newspapers and controlled the gossip of the neighbourhood. She kept a close eye on the Gun Range too as being a fruitful source of rumours. She claimed she could hear the shots, but Coffin knew that all departments were soundproofed.

He went down there now with Chief Superintendent Archie Young who was a good marksman, better than Coffin.

'Time I had a look round here,' Coffin said. 'I've had guns on my mind lately.'

On your right as you went in was the firing range with booths and electronic targets for the police to shoot at. The Second City Police was proud of its marksmen and had sent a team to Bisley. There was a baffling range of targets to choose from: a film at which they could aim, the target being a moving car, their success being checked by a sophisticated arrangement of screens divided by a stroboscopic light to a beer top hanging by a thread. The thread being the target.

The latter target was the one most used by Coffin.

There was a third target, one in which the marksman had to run, fully togged out, for several hundred yards, before entering a darkened range where a target would be illuminated suddenly for just two seconds in which time the marksman had to decide if it was friend or foe and then take aim. This was known among those who used it as the Kiss me Quick.

But not by Coffin, who had drawn his gun, and shot and killed his mark. In his case, a woman, which ought not to make a difference but somehow did.

Another department was where the officers tested out the guns to see if the riflings tallied with those on a bullet extracted from a body. Armed with practice earmuffs plus earplugs, the officer fired into iron boxes filled with sawdust or nylon padding.

The third area, locked behind metal doors, and electronically protected, was where the main supply of guns – hand guns, rifles and even Kalashnikov repeating rifles – was stored.

Archie Young had already been consulting with Sergeant Draper in the testing department.

'Definitely the same gun used in the three shootings,' Archie announced. 'Draper tells me that our chap is not one to make mistakes . . . in the three instances in which this gun was used he picked up his cartridges.'

'And what about the gun?'

Archie sighed. 'Not as straightforward as you might think. We all know that most ammunition, from the cheapest Yugoslav bullets to the choicer K & T and H & N, are 'meant to fit a wide range of automatics. They threw the list at me: Smith & Wesson, Rossi, Walther, Beretta . . .' He paused. 'And Heckler and Koch.'

'That's what the German police went over to in 1980.'

'Right, and this one they think . . . only think, mind . . . was used here. A P7K3.32 pistol.'

Coffin sighed. He knew the gun: it was small, hammerless, semi-automatic. It could be fired by either hand even with gloves on. He looked back wistfully on the days when the perp hired a gun, for several hundred pounds, and returned it to get most of his money back.

Now you could easily smuggle such a gun in from the continent.

It was a daisy of a gun, light, easily stripped down in seconds and the parts chucked into the River Thames running so obligingly through the Second City.

'Bugger,' he said. 'He knows what he's doing, our chap. May have ditched the gun already.'

'No,' said Archie Young slowly. 'I reckon he's still got it. He likes this gun, he's used it three times at least . . .' He paused.

'And he may have another use for it,' Coffin finished for him. 'Yes,' said Archie Young. 'He's on the boil. I reckon he plans to use it again.'

'I hope it's for his own head then,' said Coffin savagely.

Archie Young drove them both back to Central Headquarters through the late-afternoon traffic. Mimsie Marker saw them drive past and gave them a wave.

It's an ill wind, and events in the Second City were selling her papers well.

Coffin remembered another worry: 'Anything new about the Gilchrist girl?'

'No, not that I've heard. But I do know that Edith Lodge is of the opinion the girl will turn up. She is usually right.'

Inspector Lodge was head of the unit that dealt with missing teenagers and runaways. Experience had suggested that the Gilchrist girl would come home. She did not regard the case as urgent or high priority.

'I hope she comes back in one piece.'

Archie Young looked at the Chief Commander but decided not to say anything. They drove along in silence. He did speak in the end.

'You don't like Gilchrist.' It was a statement more than a question.

'He's preferable to Freedom. But what do you make of a stepfather who can't be sure how old his daughter is? What's the girl running away from? Perhaps she knows what she is doing.'

'Abuse, you think?'

'Well, Gilchrist never made a direct report of her being missing. Told my wife he was anxious and saw to it that she told me. Kind of back-handed.'

Archie Young was not enjoying this conversation. His own fourteen-year-old daughter had left her home and he had not told his colleagues. Nor reported her missing.

And why not?

For precisely the reasons that must have held Gilchrist back: what people would say. His girl had come home soon enough, and yes, there had been some trouble behind it: she had had a drug problem. He had managed to keep it hidden, she had taken treatment, come to her senses, as he put it to himself, and all was well. He hoped.

'It's always there in the background of your mind, isn't it, when a girl runs off?'

Young played a prevaricating card: 'I think Phoebe Astley has been in touch with Edith Lodge.'

He knew that Astley had been asked to take action on the disappearing girl, and that, this not being her speciality, she had gratefully handed it over to the right person. It was true enough, as the Chief Commander was suggesting, that the case of the missing girl had not been taken seriously and had been handed from person to person.

'Edith Lodge is good and conscientious.'

'I think I'd like to see her myself.'

Young parked the car not far from the block in which Inspector Lodge had her office. He recognized her car, they knew each other well, she had been at school with his wife, which relationship had enabled them to know they liked each other but precluded them from doing anything about it. Her red Metro told him she was there still.

'Shall I come with you, sir?'

Coffin looked at him as if he had not noticed he was there, a trick that had appeared lately and which annoyed Young, although he knew it meant nothing.

Edith was packing up to go home as they came in. She looked pleased to see Archie but surprised to see the Chief Commander.

'Afternoon, sir.'

Coffin looked at the papers she was gathering together. 'You're off to give a talk?'

'Yes, sir. I go out once a month to a different school to talk about what help I can give a runaway. I give telephone numbers, explain what will happen if they call. That sort of thing.'

'Gets results, does it?'

'Yes, it does.'

'So what about the Gilchrist girl?'

'She hasn't been gone very long,' said Inspector Lodge. 'I think she will be back. I have seen Mr Gilchrist and I think it's one of those family situations. The girl will come back if and when it is resolved.'

'I don't suppose Gilchrist told you what the situation was?'

'She's clearly an attractive girl, that comes into it,' said the inspector obliquely.

'I hope you're not hinting what I think you are hinting?'

A thoughtful pause. 'Not Mr Gilchrist, I wouldn't say. But someone within the family circle. She is probably just giving herself freedom, that's how I see it.'

'Bloody freedom,' said Coffin, half aloud.

'Sometimes it is wiser for me not to probe too deeply. I don't know the girl, I have seen her photograph, she is clearly disturbed. But I think this girl will be back.' She consulted her notes. 'She was last seen by friends six weeks ago, on the thirtieth of last month. She has not been in touch with her mother or friends, but she has been withdrawing money from her bank account . . .' She looked up from her notes. 'No money problem. Another reason for thinking she'll be back.'

'Good,' said Coffin, without conviction.

'She's training to be an actress, don't forget.'

Coffin managed a smile.

Coffin was tired, it had been a long and draining day but there was still work to be done, reading reports, signing them, and dictating a letter or two into his machine.

At intervals, he thought he was hungry but he pushed hunger away. He was conscious of drinking a cup of coffee that his secretary Sheila Heslop brought in. It was lukewarm by the time he got it down.

He was interrupted by a telephone call for him from the hospital. By this time, the officer sitting by the bedside was PC Terry Dane.

'Mr Touchey has surfaced a bit, sir. No, sir, can't say more. He spoke a few words . . . couldn't make them out, sir. Doctor was with him, he couldn't grasp what he was saying. But he says it's a good sign.'

'Thank goodness. Thank you. Keep on listening.'

He rang Stella, who was in her theatre office. 'Albie has come round and spoken . . . No, just a mutter that no one could understand. I'm going to the hospital.'

'I'll join you there,' said Stella at once.

Coffin was there before she was, sitting by Albie's bed.

'What a day.' He reached out for Stella's hand. 'I am still thinking about that cat.'

'I'm sorry it was my fault he got in.'

'He – whoever *he* is – would have got in somehow. Don't worry . . . I have upped security and had the locks changed. Perhaps we should buy a bigger dog.'

'Gus wasn't there, he was with me.'

'Just as well, it might have been his head on the stairs.'

'Head,' came a mutter from the bed.

Coffin swung round. 'Albie . . . you're with us again.'

'Head . . .'

'Yes, you got a bash on it.'

Albie closed his eyes.

'They miss you at your place of work . . .' It seemed right to talk about prison here in the hospital. Albie was sorely missed although his two assistants did good work.

Nurses no longer rustle in starched skirts nor do doctors necessarily wear a white coat, but when they move together, they make an impression.

Stella went to stand beside her husband. Coffin was too intent on reading Albie's face to turn towards the doctor.

'Albie, what did you say?'

'Mr Coffin –' began the doctor.

Coffin waved him quiet. He leaned forward to put his face near to Albie's. 'Come on, Albie, say it again.'

Albie opened his mouth and a dry kind of mutter came out of it.

Coffin listened. 'Thanks, I heard. Freedom, he said, Freedom.'

'I hope you haven't killed him,' said the doctor, pushing the Chief Commander aside.

'No, not Albie. He'll live forever.'

As he left with Stella, he reminded himself that Freedom could be a concept as well as a man's name.

9

Tony Davley soon located Mr Copley, he was where he almost always was, sitting against a radiator in the City Library, reading a newspaper. A slender, grey man just going bald, he wore his very thick spectacles with panache, as if they were a decoration, taking them off and putting them on with a flourish. But Tony could tell from the way he held the newspaper right up to his nose, assisting himself with a magnifying glass on a ribbon, that anything more than a few inches away from his nose was a blur.

As a witness, he would be hopeless. But he might, all the same, be a pretty good informant.

Since he spent most of his day with the newspapers, both local and national, and the evenings almost attached to his television set, he was remarkably well-informed. He knew at once what was behind the query.

'It's this business of the legs and arms in Barrow Street, isn't it? And then the girl shot dead in the car park and then poor old Albie.'

He'd only missed out the poor cat. 'Quite a list you've got there,' said Tony. 'What makes you think they are connected?'

'Me and my mates at the Wellington Arms. We've talked it over. Connected with Drossers, somehow. Drossers Market is the real sink in the Second City.' He sounded interested and excited at the thought. 'Don't go there myself, of course.'

Tony nodded. She knew all about Drossers Market.

'Besides, one of your lot, drinks in the Wellington and he lets things slip. Radley something.'

'Bloody Radley,' Tony thought. She knew him too and

disliked him. Tony considered going into the question of the talkative policeman but decided against it for now. It could be gone into later and the wrong sort of question would cause Mr Copley to dry up. 'Protect a mate' was certainly written into his cortex from whence it gave out behaviour instructions.

'So what can you tell me about the man who handed over the bag?'

'I didn't know it was Miss Pinero's bag, then, of course,' he said conversationally. 'I soon heard though.'

'You soon heard?'

'She's a famous lady, I could hear the girls that work here going on about it.' He nodded towards the desks. 'They don't half talk, I listen on purpose when I can. Can't always catch what they say.'

'And the man who gave you the bag, would you know the voice again? No? Anything that struck you about it, anything you noticed?'

'It must be important, that bag,' said Mr Copley with a shrewd look in those short-sighted eyes.

Tony nodded. 'So what about the man's voice?'

'It could have been a deep, husky, woman's voice.' Copley was provokingly thoughtful. 'But no, I don't think it was.'

'Good,' said Tony. 'Anything else that it was as opposed to what it wasn't?'

'Temper, temper now, missy. You're just like my grand-daughter. Grandpa, she's always saying, get on with it.'

Tony felt instant sympathy for the unknown young woman.

'He only said a few words like, "Found this bag in the hall. Hand it in for me, will you? I'm in a hurry."' He thought about it. 'A nice voice, though. Educated.'

That's something, thought Tony. Knocks out about half the population of the Second City. Or more.

Copley was still considering the voice. 'But I tell you what: underneath he was local. Yes, he came from round here, a Docklands special.'

The library was now closing for the day, so he detached himself from his cosy seat, accepted a lift from Tony Davley and went home to his flat behind the tube station.

*   *   *

DS Tony Davley reported back to Phoebe Astley who telephoned the information to John Coffin who was now back at his desk, trying to catch up with the neglected letters and files of papers.

'Not a lot of help, sir,' said Phoebe Astley, who was also working late. She had promised to look in to the Serena Seddon Refuge that evening, where anxieties had not subsided, and where Etta Duval was grieved.

'No, but Albie became conscious and spoke one word: Freedom. That could be George Freedom. He may have recognized him as his attacker.' And therefore probably the killer of Etta and the depositer of the limbs on the doorstep of the refuge.

Not to mention the man who seemed to have a grievance against the Chief Commander.

Grievance, Coffin said to himself. Grudge is more like it. What have I ever done to George Freedom?

Once failed to find amusing a comedy he had financed in the Sarah Siddons theatre off Piccadilly. Me and several thousand others, Coffin reminded himself, his part being perhaps more noticeable in that he had been sitting next to Freedom at the time.

Answer came there none.

'What have you got on Freedom?'

'Nothing much that you don't know about. He was in trouble over a so-called accident, nearly killed a girl, she's still having treatment, he did serve a short sentence.'

'I know that,' said Coffin irritably.

'He's a man who has accidents, hit a man with his car, that was an accident. And before that his current wife nearly lost an eye. All accidents. Now his stepdaughter is missing.'

'I know that too.'

'Then you know that she's also the stepdaughter of Robbie Gilchrist.'

'It's a complicated relationship,' said Coffin. But not unknown in theatrical circles.

Phoebe ran over it. 'Her mother, the lady of the damaged eye, is a kind of serial wife. The girl is fond of Gilchrist, less so of Freedom, I'm told. Her real father is off the scene.'

Coffin knew that too. 'He's in Hollywood,' he said. 'He makes monsters.'

Even Phoebe was silenced. She liked a good horror movie. 'Like Godzilla?'

'No, more like Frankenstein's Monster and Jack the Ripper . . . And Jekyll and Hyde. He does the faces.'

What a family. Blood for breakfast, it would be.

'Anything else?' Coffin asked while she considered this.

'He's not completely clear on anything but he always steps out of the shit. He certainly knows Albie, and probably doesn't like him. I'd say that was mutual.'

'I think he may be our killer.'

You want him to be, thought Phoebe.

'See what you can find, where he was on the days and times in question. Does he have a gun? Did he know Duval? See what you can get. But try not to let him know. He's a clever devil.' And Coffin had a last thought: 'Check who his lawyer is, it is going to be worth knowing.'

'Certainly, sir.' Definitely not the sort of conversation in which to call the Chief Commander by his Christian name, even although she had done once. In the past in which they were both younger. And he was less fierce; he was very fierce at the moment.

I hate this business as much as he does, but it isn't making me fierce. That's the difference between men and women for you: they are aggressive animals.

Coffin hadn't finished. 'And while you're at it, check on Gilchrist as well.'

'Right.'

'You never know.'

'We'll need extra help, sir.' Certainly sir, this time. 'We're stretched now.'

Her unit was looking for the head and torso of the limbs deposited in Barrow Street, they were checking on all known contacts of Henriette Duval, and they might even be looking for a headless black and white cat.

Etta had moved around a lot. Phoebe had the latest report beneath her hand now. After leaving the Serena Seddon Refuge she had gone to live in a street near to the tube station where she had a room. She took a job in a dress shop near by, then when it closed down, she went to work in a coffee shop, managing it. At this time, it seemed she was running an affair with one Joseph Abraham, and it was apparently for him that she had stayed in the Second City.

That relationship apparently ended because she took to working in a restaurant near the tube. Here she had another boyfriend. Only known by his nickname of Big Boy.

Note: informant for most of this is Mimsie Marker.

'I guess you've seen the report on the Duval girl?' Very quickly, she added, 'sir'. Not because she wanted to be servile but because the Chief Commander was touchy today. And who wouldn't be with what had been happening to him and around him from the first bloodstained message and initials J.C. in Barrow Street down to the cat's head.

And I like cats, she said to herself, and so does he.

Coffin agreed he had seen the report. 'Wants more detail, Phoebe. There must be some indication of what or whom she was frightened of.'

'Got to be a man.'

'Yes, Phoebe, but what we want is his face, his name, his whereabouts.'

'We are working on it, sir, that's why I said we were stretched.'

She paused, then added:

'There is something else: it may be nothing. One of the uniformed lads has a father who lives in Blenheim Street, it's not far from Barrow Street. He's been away; when he got back everything in the garden looked as normal, but his terrier keeps wanting to dig up the potato patch . . . He told his son.'

'Dig it up.'

'Just on chance?'

'All right, you're stretched. Get the chief superintendent to find the men for you.' He and Archie Young had worked together so often that they trusted each other to do what was required. It worked both ways, they helped each other out. 'Get the potato patch dug up and' – he put the emphasis here – 'check on Freedom and Gilchrist.'

Coffin put the telephone down. Time to get home. He could be in trouble. Freedom and Gilchrist, eh?

Stella will kill me if I put 'em both away.

She was home, looking at the staircase from which an area of carpet had been cut.

'Forensic tests,' she said gloomily. 'God knows why. No, don't tell me.'

Coffin looked at the carpet which was pale grey and expensive. He had said at the time that they should leave the stairs uncarpeted and stone, but he knew better than to say so now.

Gus, the dog, was fussing around their feet while sniffing at the staircase with the anxious air of a dog who knows that strange goings-on have trespassed in his home, his kennel, his safe place.

Also he could smell both cat and blood. This was worrying.

The only sensible thing to do was to attach himself firmly to one member of his family; he chose Coffin whom he always regarded as his protector.

The glass in the broken window had already been restored. One thing about being a high-ranking police officer was that people jumped to your orders.

Stella broke into this comfortable reflection. 'Of course, Jimmy Jones did the window at once because it was me. He's devoted to me, runs my fan club, or one of them.'

Stella's mobile telephone trilled away in her handbag.

'You answer it,' Coffin said quickly, 'while I get us something to eat.'

They had a quiet dinner which Coffin put together, he had learnt a few domestic skills when Stella was off on one of her trips and had discovered that made-up soup and a sandwich was not beyond his skills. He could open the packet in which both foods were sold with the best.

The important thing, he said to himself as he heated the soup and drank some wine, is to know where to buy the best pre-cooked foods.

He carried it to the sitting room on a tray. There was still a lot of things unsaid between them but now was not the time to start. Stella had finished her telephone call, but she was still clutching the telephone.

'I think the battery is running down,' she said absently. 'The sound was poor.'

'Have some food and a glass of wine.'

'Thank you.' Stella took the wine, drank the soup and ate whatever it was, Coffin could hardly remember himself, as he stared at his wife. She was pale and pensive.

'Anything wrong?'

'You mean more than we've had already?'

'Yes, I suppose I do.'

Stella didn't answer. She held out her glass. 'I think I need another glass of wine, and if I end up tipsy that is probably what I need too. It has been a lousy day.' She drank some wine. 'Has it been just one day? It feels longer.'

'What was the phone call?'

'You don't usually ask who I speak to.'

'You seem upset,' he said simply.

'It was Robbie Gilchrist, he wants to talk to you.'

'Ah.'

'Yes, ah. He thinks you want to talk to him.'

'I do.'

There was a short pause. Then Stella said, almost humbly, as if she was asking to be forgiven: 'Do you think he is the killer?'

'I think he might know who it is.' A pause

'How much does he matter to you, Stella?'

She looked surprised. 'Only as a business partner, nothing personal. I'm not sure if I even like him. He's better than Freedom, though.'

'I'm glad,' said Coffin gravely. 'When does he want to come?'

'Tonight. Now.'

He stood up and held out his hand to her. 'Let's hope we have a quiet night.'

Stella smiled at him. Perhaps not too quiet.

Coffin said: 'Gilchrist can wait till tomorrow. We might know more by then.'

The torso, for instance. Dug out of a potato patch.

*　　*　　*

It was a quiet night around the St Luke's Theatre. The big theatre and the Workshop Theatre were soon to be dark, part of the reason that made Stella anxious to work with Freedom and Gilchrist. But she had a new big show coming in, a singing and dancing comedy, things would look up.

It was noisier in the city centre as homecomers returned from a visit to the shops and theatres of the old West End in the old city beyond the Tower of London, flooding in on the tube as midnight approached. Mimsie Marker's paper stall was boarded up, but the club in the basement behind her was crowded, while the all-night coffee shop down the road (famous for a lot more than coffee) was full of light and movement.

One of the couples on the last tube train back from Leicester Square was Evelyn and her husband Peter Jones. Then they walked towards the block of flats where they had a top-floor apartment. Bodichon Street was close to Drossers Market where Evelyn had caught a glimpse of Etta Duval.

Drossers Street Market was just folding itself away for the night. One or two stalls were still operating.

'Good film, wasn't it?' said Peter to Evelyn. They were comfortable together. They both agreed that you had to get out of the Second City occasionally. This had been their night out. 'Cup of coffee? Tiger's Stall is still serving.'

'We're nearly home.'

'Let's live dangerously.'

They lined up at Tiger's counter to get a mug of his coffee, which was hot and strong.

'We your last customers?' asked Peter, as he paid for the coffee.

'Not quite.' Tim, such was Tiger's given name, nodded to the end of the stall. There in the shadows, leaning against the corner of the counter, back towards them, was a tall, thin girl, her hair falling over her shoulders. 'She's been there too long and I wish she'd move off.'

Peter stared at the girl, then turned to his wife. 'You know who that is?'

Evelyn stopped him. 'Leave this to me.' She walked up to

the girl, and touched her gently. 'Alice, you don't know me, but I know you.' She got no response at first, so even more gently she said it again. 'Alice?'

When Alice turned round it was to show a great blue bruise down the side of her face.

Evelyn put her arm round the girl's shoulders and led her away. 'Come along, Alice, I know where to take you, my dear.' Over the girl's head she looked at her husband. 'This kid's in trouble.'

'The refuge always opens its doors to those in distress,' said Mary Arden philosophically to Evelyn, but taking care not to let the girl hear. 'But why me?'

'There's no room in our flat, and I couldn't leave her on the streets. I know there's room here.'

Several families had moved out, as Evelyn knew, so yes, there was room.

'We're meant to help with family trouble, and I'd call her troubles family.'

Mary looked at her. 'Reckon so?'

'I do.'

'Well, she can't stay. Not for long. Just for a night.'

'While we work things out,' said Evelyn, who now felt responsible for the silent, weeping girl with Peter in the small waiting room.

'Did she say where she'd been?'

'Haven't asked,' said Evelyn.

'No clothes or anything with her?' said the knowledge-able Mary.

'She seems to have a small bag with her.'

'That'll have her make-up. They always bring their make-up,' said Mary. 'So she's not so bad, the really worst cases don't do that, can't stop for lipstick, but the medium-bad, the let's-get-out-of-here-and-take-over-my-own-life, they do. She'll probably have a nightdress and some money. That doesn't mean she didn't need an exit. You go. See you in the morning.'

When Evelyn had gone, Mary attended to Alice. She was kinder to the distraught girl than her brisk manner to Evelyn had suggested. She took her to the small bedroom which was free, and showed her the bathroom. The girl looked grubby, but it was late.

'Would you like a bath?'

Alice shook her head.

'In the morning then.' Mary was busy unpacking the small bag which did hold make-up and also a light cotton nightdress. Mary noticed that a thin band of blood ran along the hemline. She considered offering the girl a clean nightdress but decided to say nothing about it. 'I'm glad you are back.'

'I was coming back,' said Alice. 'I had to think about things . . .'

Mary looked at the bruise on her cheek. 'I bet you did.'

Family or boyfriend, either could be the problem. Sex was there too, somehow, sex gone wrong, you didn't get a blow that large out of love.

Coffin heard of her return the next morning; he knew before Phoebe Astley and Tony Davley.

Peter telephoned Stella to tell her. 'I thought you'd like to know.'

'He was right,' said Coffin.

'She worked with him in the theatre, part time while she waited for a part.' Stella looked thoughtful. 'I'm not sure if she was ever going to make it, not clever, you see, although with her connection she had a head start. Peter liked her, I think, probably a lot more than he wanted to admit. I have wondered if that's what she ran away from.'

'In part,' said Coffin. 'I shall want to talk to her.'

'No bullying.'

'Do I ever?'

Stella shook her head. 'You call it getting the right answers.'

'It's the job, the wrong answers are killers,' he said absently.

'We must tell Robbie the girl is safe.' As far as she can be, Stella thought with some cynicism.

'I will be seeing Gilchrist and Freedom this morning. They will both be told then.' At the moment and in the way that suits me best.

Stella looked worried. 'I think George was going to the airport, Robbie said something about New York.'

'I'll get him,' said Coffin, with conviction.

He finished his morning coffee, avoided food, because when there was any digging up to do he preferred not to eat, and told Stella that she must have Gus for the day. His reasoning here was the same. He had no desire to see a white Pekingese help dig up a body. Or what was left of it.

'Shall I tell Robbie you will be in touch?'

'Leave it strictly to me.'

'And if he rings here?'

'Tell him . . .' Coffin considered. 'Tell him nothing. Just say he will hear from me.' And he can sweat it out.

In the car, his mobile rang. He drew into a lay-by. 'Hello.'

'Phoebe Astley here, sir.' Her voice was tense. 'We're digging up the potato patch . . . I think you'd better come, sir. We think we've got something.'

'Hold on till I get there.'

Phoebe turned back to the small patch where Mr Jones had grown a few potatoes.

There was a brick wall with a door into the lane beyond, which was dominated by the blank wall of an old factory no longer in use but not yet turned into luxury apartments which was the fate of most of the early-nineteenth-century buildings in the Second City.

A narrow lane, one person wide, ran between this building and the next, equally tall and dead-looking. The map of the Second City which Coffin carried in his head told him that this lane must run out somewhere in the middle of the Drossers Lane Market.

If you wanted to bury a body then the garden was easy of access and at night would be quiet and dark.

And Mr Jones and dog had been away for over a month.

Phoebe Astley came up to him. She was one of the group standing by the patch of bare earth. He could see where the digging had begun.

'The spade hit something,' explained Phoebe, 'which is why they are using those small spades and sieving the soil.'

He nodded. 'Let's get on then.'

Two men were digging, doing so slowly, and carefully watched by one of the forensic team. Every so often this man would ask them to stop while he got down to examine the soil they were moving. He was on his knees when he held up his hand.

'Here we are.'

Mr Jones appeared at his back door, plus dog. The thin rangy mongrel, the dog who had started it all, lifted his head and began to howl.

'Get that dog inside,' snapped Phoebe. Mr Jones made a minimal movement of pushing the dog inside, but they both stayed where they were. However, the dog stopped howling.

Coffin moved nearer to the excavation, as did Phoebe. The diggers stopped, they all stood looking down at the small, plastic-wrapped object.

Must be the head, thought Coffin. He felt both excited and depressed at the same time.

Phoebe nodded at the photographer who came forward to take his careful pictures, then he stepped back and the forensic man slowly and meticulously undid the layers of plastic.

What was inside was looking smaller and smaller.

Not the head, must be the cat.

One last layer of plastic came away.

It was not the head. Not the cat. It was a baby, a small, very small bloodied foetus.

'About twenty-two to twenty-three weeks, I'd guess,' said the forensic man. 'Born dead, probably. Not viable anyway.' He got up from his knees. 'Not been out in this hard cold world long . . . twenty-four hours, thirty-six . . . Postmortem will tell.'

The dog no longer howled but started up a melodious whine almost like singing.

From the door, Mr Jones was shouting: 'This has nothing to do with me.'

Coffin looked at Phoebe Astley. 'Nothing to do with us either, do you think?' he asked.

She shrugged. 'Don't know.'

'The Gilchrist girl is back . . . you do know that?'

'Mary Arden phoned me just before I came out. She is worried about her.'

Coffin stood in thought. He could be all wrong about this, it was just guesswork.

'Look,' he said. 'I don't know where it all fits in. If it does, I'm doing one of those mad leaps that come occasionally.' Then as he turned away to his car: 'Get the girl into hospital. I think she may be in urgent need of medical attention . . . that's how they put it, isn't it?'

Phoebe said doubtfully that she would try.

'But do it as a friend.'

'And get Gilchrist and Freedom in. We will run a few things over them.'

10

The household at the Serena Seddon Refuge rose early, and there was already movement when Mary made a pot of tea and some toast to take up to Alice. Poor child, she thought, poor child.

On the stairs she met the boy Billy and realized that the quality in his eyes she and Evelyn had so meanly called evil was really sharp intelligence.

'Morning,' she said. 'And look after yourself. That quality you have got there is dangerous.'

The lad put his head on one side and grinned. 'Dunno what you mean, Mrs Arden. We're moving out.'

'I know.' Mary had been instrumental in finding the new home. 'And it's *Miss* Arden.'

'Mum says we've got a bit of luck at last.' He grinned. 'Miss.'

'Hang on to it then,' said Mary as she passed on up the stairs.

Without knowing it, she was about to do what the Chief Commander had asked. Not telepathy or anything such, each faced a question and found the right answer.

The nearest hospital to the Serena Seddon was the University Hospital. One way and another, Mary Arden had come to know it well. It was, alas, true that some of the women who came to her also needed medical help.

The Emergency and Accident Department respected and liked her because of the gentle and good-mannered way she dealt with her hurt and angry visitors. On occasion she had been the victim herself. Not all the scars she had come by showed on her skin.

Now she showed all the kindness and tact she had learned. Alice sat up in bed as she came in. She looked better.

Mary planted the tray on her knees. 'I've brought you breakfast.'

She sat down by the bed and watched Alice and saw a little more colour come into her face.

'Come on, Alice, we have to go and get you looked at. I could get a doctor here, but I fancy the hospital would be best. You are bleeding too much, and don't tell me it's your usual heavy period.' She touched the girl's hand. 'I've had a child.'

'What happened to it?'

Mary looked towards the window, towards light and air, and the living world. 'She died.' It was not something she talked about, although forgetting never.

'So did mine,' and Alice began to cry. Mary put her arms round her.

Evelyn arrived by the time they were ready to go to the hospital. Mary told her where she was going.

Evelyn nodded. 'I'll get on with things here. Anything to report?'

'No, all quiet.'

'That's because we are almost empty. It'll fill up again,' she said philosophically. After all, she wouldn't have a job if it didn't and she needed to earn.

'Any minute now,' agreed Mary. 'Goes in patches, doesn't it? If anyone rings like the police or such, say I am at the hospital.'

Phoebe Astley got the message when she rang. 'Right.' She was relieved because it meant she could get back to some of the more routine problems of the day, like checking that the poor little scrap they had dug up was on her way to the pathology laboratory, that the reports on the search for the head and torso were coming in as they should do, and that no one but no one took any more time off than was strictly necessary. And what was necessary she would decide.

On the telephone, she despatched DC Geoff Little and WDC Eleanor Brand to call on George Freedom and Robbie Gilchrist and bring them both in.

Politely mind.

She anticipated no trouble in this quest.

After a moment's thought, she decided to call at the hospital herself. A good career move, she thought. Coffin liked you to be hands on.

She went into the University Hospital just as the small body was being received in the pathology department, and while Alice Gilchrist was telling the story of her birth and death.

She was counted as an emergency and was being attended to by a young nurse and an equally young registrar. Mary Arden had not intruded but had left Alice to tell her own story.

Dr Martin had listened and examined Alice and then said that he would like her to see Dr Edith Brent who was the gynaecologist who would give her another thorough examination. His own examination was more superficial, he explained.

He did not explain that he found Alice puzzling. He could see she was a girl who would find the world puzzling, a girl who would accept the things that happened to her. But even so, he shook his head.

He was gentle and quiet so that Alice had found it easy to admit to the quick and unexpected early arrival of the child.

'Were you alone?' he asked.

'I was with a friend. She looked after me.'

'And the baby, the foetus? You are sure it was dead?' From what he had gathered it was twenty-two to twenty-three weeks, and not viable. But there might be a worrying point here if the police asked.

There was a long pause.

'My friend said she would deal with it.'

After a moment's thought, he left it there. After all, he thought, I am a doctor, not a policeman or a social worker. Then he sent her with a nurse to see Dr Edith Brent. Alice had to wait some twenty minutes before she saw her.

Dr Brent was a large lady with a generous bust and a froth of white hair. A small nurse was in attendance. Once again, Alice was examined on a comfortable couch behind a tactful screen. Dr Brent was slow, careful and gentle. She was silent at first, then asked Alice to get her clothes on and come and sit on the chair by her desk.

'You seem all right, my dear. No damage done. There could have been . . . these quick births can be tricky. No time to get into hospital?'

Alice shook her head.

'Which doctor are you registered with?'

Alice shook her head again.

'You didn't attend a prenatal clinic? You didn't visit your GP when you thought you were pregnant?' She already knew the answer to that question. One of those, she thought. Why, why? You don't get sent to a nunnery these days.

But she knew also that there was always a background, a reason for secrecy like this.

'I've been staying with a friend,' said Alice quickly. 'Here in the Second City. My own GP is in Kensington, I am registered there, but I have never seen him.' She seemed to have it off pat like a learned lesson.

Dr Brent studied some notes that had been handed on to her. 'So a friend was with you. Who was that?'

'Katy Cameron. I was staying with her.'

'And she dealt with the afterbirth and the baby? What did she do?'

Alice was quiet. Then she said: 'She told me she would do what was right.'

'I see.'

Dr Brent did not see, but at that moment, Alice was her patient. 'I expect Katy can tell us.'

Alice licked her lips. 'Well, yes. But she's gone home . . . to Jamaica.'

'Oh, is that the case?' Dr Brent considered. It couldn't be left there but she knew already, having spoken to Mary Arden, that DCI Astley was waiting in the wings.

She bent her head to the desk and wrote on a pad.

She rose and held out her hand. 'I must see you again, my dear, but meanwhile Nurse here will take you out to the desk to make an appointment. She will take you to get these tablets. Is anyone with you?'

'Miss Arden.'

'Oh yes, I remember you are staying with her. Where is she now?'

Alice looked vague. The nurse answered for her: 'In the private waiting room, Doctor.'

When the two had left, Dr Brent dictated some notes about the case on her machine, then she walked down the corridor to where Mary Arden was sitting.

The two women knew each other, having met in the past over the case of a resident at the Serena Seddon Refuge who had a difficult labour and produced twins, interestingly, of different colours.

Dr Brent outlined to Mary what she had learnt from Alice.

Mary nodded. 'More or less what she told me.'

'Did you believe all that?'

Mary considered. 'No,' she said.

Dr Brent said that she guessed that Alice had been classed as educationally subnormal. She looked at Mary with enquiry.

'Alice, Alice, sit by the Fire. That was Barrie, wasn't it? And Sam Pepys had a servant called Alice. Nice name, really, always sounds innocent.'

'Our Alice is not a liar,' said Mary at once.

'No.' A nod of acceptance.

Mary said carefully, 'All the same, I don't think it is quite the truth. She's holding something back.'

Phoebe Astley was waiting for her, she had been walking up and down the corridor impatiently.

'Didn't like to come in.'

'I'm not sure if I'm surprised to see you or not.'

'I'm here because we found the body of a baby, it was buried in an old man's garden and his dog tried to dig it up.'

Mary drew her breath in. 'You think it is Alice's child?'

'That's why you are here, isn't it? Tests will show if the girl is the mother,' said Phoebe bluntly. 'What does she say?'

'Not much.'

'I'd better come back and talk to her.'

'Keep out of it, Phoebe.'

'This might be a police matter.'

*   *   *

During all this time, DC Geoff Little and WDC Eleanor Brand were trawling the area around and behind Drossers Lane, trying to find Robbie Gilchrist and George Freedom; they had addresses for both men, but they were elusive. They lived in apartments in the same converted factory but on different floors and on opposite ends of the building. This, as Stella could have told them, was the epitome of their relationship. Near each other but not too near. Was either man here? Or had both taken a move to somewhere? This was a check.

There were several such buildings, one or two derelict, another used by temporary tenants for storage, and yet another, which had once been a frozen meat store (it had its mini-railway to the docks) and was now empty, condemned by the Health and Food officers. It was well-decorated with graffiti. The block where George Freedom and Robbie Gilchrist lived was painted and clean. Sophistication stopped at that point.

There was no doorman and no obvious security, you just walked in.

They tried the Gilchrist door first; DC Little rang the bell, and getting no answer hammered on the door. Still no reply.

'Out,' said Eleanor Brand. She bent down and looked through the letter box. 'No post lying there, and no newspaper.'

'Maybe he had no letters and doesn't take a newspaper.'

''Course he does, he's a writer, he'll want to know the news.'

'You seem to know about him.'

'I do my homework, Geoff. You never know when a bit of knowledge will come in.'

DC Little sighed. It could be wearing working with an ambitious woman.

'Bang again.'

Little did so, and with greater force, keeping up a sort of fusillade.

Along the corridor a door opened and a woman's head peered round. 'For God's sake,' she said. 'He'd have answered now if he wasn't dead. Or even if he was dead, I should think.'

With interest, Little said, 'You don't think he is dead?'

'I shan't answer that.' And she closed the door.

Eleanor moved down the corridor. 'Let's try Freedom.'

This time, she rang the bell, leaning on it somewhat heavily.

Speedily the door swung open. A tall, thin woman wearing an apron made of sacking and thick rubber gloves appeared. She carried a mop in one hand and a scrubbing brush in the other. She was clearly one of the old school of cleaners, not prepared to use any modern pieces of equipment like vacuum cleaners and floor polishers. 'No need to break the bell.'

'Mr Freedom?'

'Not at home.' She was preparing to close the door.

Eleanor Brand asked politely when he would be back.

'Gone. Paid my wages, packed his bags, and gone.'

'What? For how long?'

'I dunno, do I? I'm not his nursemaid. He's a fly-by-night, anyway, theatricals often are.'

The door closed.

'Don't relish going back and telling Chief Inspector Astley we haven't got them.'

'Not our fault.'

'It will be somehow, in the end, you'll see,' said Little with a glum face.

'She's not like that.'

'Not one of the worst,' admitted Little. 'Let's go and have some coffee in that café place in the market. They may know something.'

'They won't.'

'We can say that's why we went in. Use your brain.'

The first and best eating place in Drossers Market, which they both knew, Stormy Weather, just offered: FOOD ALL DAY.

This included, as they well knew, drink and possibly drugs, but that had proved very hard to establish.

DC Little went to collect two cups of coffee and two doughnuts, he was not on a diet although probably Eleanor Brand was. Another man was leaning against the counter, and he gave Little a quick look before turning away.

'Jam or chocolate?' asked the truly large lady, almost the largest he had ever seen. 'Doughnuts, jam or choc?' she prodded him.

'Jam.' She did not seem the most approachable of women, this large lady, and yet there was a look in her eyes imbedded in her flesh which suggested she knew the street scene.

She's been more than once up and down the street, he thought.

'I called on Mr Freedom, lives in the new block of apartments, he wasn't home. I wondered if you knew him and if he'd been in . . . I know he pops in here to eat.' A lie, this, but there you are, he had to say something.

She did look at him but said nothing, just a shake of the head.

Little went back, and planted the two cups with the plate of doughnuts in front of Eleanor Brand.

'No luck there.'

In a corner table was a man with red hair and a twisted nose who seemed to be discussing his supper with his neighbour, tall and thin with spectacles. Beef seemed on order.

'Who's that?' Eleanor nodded towards the red-haired man.

Little took a quick look. 'Oh, that's Hamish Scott. Not a bad villain as they go.'

'Is he a Scot?'

'Not as far as I know. It's only his name. Beef, did he say? He's always been a big eater.' He embarked on a doughnut with some satisfaction.

The man who had been at the counter came across. 'You were asking for Mr Freedom.'

'Yes, do you know him?' Little put down his coffee.

'Not to say know. Know who he is. Seen him around the theatre.'

'You're an actor?'

'When I can be,' said Dave with a grin. 'And if you want Mr Freedom, I saw him go off in a taxi with a suitcase.'

'Ah, thanks.'

Dave went back to the counter, where he said to the large lady that he'd told 'em Freedom was in a taxi and off.

'Best to keep away from the police.'

'If you can,' he said, but without emphasis. 'I saw Freedom hit a girl across the face, kid that works in the theatre a bit . . . I like to help a woman when I can.'

'You're an attractive man, Dave,' said the fat lady. 'Not a good man, but attractive.'

'And you're attractive too, my dear, and not good either.'

Eleanor, who had watched this byplay, said nothing, and leaned across to Little. 'And I know him . . . Saw him when he came to make a statement . . . he's the one who found the cat's head.'

'He's been a bit helpful.' Little drained his coffee.

'Not because he loves us,' said Eleanor thoughtfully.

Alone in his office, Coffin called Stella. He had had a phone call about the state of the girl Alice.

'I'm with them,' Phoebe said. 'Just going back to the Serena Seddon with them. I'm not wanted but I am going.'

Phoebe was a friend of Mary but she was not always tactful. They did not know each other that well.

'Have you got time to go round to the Refuge Seddon to talk to Mary Arden?'

Stella sighed. 'You'd better tell me: what is it you want me to do?'

'Get round there. Check if all is well?'

'What is it all about?'

'No. Later.'

'No – not even what all being well means?'

'You'll discover. But be tactful.'

'If it's of interest to you, I have George and Robbie here now. No, they did not go to New York, just wanted out. They heard on the grapevine you want to talk to them and they are undecided whether to stay around and be talked to or to take Concorde out on its next flight to anywhere.'

'Are they in the room with you?'

'No,' she said smoothly. 'I have parked them in that little room where I put actors who want a part that I am not going to give them. They thought I was a safe pair of hands.'

'Leave them then, and pop round to the Serena Seddon.'

'Suppose they break out?'

143

'They won't break far,' said Coffin grimly. 'And say nothing to them, nothing. Will you do this for me?'

'Yes, that part is easy because nothing is what I know . . . But I can't see why one of your nice cosy policewomen can't do it.'

'You may not believe me, but I am thinking of the girl.'

Accordingly, Stella put her head round the door of the room in which Freedom and Gilchrist were walking up and down impatiently. 'Be with you in a sec, boys. Hang on.' She returned to the phone to finish her conversation with Coffin.

George Freedom made a kind of sideways dancing step across the room as she left. 'Goodbye, lady, goodbye . . . Not a bad idea for a song, Robbie. Perhaps we could do a duet.'

'What part do I get?'

'You can be soprano.' Georgie was still tiptoeing here and there. His line was unsteady.

Robbie looked at George's dancing feet.

'My footwork is better than yours.'

George stopped dancing. 'We ought to be on the stage.'

'Ha, ha, you always were the jokes man.'

'And the money man, don't forget that.'

'I'd like to continue this conversation on that account,' said Robbie, standing up, 'but you are boring me. That's one thing: two, is don't you wonder why the police want to see us, both of us, together, and why we are put in cold storage.'

'Yes,' said Freedom, sitting and taking off his shoes. 'God, these shoes pinch . . . Something has happened.'

'And what is it that links us together?'

'Money, the theatre, Stella Pinero.'

'They are all one and the same thing. What else?'

After a pause, in which he put his shoes back on, Freedom said: 'The girl we share in common: Alice.'

'I don't like the way you put that,' said Gilchrist, 'but yes, Alice . . . When she turns up – if she turns up – I hope she tells us what you've done to her.' He began to shiver.

'You too,' said Freedom.

Robbie hurled himself at Freedom and began to punch him.

A drop of blood appeared down Freedom's nose and ran down his shirt collar. He swore and kicked at Robbie.

Stella heard them while she was still talking to Coffin. 'I must hang up. I can hear those two men fighting.'

11

Parted by Stella, who displayed her usual determination and control, and advised to calm down, Freedom and Gilchrist were driven round to Coffin's office.

Stella called Coffin and told him she would be bringing them in on the way to the refuge.

'I'll send a car,' he said at once.

'They will hate that. Like being arrested.'

'Freedom has been arrested once, he ought to know what it feels like.'

But Stella, as shrewd a psychologist as her husband, drove them herself. If they survived, she still wanted their money. Also, and this was where the psychology came in, she did not believe that either of the men, even Freedom, was guilty of the sort of crimes that had happened. The bloody man even liked cats.

Also, and she faced this fact: her husband wanted to get Freedom, he wanted him to be guilty.

When they arrived at the Headquarters of the Second City Police Force, a new and architecturally fierce building created by an architect who was into brutalism, she stopped the car and sat there, letting the two men see the force of the building and know apprehension.

She could see it in Freedom's face, although he tried to hide it. He had had one stay in prison, and did not desire to go back. It's not the inmates, he was thinking. It's the warders. They hated me. They hated him because the charge against him was of attempting to kill a young girl. She was very badly hurt. Only but for the grace of God was he a murderer, was believed of him.

'Go in, boys,' she said, 'and unburden your soul.'

'We have got one each,' snarled George. 'Not one soul between us.'

'I've often wondered,' said Stella, departing. 'Someone in uniform will see you up. There is no lift, you will have to walk.' She was lying, but she thought a walk up a flight of stairs was just what they deserved.

By now, Coffin had spoken to Phoebe Astley again and she had passed on the speculation that George Freedom was the father of the child born to Alice and that he had hit the girl on the face, which had brought on the premature birth. No details, though, Phoebe had said regretfully, the girl is not yet talking. She had added, But Mary Arden and I will get the full tale, no fear.

This had all happened after he had decided to ask Stella to call in on the refuge.

Robbie came in silently, and George Freedom flounced behind him, and delivered himself of a loud judgement:

'So you want to talk to us? I should think you'd got something better to do than that.'

'Yes, I have. I have. But Albie is a friend, someone I happen to like and he was gunned down on my doorstep. And not the only thing on doorsteps round here.' Arms, legs, a handbag. 'I take a sharp interest in all that. A personal interest.'

Robbie remained silent, while Freedom grunted something under his breath.

'You know Albert Touchey, I believe,' said Coffin.

'We've met.'

'Of course you have. He has come round, he is able to speak and name his attacker.' Not quite true and Coffin knew it: Albie had said one word: Freedom. After this he had relapsed into unconsciousness again.

'If he named me then he was wrong.'

'I didn't say so.'

'You didn't have to; I know you lot. It's what you are hinting and you want me to react.'

Which you are doing, thought Coffin. He looked blandly at his foe. Yes, he felt Freedom was his enemy. Then he stopped himself in mid-thought: he was professional enough to know how dangerous the concept was. He swallowed back the thought and it went down like a hard, hot pill which went cold as it passed down his gut.

Coldness was much less dangerous.

'If this is how it is going, then I want a solicitor.'

'Of course.' Coffin was all courtesy. 'And I will not be questioning you myself.' He stood up, he was tall and Freedom was short, he could look down on him. 'But I will take you down myself.'

For a moment, Freedom hesitated, as if he would not move unless forced. He turned to Gilchrist. 'What about you, then?'

Robbie took a step as if making for the door. 'Not you, Mr Gilchrist,' said Coffin. 'I want to talk to you.' At the door, he paused and said to Gillian, his secretary: 'Make Mr Gilchrist comfortable and give him some coffee.'

Gillian came forward with the nervous smile which afflicted her when the Chief Commander was in an awkward mood. He was always polite, but when he was like that, you had to watch your step.

Here, she rightly interpreted the Chief Commander's words as, Keep an eye on Gilchrist and make sure he doesn't see or hear anything that he shouldn't. So she gave Robbie a cup of strong coffee in the best china while watching that he didn't read anything that was on the computer screen. The telephone she would not answer while he was there and listening.

He was listening and watching, for which she could not blame him.

'Might get a scene or two out of this one day,' he said. 'Comedy. Oh yes, it has its comic side.'

'Not everyone would find it funny,' observed Gillian.

'Depends where you stand, comedy, tragedy, thin dividing line.'

'I've heard people say that and never believed it.'

'Take it from me.'

He was the tiniest bit drunk, she decided, an opinion reinforced when he poured something from a hip flask into his coffee. 'Medicinal,' he said.

Coffin came back, he nodded at Gillian and swept Robbie before him into his own office.

Why am I nervous? Robbie asked himself. I haven't done anything. I HAVEN'T DONE ANYTHING.

'All set up,' said Coffin.

'He's being interviewed?'

'He will be. He may have to wait some time.' There was a delicate cruelty here that made Robbie understand why he was nervous. This man here was more formidable than when met at dinner with Stella Pinero. And it was anger that gave him force, Robbie suddenly grasped, not cruelty.

He remembered what he had read in the newspapers and heard on the television news and picked up from the gossip of the theatre.

The limbs, arms and legs of a woman, left on the doorstep of that house in Barrow Street. A house in which Coffin had once lodged.

The woman shot dead in the car park. She had lived in that house too.

Albie Touchey, Prison Governor, shot and seriously wounded outside the tower in St Luke's.

And there was something else too, not yet in the papers or on TV but talked about, all over the theatre, the head of a cat left inside the tower home of Stella and John Coffin. There were other rumours going round the theatre too, some wilder than others.

Make a great Gothic, he thought, a play or film.

He shook his head. Not his style. Not really Freedom's style either. Too *Grand Guignol*.

'He's a skunk, a bloody good writer but a skunk. Not a murderer though, anything else, rapist, seducer, wife-beater, oh yes, but not that, not a murderer . . . A coward, you see, in the final countdown.'

Coffin did not answer.

'And if he did do it, you'll never get him, he's as cunning as a fox. I ought to know.'

'I asked you to stay behind because I wanted to tell you about Alice, your stepdaughter. She's turned up.'

'Everyone's stepdaughter,' said Robbie, 'with a mother like

that, always moving on. I'm glad the girl is back. I'm fond of her.'

'I thought you were.'

'She's all right?' Robbie had caught a note in Coffin's voice. 'Turned up . . . you don't mean she's dead?'

'No, she's safe enough and well enough. She's at the Serena Seddon being looked after by the people there.'

'Come on, there's more than this. What is it?'

Briefly, Coffin told him what Phoebe Astley had passed on to him.

'She's an innocent,' groaned Robbie. 'Couldn't take the pill, made her ill. Wouldn't remember anyway. Some bloody man took advantage of her. Did she say?'

'She's a bit confused. And frightened.'

'It's Freedom, that's what you think. I'll kill him.' And then: 'What happened to the baby?'

'It was buried,' said Coffin in a neutral voice.

'There's a lot you're not telling me.' Robbie glared at him.

'She can't stay at the refuge,' went on Coffin, ignoring what Robbie said. 'Can you arrange to take her away . . . not far, because we shall need to talk to her.'

'Now I know there is something,' cried Robbie.

Coffin suddenly felt very tired.

Robbie stood up. 'I'll get off to see Alice. That's allowed, I suppose? I'll find out what went on from her, she trusts me. And I'll look after her.' He got to the door unchecked. 'And what about Freedom?'

'Leave him to us,' said Coffin. 'We will look after him.'

George Freedom sat for over an hour, alone, in the room where questioning went on, while he waited for his solicitor to appear. His solicitor, Edward Tremain, had offices in the city of London off Fleet Street, though near to the Law Courts, but lived in Epsom. He was working at home that day so he took some time to arrive. Traffic hold-ups, he explained when he arrived in the Second City.

Freedom, increasingly angry as time went by, was offered coffee and tea but refused everything. He accused the police sourly of delaying things on purpose.

'He's on his way, sir,' said the constable who had brought the tea. 'He rang through on his mobile to say he was held up on the motorway, and would be here soon.'

Freedom glowered and managed to upset the teacup so it went over the constable's trousers.

'Sorry,' he said. 'Oh dear, did it burn you?'

When Edward Tremain hurried in, Freedom swore at him and demanded the police get on with it.

'Glad to, Mr Freedom,' said Phoebe Astley, who had come back from Serena Seddon, leaving a sleeping Alice and an exhausted Mary Arden.

She questioned Freedom for a couple of hours about his movements in the Second City on the four days which were important.

The evening on which the legs and arms were deposited on the doorstep of the refuge.

The morning on which Etta Duval had been shot and killed.

The evening on which Albie had been shot, possibly in mistake for the Chief Commander.

And the afternoon on which a cat's head had been left inside the home of the Chief Commander.

Freedom, after a quick look at his solicitor, denied any knowledge of these events. Couldn't even remember the dates.

Phoebe had thought of this. She pushed over a sheet of paper with the dates on them.

Freedom pushed it back.

The solicitor started to make a deprecating noise.

'And don't you say anything,' said Freedom, rounding on him. He produced his diary from his pocket and threw it at Phoebe. 'Here you are, read it, see for yourself where I was and what I was doing. Damned if I can remember.'

The solicitor made a quiet, moaning noise.

'May I keep this?' Phoebe asked politely. 'I will, of course, return it to you.'

She then questioned him about any knowledge he had of Henriette Duval.

'Didn't know the girl.'

'Are you sure? Be worrying for us if we found you did.'

She showed him a photograph, procured from Mary Arden, showing the girl in a summer dress with her hair flowing over her shoulders.

He looked. 'Might have seen her around. Seem to know the face.' He returned the photograph. Then he reached out to take the picture back. 'Might have seen her around.'

'Thank you.' Phoebe made a note, carefully and deliberately, since she had observed that the sight of her making notes made him jumpy. Jumpier the better, she thought.

'You know Mr Touchey, of course.'

'Of course I do, you know that. I've been asked it once and said I knew him, and I didn't shoot him. I don't like him but he's a fair bastard and I wouldn't and didn't shoot him. Haven't got a gun.'

He looked at his solicitor, who murmured that the chief inspector had no evidence.

Phoebe made an excuse, suspended the interview, and went back some twenty minutes later, to take him through it all again. She kept a wary eye on the solicitor and framed her questions carefully. 'Just checking.'

Then she let him go. 'Your stepdaughter Alice has been found,' she said, as he left. 'I expect you will want to see her. And I believe Mr Gilchrist wants to see you.'

'And he went white,' said Phoebe as she reported to Coffin later.

Coffin raised his head from the sea of papers on his desk, then switched off his computer which seemed to be telling him things he did not wish to hear about a bomb in Central London. His turn in the Second City next, he thought.

He was glad to give his attention to Phoebe Astley who had pushed her way past the protective Gillian.

'What did he say about the girl?'

'Just: silly bitch.'

'Charming.' He added thoughtfully. 'Someone will beat him up one day and I think it will be Robbie Gilchrist.'

'I don't think we will get him for anything, more's the pity. He's in the clear. Still, we put the wind up him.'

'Do you think just one person did all three crimes?'

'Four, if you count breaking and entering and leaving the feline head.' The dog, Gus, had not settled down yet after this intrusion and still went around snuffling and whining gently. 'No. I'm not sure about that.'

He had three teams working on the different crimes, each of them throwing specimens at forensics and begging for answers.

'I keep hoping forensics will come up with something,' said Phoebe Astley. 'So far nothing.'

'I had noticed.

'Anything else?'

'There was one thing,' said Phoebe slowly. 'At first he denied knowing Henriette Duval. Then he said he might have seen her around.'

'So?'

'Just as he was leaving, he told me he associated her with food, with eating.'

Coffin looked doubtful. 'Invention to get you going?'

'He'd got me going already, he knew I disliked him . . . No, the thing is, I think he believed it.'

Phoebe went off on her next mission; find out where Freedom eats. Start off by asking him, said common sense.

He had left the building, in the company of his reluctant solicitor. He had left behind him a threat of an action for harassment, using language which made his solicitor pinch his lips.

Called by Tony Davley on his mobile phone, he answered in a thick voice. 'Hello.'

Sloshed, pissed, drunk, thought Tony as she introduced herself.

'God give me strength,' said Freedom. 'What is it now?'

Tony put her question.

'Where I eat, damn you? I eat in New York, Paris, London, and this bloody Second City. I eat wherever I am, and no, I can't remember where I saw that face. Maybe I didn't.'

Tony ground her teeth. Over the line, she could hear the solicitor making plaintive noises, and Freedom shouting, OK, OK. Then he came back to her:

'It seemed cheap and cheerful, so it was round here some-where. Best I can do and you're lucky to get that.'

John Coffin, Chief Superintendent Archie Young (called away from his preoccupation with the Russian visit) and DCI Phoebe Astley met for a drink in the bar in the basement of the building. It was an egalitarian bar in which rank got you a drink no quicker, but there was a certain corner which was left for the Chief Commander and anyone he might be drinking with. Now in a crowded room, they were left alone. Watched but not spoken to. This was a democratic force, but few went up to the Chief Commander with a breezy Hello.

'Got a face of doom on him,' said one uniformed coffee drinker. 'And don't I know why.' There was plenty of specu-lation and bawdy jokes about what the Chief Commander knew about the owner of the legs and arms left where he had once lived.

The mood of all three in the select corner was depressed. Stella had spoken to him from the refuge, saying that the girl Alice was recovering and it was a lousy business.

'Stella,' he had started to say, longing to speak to her, but she had put the receiver down pretty quick. Not a good sign for future relations.

He himself had telephoned the hospital to see how Albie Touchey was, and the answer was, No change. He was murmuring odd words and was coming round, but not yet.

Not yet, words of doom, thought Coffin gloomily.

'We've been at it for some time,' said Phoebe. 'And we don't have a suspect.'

She hated this thought: she usually had a suspect in her mind, even if later it turned out to be the wrong one, that was police work, you worked on.

'Even George Freedom didn't qualify. I don't like him, but I don't see him as guilty.'

Knowing that the media was yapping at their heels, Coffin ordered Phoebe: 'Get a notice in the papers saying we are pursuing an important line.'

'And hope for an announcement soon?'

Coffin was a realist. 'No, that would be pushing our luck.'

He gave Phoebe a sharp look, and to her that look said, Get on with it.

He had given her quick promotion and now he wanted results.

Phoebe Astley went back to her office, she felt lonely and lost, she had few friends in the Second City and now it looked as if her career was going down the drain fast.

In the big incident room she had two separate teams working, one searching for the torso and head, still missing. The second team was working on the shootings. The break-in at the Chief Commander's home, and the depositing of the head of the cat, was shuttled between the two as officers completed one task and reported on it and moved on afresh. The third team sat at desks and computers and collated everything.

The total result so far was a pile of reports and photographs, all carefully studied by Phoebe who also discussed them with the officers concerned.

She was summarizing her thoughts aloud, bemoaning Freedom's regrettable way of giving information. 'You can tell he writes comedy,' she complained.

'I've had some good laughs from him on TV shows he's put on,' said a constable, handing her yet another bundle of reports.

'Chopping Tree Lane.' A voice spoke up from the table in front of Phoebe. 'Cheap and easy eating there. And everything else,' the young woman added thoughtfully. 'Samuel Pepys said it had the most liberal stews and pimps and whores in the whole of East Hythe. The lane that runs between Drossers Lane Market and where Freedom lives is the old Chopping Tree Lane.' She stood up to face Phoebe, a tall, solid girl, not beautiful but taking. 'I don't think its character has changed all that much. It's called Pepys' Alley now.'

'I thought that was Inches Street,' called a cheerful baritone from across the room.

'It was until that Know Your Own History Month last year and then it was changed to commemorate Pepys.' She added thoughtfully, 'He called it Piss Alley.'

'You seem to know a lot about it, Liz,' came from the baritone. 'Go there a lot, do you?'

'No, clever clogs. I'm just interested in the past. More your sort of scene than mine.'

Phoebe was remembering that where the child's body had been buried and where George Freedom lived in the old warehouse were close together too, both near Chopping Tree Lane and both near Drossers Market.

She made a decision: 'Concentrate on that triangle; Drossers Market, Pepys' Alley or whatever it is called and the road where the child was found. Question people, search it, photograph it, dig it up.'

The room went quiet.

'Anything from pathology about the child yet?'

'Natural death . . . report is on the way,' called a voice. 'It's being faxed. Coming through now.'

Phoebe walked across to pick up the pages as they appeared. Her eye fell on the comment that DNA specimens would be necessary if there was an attempt to prove paternity.

Back to Freedom again, then.

A few hundred yards from Chopping Tree Lane was the canal, now unused, built by Irish labourers before the railways came. It had had an industrial life until after the last war when the factories along its banks closed one after another and fell empty or were converted into luxury apartments. The canal then became a selling point and the word Venice was mentioned. Freedom and Gilchrist had debated using the scene for a television comedy: *Watermen at Play* . . . provisional title only. Both of them could see the canal from their bedroom windows.

Now it was occasionally used by pleasure barges, and there was talk of 'kind of a marina' being constructed further down the canal towards the Essex coast, but at the moment children played on the canal path and rats lived there in some peace. It was a health and safety hazard by any standard.

This being so, a police constable patrolled the path at irregular intervals. Irregular because if the kids knew the time you were coming, they stopped whatever wrongdoing they were up to. It was a favourite police walk because you could stop and have a fag.

WPC Winifred Darby was just about to do that when she saw a cluster of kids on the canal bank. Experience suggested she go to look. WPC Darby was a sturdy, matronly lady with a family of her own.

'What have you got there?' Once a bag of drugs had surfaced. As she walked towards them, she did just hope it wasn't that head they were all being encouraged to find. She didn't fancy a decomposing head when she was hungry. (Lose some weight, Win, her husband had suggested, I like an armful of woman in bed but not a sackful. Hurtful but true.)

But not this evening.

'It's a gun,' said the leader of the troop, a boy like a bright-eyed monkey. 'I reckon we ought to get a reward . . .' He read the newspapers and watched the TV news. 'I reckon it's the one that killed that woman.'

Win Darby knew what to do. 'Leave it where it is, don't touch it.' And she got on her mobile to phone in the news.

She hoped the incident room would be pleased and give her and the young monkey a good mark.

A long working day over, Coffin went back home, walking to give the dog some exercise. He let himself in, checking that the new alarms system was working. Certainly made enough noise, he thought as he switched it off, and if the noise went on beyond three minutes then Police Headquarters were alerted.

Today there was a police car parked outside. That mustn't go on, police money must not be used too freely on him.

Stella was at home, waiting for him. She seemed more cheerful than he had expected in view of the fact that she might be losing George Freedom's money and possibly also the comedy sketches he and Gilchrist were going to produce, using the small Theatre Workshop, and selling it to one of the big television companies, with possibility of US transmission.

'Sorry about all this, upset your plans with Freedom and Gilchrist.'

'I couldn't use him or his money if he has behaved the way he seems to have done.'

'He may not be the killer.'

Coffin had underestimated Stella's cool practical good sense. 'I'll miss the money the comedies might have brought in, but on the other hand, TV writers don't always transfer well to the stage. And it wouldn't do me or the theatre any good to be mixed up with him. He's bad publicity whether he murdered anyone in the Second City or not.'

'No, I agree. Robbie Gilchrist is out of it.' Had never really been in view as the killer; the police investigation was floundering. Soon the media – the newspaper and the television commentators would pick it up, and then the roof might fall in.

Mimsie Marker had summed it up: Blind Man's Buff, that's what it is, and no one knowing the tune. They need a leader and the Chief is keeping his head below the parapet. She hated having to put it like this, she had admired Coffin, called him 'One of us', but on the other hand, selling newspapers was her business and a sparky comment helped to sell them.

Very gently, Stella said: 'And I hope you manage to keep your feet clear too.'

He sat in silence, this was settlement time.

'If things go down, I may have to resign.'

Stella remained silent, watching his face.

'Would you like me to do it now?'

She was still silent. Was that a smile, kindly or mocking, just moving her lips?

'It's time I put us, you, first,' he said. He had the uneasy feeling that he was sinking, deeper and deeper, water over his head soon. Oddly enough, he was still breathing and not feeling too bad.

She was laughing. No doubt about it.

'You fool. Of course you mustn't resign. If there's a war on, then I fight on your side. Always, you know that.'

This was where, Coffin thought afterwards, we should fall into each other's arms and passionately embrace.

What happened was that the telephone rang, and so conditioned were they both, that both moved to answer it. They collided, rolling together on the floor in each other's arms.

Coffin managed to reach out to get the telephone.

There was another diary written some time after Samuel Pepys's visit with his friend Dr Williams to East Hythe. This was the diary of Margery Loveheart, actress and widow.

August 3, A Sunday

Last night, being a Saturday and after visiting my daughter Sarah who is playing at the new St Giles Theatre where she is Lady Macbeth, I walked home together with my servant John through Chopping Tree Lane.

As we walked I saw that we were walking among a herd of dead cows. I knew they were dead because they were being carried in a great cart which was freezing cold. The cart was closed in with no windows but somehow I could see inside.

The cart itself was mighty and horrible, unlike to any cart I had seen before since it moved on its own strength with no horse or animal pulling it.

And behind me came another cart, this time full of sheep, bleating and moving about, which was not to be believed because they were already jointed, legs and shoulder.

I turned to John and asked him what he made of this, but he stared at me and said he saw nothing but the street and our house ahead. And then he said he was frightened for me for there was the Plague about and what I saw was a warning that I was ill.

He would not walk beside me then but moved forward to march in front.

It is true that the carts faded away as he spoke and my head ached mightily and all I saw was a couple of black and white cats.

I believe I shall be ill, but I have good girls in my house and they will look after me.

*   *   *

Editor's note: Three pages of this diary were found, bound up in a book of housewifery and cookery which is dated 1703. The paper is old, the writing looks genuine, but some doubts must remain.

From the magistrate's record of East Hythe court at this time it is clear that the 'house' of which Mrs Loveheart spoke was a bawdy house which she owned and her girls were whores.

It is a strange vision she saw of frozen meat trundling through seventeenth-century East Hythe.

Editor: Dr E. Marting. *Stories of East Hythe.*

12

Phoebe's voice was quick and anxious. 'Glad you're there, sir, thought you might not be. I thought Miss Pinero said she was taking you out for a meal.'

He looked at Stella, now tidying her hair. Had she said that? Phoebe was not likely to have got it wrong. So was it to have been the last meal before the execution or a friendly meal because she loved him?

'We might be off later.' He looked at his wife, no expression other than gentle interest on the lovely face, but who can trust to an actress's expression. He took heart from what she had said: I fight on your side. 'So what is it?'

'Earlier today after questioning George Freedom, and getting nothing from him and nothing circumstantial from forensic, I thought he really was out of the picture. Now I am not so sure.'

'Go on.'

'We had Albie Touchey's single word "Freedom", nothing else. I've got his diary and the chain of engagements in it give alibis for all-important dates . . . the limbs, he says he was with you, then in bed and asleep; the first shooting, he says he would never use a gun in anger and was in bed when Etta was shot . . . admittedly he seems to have been in the Second City when Albie was shot, but working at home and making telephone calls which prove it, so he claims. But is this the truth? It could all be a carefully constructed tissue of lies.'

'So why are you now saying he is in the picture?'

'Because he is, sir. He is all over it.' Phoebe defended herself with her usual energy. 'His name keeps coming up in the places where there's been trouble . . . And the detective firm that was hired, Geoff Fraber, gave up without pay, didn't trust either of them. I've spoken to Fraber and although he is being professional and discreet, he got out. Freedom lives pretty close to where the baby was found, he might have known the old man was away . . . Alice hasn't told the truth about the birth, and we don't know if the child died in labour or in utero. And he admits he knew Etta . . . well, he admits he saw her in an eating place. He claims to be vague but I reckon he knows he was seen there and that other people saw him too. Admitting it because he has to. We don't know where this eating place was, but I'm betting it is near what was Chopping Tree Lane. Say the Stormy Weather eating place? The sort of place he might like . . . good food and probably criminous. He permeates everywhere, Freedom does.'

Coffin considered. It was true but meant little. He disliked Freedom and certainly believed he would be a ready man with a gun. 'Not much, Phoebe,' he said. 'Motive?'

'Yet to be established, sir, but there will be one. I guess he thought she knew too much about him. Perhaps she did.'

Coffin wanted to believe it.

'But that's not all: the gun has been traced.'

Coffin sat up. 'What? Where?'

'Near the canal. Found in grass on the side.'

'Not in the water?'

'No.' Phoebe's voice suggested that she too found that carelessness puzzling. 'But there was a handkerchief with it. Let's see if it's Freedom's.'

'I'm thinking,' said Coffin. 'Where did it come from, any clues?'

'It's got to be the gun that was used, sir. I don't believe in coincidence.'

Coffin thought that he did not believe in lucky chances either but he did not say so. 'Provenance?' he asked.

'Too early to say, but it matches with one of the guns stolen from the Abbey Road Gun Club.'

Coffin said: 'Well done, Phoebe, I'm impressed.'

'Yes, I reckon he stole it from the Abbey Road Gun Club.'

'Wouldn't it be easier to have bought one. Plenty floating round the place.'

'I think he's the sort of man who likes to do things himself. If he bought a gun there would always be the chance of blackmail afterwards.'

'But did he know the place?'

'Yes. I have spoken to the man who runs it. He remembers Freedom. Freedom went in there and tried to join. Looked all over the place, inspected the guns and where they keep them. Just before the flood which may not have been an accident.'

'You need a reference to get in there,' said Coffin cautiously.

'And guess who backed him? One of ours, DC Radley.' Not Sergeant Grimm about whom her suspicions were darker and deeper.

Coffin saw that in Phoebe he had recruited someone who was as anxious to get Freedom as he was himself.

Danger there, he couldn't risk Phoebe going over the top.

'Bedworthy Radley?'

'Oh, you know that name?'

'Everybody knows it.'

'He's a good officer. On the whole,' said Phoebe, who saw Tim Radley's attractions herself but had been far too prudent to take advantage of them.

'Right, well, we're going to talk to Radley.'

He was taking this investigation into his own hands, he was involved, now he meant to make sure the killer was found.

And as for Anna, it had to be hoped she turned up alive and well. Preferably in Australia.

Tim Radley, whose day off it was, was still in bed when he got the call from Chief Inspector Astley. He was not alone in bed and was reluctant to answer the call. He rolled over and grabbed the phone. 'I must, Claudia.'

'You took your time.' Phoebe was irritable. 'Who's Claudia? No, don't answer.'

'Ma'am . . .' began Radley, draping the sheet across himself. DCI Astley did not come his way very often, or not directly, but he did not wish her to see him naked. She had been a patron of his pal Ryman-Lawson, now in deep trouble because of his connection with Mercer and Lightgate, whom he also had known. Bad news.

'She can't see you,' murmured his bed companion, dragging the sheet away and kissing him.

Radley covered himself again, he was beginning to feel he would need all the protection he could get.

'And don't tell me it's your day off, I want you round here now, and what's more, so does the Chief Commander.'

'Hell,' muttered Radley.

'I'll pretend I didn't hear that.'

'On my way,' said Radley.

'And get dressed first.' DCI Astley was reputed to be able to see through brick walls and it seemed now as if she could, and distance no object.

'Good . . . And I'll see you get some time off in lieu.'

'Thank you, ma'am,' he answered, looking sadly at Claudia, who would almost certainly not be here in his bed tomorrow or the next day. She had been hard enough to get there in the first place.

He cycled to the Headquarters, not far from where he had a house, a very small house built before the Crimean War, with a garden just large enough for one tomcat. With his way of life, a house was essential and the cat came to keep the rats out. It was just his luck that Ginger was a very active male. In truth, he admired Ginger with his perpetual lust and instant performance. A bit too sudden, possibly, but you couldn't have everything.

He arrived, hot and flushed from all his activities, and was shown into the small side annex to the incident room.

He's just a boy really, thought Phoebe, looking at him with sympathy, which she suppressed when she remembered what trouble boys could be.

John Coffin was standing by the window, his back to the light which, it being a sunny day, could fall straight on Tim Radley's face. He did not smile or offer any politeness to the constable, but just nodded at Phoebe.

Phoebe sat down and drew up a chair for DC Radley. 'Sit

down.' He was out of breath and deserved a chair, besides she wanted to talk to him, not make it an inquisition.

'You aren't a part of the inquiry now going on into a quartet of crime, but you know about them.'

Radley nodded. He did indeed, the whole Headquarters and every substation knew, passing on gossip. Plenty of that, and rumours, plenty of those too. His eyes flicked towards the Chief Commander. Good luck to him, he thought, what if he did have it away with that bird that got chopped up? Who's to blame. He stopped short of thinking that the Chief Commander had done the job on her himself, although that was one of the rumours. Of course, that was rubbish.

He looked away from the Chief Commander towards DCI Astley, whose expression was not promising. Tell the truth, he told himself, and no man can harm you. Not true, he thought.

'Do you know a man called George Freedom?'

'Is that his name? I always thought it might be made up.'

'It's his name,' said Phoebe shortly.

'I don't really know him, but I've watched some of his comedies on TV. He does them with another bloke. That one about the pair of chaps working in the glue factory, I really laughed at that one. It was what I was talking about with a mate when he came up. Told me who he was.'

'You hadn't seen him before?'

'No. I knew his name, didn't know his face.'

Coffin walked forward. 'Did you just talk about his comedies?'

'We had a drink together. The mate I was with had to go off to meet his bird so I stayed talking to Freedom. He seemed to want to talk.'

'What did you talk about?'

'Is it important, sir? Not sure if I can remember much . . . we were drinking. Wipes things out a bit, sometimes, sir.'

'Do you remember any talk about guns? Did you talk about guns? You belong to the Abbey Road Gun Club?'

'Oh yes, I do. The best club in town.'

'Sergeant Grimm belongs too?'

'Yes, ma'am.'

'See much of him?'

'No, ma'am.' He sounded surprised. 'Only in the way of work. He's on sick leave at the moment.' What he had in common with Sergeant Death was women, but best not to mention that.

Because I told him he'd better take some leave because we might be investigating him, thought Phoebe. And why might that be? We are investigating him and the dossier is filling up. Along with others, probably this boy here too. I hope to God Grimm isn't in his villa in Spain. Joke. But he's got something somewhere, must have. Money, money, money.

'Did Mr Freedom ask you to take him there?'

'Yes, we went down there together.' He had a nice smile and knew how to use it; in view of all the pitfalls in his life, he thought he had better start using it. 'It's my hobby, I hope to get into the Second City Gun Squad.' No harm in putting in a pitch for yourself.

This was well received and he got a smile back from Phoebe Astley. Coffin remained unsmiling. Radley had heard that he did smile, but he personally had never seen it happen.

But it was the Chief Commander who spoke: 'So you took him down there and he was shown round and you offered to act as his reference. Is that right?'

'He asked me to do all this.'

'How did he know you belonged . . . you hadn't met before. Or had you?'

'No, no. I suppose he heard me talking about it to my mate.'

Boasting, thought Coffin.

'And I didn't offer to take him to the Gun Club, never struck me he would be interested. A writer. But he said that was it, he was going to set a sitcom in a gun club.'

'Right,' said Phoebe. 'Wait outside, will you? I'll see you before you go.'

Tim Radley took himself off, to lean against a wall in the incident room and smoke a cigarette where the air was already too full of the mist of tobacco.

'Freedom lay in wait for him,' said Coffin. 'Knew who he

was and got what he wanted from him. They may have met before in spite of what Radley says.'

'Could be.' Phoebe nodded. She had not been too impressed with boy Radley's performance.

'Do you think money changed hands? That Freedom slipped him something?'

Phoebe nodded. 'Could be. Shall we have him back and ask him?'

'Not much point, he'll only lie.'

'What about Freedom?'

'He'll lie too.' Coffin thought for a moment. 'Might not be the same lie, though, if we can keep them apart. I want to see the Gun Club. We'll take Radley down with us.'

Tim Radley could not make up his mind whether it was a good career move to be seen going off with the Chief Commander and DCI Phoebe Astley or whether life afterwards with his contemporaries in Cutts Street would be unbearable.

Not that he had any choice.

He sat in the back of DCI Astley's car, which she drove. She did not need him to tell her the way, which told him she had been here before, since the Gun Club was tucked away in an old mews running behind Abbey Road. The front door was in the mews but the club extended back towards the main road.

'Do you have keys to this place?'

'Some members do.' He was shifty about this admission.

Not very good security then, Coffin thought, flood or not. They went in as a trio with Tim Radley leading the way, while at the same time trying to hide himself. The Gun Club was a tight unit and two extra members of the police sailing in would not be welcome.

However, it was afternoon, and not too many members used it in this time of the day.

The secretary, Bill Eager, was there. He was always there. Paid to be. Ex-army, ex-copper but from the Met, he was not known to Coffin.

He came out of his office, slowly and deliberately, pretending, as so often, to be more stupid than he was. In fact, he was a sharp-minded man, not a deep thinker but acute.

He held out his hand. 'Chief Commander, sir.' He knew why they had come, of course, since he had already had a visitation from DS Tony Davley on the subject of the gun.

Although the Chief Commander did not remember it, they had met in the past when John Coffin was already an important CID officer, while Bill Eager was a recruit, walking the beat. He'd seen Coffin working a case.

Eager ran an appraising eye over him, he himself had retired on an injury pension, and felt able to allow himself this liberty. The man had worn well, hardly gone grey and hadn't gone bald. Not fat either, but he had been a success and perhaps success kept you thin.

Coffin took his hand. 'I remember you: Kettle Street Station, wasn't it? That bank murder with arson?'

'That's right, sir, but you can't remember me?'

Coffin smiled without answering. No, he thought, but I do my homework. 'You had a flood?'

'Yes, a tap was left running in the upstairs toilet. Accidental or on purpose. We're still fighting that out with the insurers. It wasn't me, I can tell you that.'

'How did it happen?'

'Some fool pulled the piping away from the cistern in the lavatory . . . the water came pouring out, but I didn't notice till a real torrent had built up. I was downstairs in the basement.'

'Did a lot of damage?' Coffin looked around, it still had the sour damp smell of carpets and curtains drying out.

'Blew the wiring and took most of our security with it. We had a lot of trouble, took the computer where we keep all the records. The devil, it was.'

Coffin nodded.

'So you didn't know what guns you'd lost?'

'Shouldn't have lost any. The big cupboard where they are kept works on an electronic card; I got the cupboard open but I couldn't secure it again. Not properly, but it all seemed all right. All the members stayed away as no shooting was possible till we dried out.'

'But one gun went?'

'Yes, I knew as soon as I saw it. Often had it in my hands. Didn't belong to me. Not particularly.'

Not particularly, thought Coffin. Nice phrase.

'All right, it was sloppy, I plead guilty, but I was so busy mopping up and cleaning and drying. Added to which we had newish cleaners that I didn't know so well, so there was more direction needed from me.'

'Yes, I see.' Coffin was walking round the room, which looked tidy and well-run enough now.

'But when I heard about the gun that was found, and one of your officers came along checking again . . . well, I was able to put my hand up and say, Yes, sorry, sir, it is one of ours. Mine, in fact, although I haven't used it for some time.'

So that was what 'not particularly' meant, Coffin thought.

Coffin continued his slow perambulation round the room. 'Mr Freedom came in before the flood with a view to joining, I believe?'

'Yes, sure. He came in with Tim Radley. Business being what it is, we like an introduction.' He nodded towards Tim Radley, whose face remained expressionless, so much so that Eager turned away with the air of having been rebuffed.

'Did he come again?'

'No, well, we had the flood, visitors were not encouraged. No, I correct myself . . . he tried, one of the cleaners told me. I didn't see him myself.'

'It looks as though this gun which went on the loose, killed a woman and was used to half-kill a man.'

Eager muttered that he understood as much.

'Did Mr Freedom offer you any money to let him join the club?'

'No,' said Eager stiffly. 'A bribe would not have been necessary, we need members, but they must come with a backer. Someone who knows the proposed member well. And the proposer must be a member in good standing.'

'Of course,' said Coffin smoothly. 'Like a policeman.' He looked at Tim Radley, who licked his lips. 'Thank you, Mr Eager, for letting us have a look round. I expect you will get another visit.'

'Naturally, I'm glad to help. I can't think how the gun got stolen but plenty of people including firemen and members of the police were in and out when we had the flood. Oh, and the neighbours said we fused their freezers.'

'We might want to call you in for a further interview.'

'Yes,' agreed Eager. 'Sure. Whenever.'

During all this time, Tim Radley had not spoken. Now he said: 'Did you know Mr Freedom before I brought him in?'

'Never saw him before. Knew who he was, of course. Successful man, isn't he, with that string of successes. Be glad to have him as a member, thank you for the introduction.'

In the car, Tim said: 'I'm surprised he didn't make a connection between the killings and Mr Freedom.'

'Oh, he did, of course he did. Just putting up a front.' Coffin settled himself in his seat. 'As you are yourself . . . How much did Freedom offer you to get him into the club?'

Radley looked at Phoebe Astley who looked at him with a query: 'Well? Worth at least a tenner, I should think.'

Radley swallowed. 'Spot on, ma'am.'

Which means, decided Phoebe, that it was at least twice that much; Freedom must have wanted to get inside that Gun Club badly.

'You may have to swear to that.'

Radley swallowed again. 'Right, ma'am. May I ask, are you putting Mr Freedom in the frame for the two shootings?' He added nervously: 'I feel I have the right to ask as I seem to have helped him get the gun . . .'

'I'll drive you home,' was all the answer he got from Phoebe.

When they got to his small house from which he knew Claudia would long since have departed, he got out of the car, offered his thanks for the lift and then, still holding the car door, he said, to the air as much as any person, although he looked at Phoebe: 'I suppose I'm in trouble, ma'am?'

'Yes,' said Phoebe, as she drove off.

Coffin said: 'He was bribed, probably with more than the tenner, and Eager as well, possibly . . . anyway, he might have been glad to get the insurance money. Check on the club's finances.'

'I was thinking that myself.'

'Get hold of Freedom, and set up an interview with Eager. See they meet. Then they can be questioned together. I will sit in if I can.'

Phoebe returned to the incident room to check on what was going on there. Tony Davley was crouched over a computer, the room was emptying as the day shift went off. The incident room was lightly staffed at night.

Tony looked up. 'Well, any luck?'

'Seems as though Freedom worked out how to steal a gun.'

'Still think it would be easier to buy one.'

'I don't know. Not a man you can figure out.' Phoebe went on: 'Do you know where he is?'

'I know where he is supposed to be: in his flat, but he was only requested to stay there. I doubt if he felt bound by that.'

'As long as he's there now,' said Phoebe. She passed Coffin's orders on: 'Get someone to bring him in, and set up a meeting with Eager.'

Coffin went to his office, prepared to sign letters and read reports before going home. He had not taken the dog with him to the Gun Club but left him with Gillian. Gus fell upon him with the joy of a dog that has been abandoned and was now reunited with his master. He fawned upon Coffin, licking his feet.

'He does love your shoes,' said Gillian. She admired Gus but thought he was spoilt. In her world, you did not spoil animals. She had noticed that Gus had somehow manoeuvred himself into the position of honorary human.

She was getting her possessions together, which Coffin recognized as signalling her departure.

'Get off them, you fetishist,' said Coffin, giving Gus a shove. Gus clung on, eyes adoring. He stood up, perforce taking the dog with him. 'Time to go home.'

They followed Gillian down in the lift, the Peke tucked under one arm because he did not like lifts. Dangerous for paws.

*　　*　　*

In the airy upstairs sitting room, they found Robbie Gilchrist sitting on the sofa, facing the sun through the big window, drinking whisky and talking to Stella.

Stella looked cheerful, so if it was business then it was going well. Gilchrist stood up when Coffin came in.

'I wanted to tell Stella that I am taking Alice home with me . . . No, not to the place here, but to the house I have in Gloucestershire. I will leave her there with the good friend who keeps house for me.'

Good friend, Coffin thought, nice way of putting it.

'I went round to the Serena Seddon to have a long talk with Mary Arden. She agrees with me that to get Alice away will be a good idea. Physically she is better. I know she's not clever, but there's more to her than you might think. Evelyn told me her husband thinks she would work well in his department at the theatre. She's good with colour and materials.'

No doubt he had come to some arrangement with Stella, hence her pleased smile.

'She's ready to travel but I wanted to clear it with you first.'

Coffin poured himself a drink, noted with amusement that Gus, the sycophant, had transferred his attention to Gilchrist and was leaning against his leg with a wistful look. Wants a job on TV, no doubt.

'Has she said any more about what went on? About where she was while she was missing and the birth of the child?'

'I haven't pressed her.'

'Someone should, I think.'

Robbie Gilchrist muttered something about the dangers of digging things up.

Coffin, whose whole professional life had consisted of 'digging things up', said gravely: 'She might be glad to talk.'

'Do you think so?'

Coffin said he thought so. 'To the right person.'

'I don't think that's me . . .' Robbie sat thinking, hands on his knees. Then he bent down to pat Gus's head. Not looking at Coffin, he said: 'Would you do it?'

'Do you have any special reason for asking me to do it?'

'I know you are still investigating George Freedom, and if this in any way helps your case against him, I want you to be the one who does it.'

Old friends, old enemies, Coffin thought. He knew the feeling well. Goodness knows, he wanted to get Freedom.

'Yes, I'll do it. You must be there, though.'

'Yes, sure. I know that.'

'And you must in the end talk to Alice about this business,' he said gently. 'You or her mother.'

'Not her mother,' said Robbie instantly.

'You then.' Coffin shook his head. 'Don't bury it. I've buried a lot in my time, and take it from me, it lies there rotting.'

'No time like the present then. Shall we get on with it? Then I'd like Alice to go to Gloucestershire.'

Stella came across to kiss Coffin on the cheek. A public demonstration of affection that she rarely showed. He looked at her sceptically.

'Just glad to see you,' she said. 'Robbie and I will be working together when he gets back.'

'No input from Freedom?' he couldn't resist asking.

'I think we can manage.'

That dumped Freedom nicely then.

'I must just make a telephone call before we go,' he said to Robbie. He was Robbie now, not Gilchrist, now and probably forever – Coffin had a strong feeling that Robbie was here in his life to stay.

He went to his own work room, a few steps up the tower, to call Phoebe.

'No nothing special on Freedom. He was at home and has made one or two phone calls. No, we have no tap on him, so I can't say what they were, I only know he made them because he could be seen through the window using his mobile. It looks as though he means to stay there, for now at least, and not do a bunk.'

'Tomorrow then.' Coffin ran over in his mind what his diary had down for tomorrow. 'Afternoon, I think.'

Phoebe agreed.

'Nothing on the head or the torso, I suppose? We really need it. One or both. Both preferably.'

The beginning had been the dumping of the arms and legs on the house in Barrow Street where he had once lived. Where Anna had once visited him. For a very short space. It all started with Anna.

Joanna Carmichael. A woman with two names. If that had indeed been her name. How many names did she have?

He couldn't help feeling that someone wanted revenge for Anna.

But I need to see your face, Anna, I need to see Shelley plain. God, you are not like the marvellous poet, although he was a liar and a bit of a performer. Although they all were in that little coterie: Byron, Trefusis, Shelley. Not Mary Shelley, though. But then she had Mary Godwin for her mother.

Phoebe was still talking. 'You all right, sir?'

'Yes, fine. Go on.'

'Nothing found, still have a team out looking. Scaled down though.' They were beginning to give up hope. 'But there is one piece of good news: Albie Touchey is coming round. Talking more coherently. You will be able to see him.'

'Yes, that is good news. I will try to see him before Freedom tomorrow.'

But first, he had to go to the house in Barrow Street.

Well, this is it, he thought, as he followed Robbie Gilchrist in. But the place had changed so much since he had lived there for a few uneasy months.

He had expected painful, angry memories to flash back. But there was nothing.

The place was so different, it even smelt different, a mixture of lavender airspray and disinfectant. And there were children playing on the stairs. Children who gave him a hostile look. He was not to know that they were very new arrivals whose memory of the world outside the Serena Seddon was of violence and swearing. If necessary they were prepared to offer both back, but for the moment they were silent.

Coffin was able to follow Robbie upstairs to Mary Arden's room with more calm than he had expected. The ghost of Anna, if indeed there was a ghost, was not to be found here.

Mary Arden with Evelyn by her side stood up to greet them. Alice tried to rise too. 'Don't get up, Alice.'

The telephone was ringing and was ignored. After a while, it went silent. No one took any notice.

Except John Coffin who wondered who it was and who was getting the rough treatment.

Robbie, who had bent to kiss the girl, drew back.

'Do you want to stay, Alice?' Mary asked.

Alice nodded. She looked pale still, but her hair was combed and shining clean, while the blue jeans and blue shirt she wore fitted her slender frame snugly. Care had been taken over her appearance.

'I expect Robbie and the Chief Commander here will want to ask you questions, but you need not answer.'

Once again Alice nodded.

'Before you two start, I want to tell you something. First, I have talked to Alice and she has given me permission to tell you about her and to answer questions for her if she wishes. I will do it only with her consent; she may prefer to answer herself.' Mary's voice was coldly angry, her face was turned to Robbie Gilchrist. 'For a professional family, educated people, you and Alice's mother have treated her shamefully. The girl has great problems in communication but she is not stupid, she is autistic. She is locked in her own world and you and her mother did not help her to climb out of it.'

Robbie opened his mouth, then shut it again. Coffin said nothing, but he watched the girl. She may have said nothing but her eyes followed Mary.

'It took Evelyn and her husband Peter to work out what Alice's trouble is. She finds it very very hard to struggle with the world outside but she is not stupid; Peter thinks she will work beautifully in his workshop in the theatre, she has a marvellous colour sense.'

Robbie said: 'I am taking her home with me for a rest. That is if she wants to come.'

Mary looked at Alice. 'Do you?'

In a clear, sweet voice, Alice said, Yes, if she could then come back and work in the theatre again.

'Yes, sure, of course.'

'Right, agreed. But she ought not to go back and live alone in that grotty little flat she had. That is not good for her.'

The telephone rang again and was once more ignored.

Coffin raised his eyebrows. 'Do answer it if you wish.'

'It will be Mr Freedom,' said Mary. 'He has been ringing at intervals. He wishes to see Alice. We made a joint resolution not to answer his calls.'

Coffin looked at Alice. 'Is that so, Alice?'

Alice nodded.

When almost at once the phone rang again, she shivered. A long, painful movement. Fear personified, which Coffin saw and understood: she was terrified of Freedom.

'He's a bully,' said Evelyn, who hadn't spoken before. 'Violent with it.'

'What I want to know from Alice, if she wants to tell us, is: Who is the father of the baby, where was she living when she disappeared, and who was it that was with her when the child was born and then buried the child?'

'A lot of questions.' Mary spoke dryly.

'Short answers will do. Do you know the answers?'

'Yes.'

Coffin looked at Alice. 'Can you do it? No one will blame you if you can't.'

Alice was silent, then she stood up, hands clasped in front of her. 'My stepfather,' she began, then she looked at Robbie, who seemed frozen. 'Not you.' She gave him a sweet, affectionate smile. 'The other one . . .'

In the pause, Coffin noticed that Robbie was crying.

The words came in little bursts, bundles of words, gasped out.

'My stepfather liked to make love to me. He always liked to make love to me.'

Coffin heard Robbie make a hissing noise.

The words came squeezing out like toothpaste. She had enjoyed working in the theatre . . . Her mother had got her the work before going off to America, she loved working there, no one told her she was stupid . . . she liked her little room. Peter was kind to her. Her stepfather did not visit her there. Then he did.

There was a pause.

Mary said she could stop, if she liked. No need to go on.

But Alice went on: she did not bleed as often as some girls, she knew this was how she was. So it was some time before she understood that there was a baby inside her.

She told her stepfather, and he hit her, she fell. At this point she began to cry; he always hit her, she expected it. 'I must never say anything, I must never say anything.'

Mary stopped her. 'Alice does not remember much after that. I think she was unconscious. When she came round, she was being looked after by a woman she did not know but who was kind to her, in a place she did not recognize. Time seemed to have lost its meaning for Alice, then. Then one day, she was standing by the window looking out, this was what she did most of the time, when the birth began . . .' Mary paused. The phone was ringing again. 'Someone ought to kill that man,' she said in a gentle voice. 'Alice could not talk about it, which we must respect, but the woman took the child and said she would do the right thing . . . The rest you know . . .

'She is not sure why she was wandering on the street, but she said she was told to go home . . .'

The room was silent. Robbie went over to put his arm about Alice. 'I'm here, kid, you've got help.'

'If you want my opinion,' said Evelyn, 'I think she was drugged.'

'What did she see from the window when she looked out?' asked Coffin. 'What did you see, Alice?'

Alice rested her head on Robbie's shoulder. She thought, her eyes looking towards the window in Mary's room in Barrow Street. 'A roof, a long roof, and a wall, a wall without windows.'

After this no one spoke for some time. There seemed nothing worthwhile to say.

'It was a *Grand Guignol*, a Gothic tale,' said Coffin to Stella when he got back. 'Unbelievable.'

'And did you believe her?'

'Yes,' said Coffin. 'I believed her. Except the ending . . . I think she knew where she was.'

13

The University Hospital into which Albie Touchey had been taken had benefited from a large grant three years ago. The core of it was pretty much what it was when it was the Poor Law Hospital for East Hythe, but its face was greatly improved.

It had also added a suite of private rooms, in one of which Albie Touchey was resting. If resting was the word, for he was in a chair, drawn up to a table.

When Coffin arrived to see him next morning, he was working at his portable computer, listening to a caller on his mobile and interviewing the assistant governor of the prison.

'Glad you're up and about,' said Coffin.

'Those doctors . . . I'm a strong chap.'

It didn't seem the moment to say: You nearly died, Albie, and you were unconscious for a long time.

'I heard you'd been asking, hoping to see me stretched out stiff as a board, eh?'

'You know that's not true.'

'Yes, sure, of course I do. You get to make silly jokes after a week or so in this place.' Then he went on: 'No, seriously, I did wonder if I was going to die, it was the morphine they plugged into me. Gave me terrible fantasies. I thought this is how it is going to end: Not with a whimper but a bang. You're supposed not to hear the shot that kills you and that was the only thing that kept me cheerful, I swear I heard the shot.' He leaned forward. Stiffly, revealing the bandages still taped to his chest. 'So, what's been going on? Jonesy here' – he nodded towards his assistant – 'won't tell me a thing. Got to keep my blood pressure down.'

'I didn't say that.' This from William Jones. 'The doc just said not to worry you.'

'There's been a lot going on around here,' said Coffin. 'I think most of it you know.' No need to tell him about Alice.

'Thought you'd killed me, did you?' Albie joked.

'I thought you had been attacked instead of me.'

Albie gave Coffin a sharp look. 'No,' he said. He turned to William Jones: 'Give me those letters and I'll sign them. Then you can push off.'

He began the signing at once.

'Anything else?'

'No, Bill, but keep me in touch and tell the lads I'll be back with them all soon. Too soon for some, I daresay.' He handed the signed letters over.

Bill Jones gathered up letters and reports, then took himself off. 'Look after yourself, sir.'

When he had gone, Albie said: 'I wasn't shot instead of you. I was the one that gun was aimed at. Take it from me. I was the one he wanted. We all have enemies and mine found me.'

'You think so?' Coffin kept his tone neutral.

Albie patted his chest. 'I know so.'

'Any idea who did it then?'

Slowly Albie shook his head. 'That's your job.'

'When you came round first you said Freedom.'

Albie frowned. 'Ah yes, that name was on my mind, not surprising it came popping out. I was anxious about Freedom and his stepdaughter . . . I was frightened he would harm her.'

'Why do you say that, Albie?'

Albie motioned towards the cupboard. 'Like a drink? 'Fraid it's only fruit juice, all you're allowed here . . . About Freedom, just the way he was. The way he talked about the girl, about girls. Women.'

'I know what you mean. He has harmed her.'

'Oh?' Albie looked sharply at Coffin. 'Where is he now?'.

'He's living in something called the Argosy, one of those

new blocks made out of a disused factory or warehouse. I think this was a warehouse for a firm making naval uniforms . . . I suppose that's why they called it The Argosy. It's in Rickards Passage.' He was talking too much and he knew it, loading his conversation with inessentials because he did not wish, here and now, to talk about Alice.

'So what did he do?'

'Tell you later. On which subject . . . you were coming to tell me something. Urgently. Or I got that impression.'

'Yes.' Albie took a deep breath. 'I had been told that someone was out to do you damage. I get a lot of stories told me, some of them false. I believed this one, the man who told me was dying. Sam Sears.'

Coffin nodded. 'Know the name.' Sears had been a sick man when arrested for attempting to kill his wife, Coffin had seen he got the right medical treatment, secretly sympathizing with him for the attempt on the wife. A bitch of the first order.

'You helped him.'

'I remember.'

'He wanted to help you back.'

'And did he say who was after me?'

Albie sighed. 'I think he did. Must have done. But it's gone.'

Coffin said: 'Well, thanks.'

'Shock, I suppose. Or the morphine and other drugs they pumped into me. Blank. Only patches. I daresay it will come back.'

'Sure. Take it easy, Albie.'

'Wait a minute . . . there was something about a wife, yes, I remember that much.'

'He was in trouble over his wife,' said Coffin.

But Albie was talking on, not listening: 'Was it a threat to her? No.' He shook his head. 'More later if I remember.'

The conversation had not gone uninterrupted, all the time nurses had been popping in and out, putting out pills on little saucers, bringing in carafes of water or just standing at the door and looking.

Coffin walked away and got into his car to drive back to see George Freedom.

Any threat to Stella I take seriously, very seriously. Is that what I was hearing?

So what do I do now? Tough it out.

He went back to St Luke's Tower before visiting his office, on the pretext of collecting the dog. Stella was at home, shuffling scripts and making telephone calls. She said she was less disturbed working at home than if she went into her office in the theatre.

'What are you doing today?' he asked.

'Working. What are you doing?'

'Working.'

'That's established then.'

He stood by her desk, looking down on the neat, well-cut hair, the pearl earrings and the necklace, also pearls, nestling in the curve of her neck.

'Thank you for staying with me in this business.'

She took off the spectacles, chosen to match her Ferragamo shirt and trousers. 'Of course, what else would I do? We've had this conversation before.'

'I think we may be drawing to the end.'

'You mean you'll get Freedom?' She sat back. 'I'll be surprised. He's a cunning bugger. Well, well. Just let me know in good time, will you? In advance of the rest of the world.'

'Yes, anything special you would like me to know in advance?'

'He was never my lover, if that's what you mean.' She laughed. 'But you don't mean that, do you?'

'He doesn't seem your style somehow.'

'There's a lot of sex there all right, but not too straightforward and I have always been that. As you know. No, and I never accepted any money for this or that in the theatre, tempting as it would have been because I always wondered what he would have wanted in addition. He and Robbie made a very good team, though. I don't know how Robbie will go on without him. I suppose he has lost him?'

'One way or another, yes.'

Stella put her spectacles back on, to return to work. 'Take Gus with you, he's ruining my new Prada shoes.'

181

Gus was dragged from the top of her feet. 'Beast,' said Stella lovingly as they departed, and Coffin asked himself which one of them she meant.

There was a message from Phoebe awaiting him. It said:

I have George Freedom here and also Bill Eager. Not together. Both impatient.

She had clearly been waiting for his arrival, because soon Gillian appeared to ask if DCI Astley could come in.

'Yes, just give me ten minutes to go through what is on my desk. Then bring the chief inspector and some coffee too, please.'

He was longer than his ten minutes, but Phoebe filled in the time talking to Gillian. She knew from experience that Gillian was very well-informed on everything that went on in the Second City police, uniformed and plain clothes, and although discreet would pass on what she thought you should know.

The room she worked in was large with a recess in which another secretary worked, and a large bay window where Inspector Paul Masters had his own desk and telephone. But Gillian had her own territory, near to the Chief Commander's door and a desk with a pot plant on it.

'He won't be long. I'm just making some coffee.' Gillian moved to a corner of the room where she had a coffee grinder and a coffee filter machine. This arrangement was for her own comfort since she knew that the Chief Commander downed whatever she offered him without comment. The coffee was hot and good and prestige demanded that the china was thin, delicate Worcester. She did not allow him either cream or sugar, since Miss Pinero had advised her not to. She had started by cutting down both by degrees until she realized that the Chief Commander never noticed and drank what was offered.

Phoebe also got black coffee. Gillian herself took it with added cream and sugar.

'Nice to have the Chief Commander back,' she said, handing the cup to Phoebe. 'I think he ought to take a holiday, but he always says that when he can take a holiday then Miss

Pinero can't and when she can, then he is too busy. It's been a tough year.'

Phoebe agreed it had been, wondering what Gillian was leading up to.

'Of course, he's got lots of problems, especially at the moment.'

'I know,' said Phoebe.

'It's amazing the people who do get away.'

'Isn't it?' She felt the prey was coming closer.

Gillian shook her head. 'I saw Sergeant Grimm dashing for the train to Paris when I was rushing through Waterloo the other morning. He didn't see me.'

'Was he on his own?'

'Yes, although he's not what I'd call the monastic type.'

'No,' agreed Phoebe. 'So they say, just gossip.'

'Usually right, though, aren't they? I always say if you want to know what's going on in the Second City, ask Mimsie Marker.'

'She is well-informed.'

'Keeps her eyes open. Now, I expect if I told her about the sergeant she'd say, Oh, that's where he keeps his money.' Gillian giggled.

Phoebe drank her coffee, appreciating the nugget of information thus passed. 'Make a good detective, Mimsie would.' And not so bad yourself, Gillian.

Gillian smiled. 'Of course, that train is so fast, you can come and go in a day and no one knows you've been away.'

The buzzer sounded from the room beyond; Gillian gave a friendly nod. 'For you.'

As Phoebe made her way into Coffin's room she made a mental note to pass over to him the information about Sergeant Grimm. Meanwhile, she would keep it to herself, think about what it meant and consider what to do. There might be merit marks here.

Coffin stood up, dislodging Gus. 'I didn't get much out of Albie, if that's what you wanted to know. All he meant by muttering Freedom, so he says, is that he thought Freedom was a menace to young girls, and we already know that.'

'Someone will kill Freedom one day,' said Phoebe. She

had been told in full what had happened to Alice and at whose hands. 'Unless he develops some mortal disease first. He might do. There's always hope.'

'Robbie wishes to take the girl away to his house in Gloucestershire. I have asked him to wait till we clear some matters here.'

Phoebe raised an eyebrow. 'Such as?'

'I don't think Alice told us quite everything. She says she was in a daze, drugged, so Evelyn thought. Maybe, she may well have been drugged, but all the same, I think she knows where she was and with whom. She did murmur something but later seemed vaguer.'

'Why keep quiet?'

'Yes, that's what interests me.'

'Frightened again?'

'Could be. She was somewhere near where she was found, I swear. She told me what she could see from the window of the room she was in. And it sounded to me like the area around Drossers Lane Market. And that wasn't so far away from where Evelyn Jones found her. Walking distance, anyway. But we'll find out.'

'Important?'

'Well, it's a funny story, and I'd like to get more sense into it.'

He pushed Gus aside, noticed that he had not drunk his coffee so he politely finished it, cold, and motioned Phoebe to the door.

'I hope Freedom and Eager are getting nicely irritable. Men talk more loosely then.'

'Don't women?' she asked as she led the way down the corridor. Coffin just grinned in reply: not nice women, said the grin. 'I have Freedom in interview room A and Eager in B. Which do you want first?'

Coffin didn't have to think. 'Freedom first, we will see what we can bounce out of him about the gun. He's bound to lie, so then get Eager to put the pressure on.'

'And I have the handkerchief which was found round the gun to produce to see if we can tie it to Freedom. Nothing memorable about it, so he will resist it, but worth a try.'

Room A first then.

A young WPC was standing politely in one corner while George Freedom paced the room, swearing. They could hear him as they went in.

'You've taken your bloody time.'

'Sorry, sir.' This from Phoebe. 'Please sit down.'

Coffin slid into the seat beside her. Freedom turned his anger this way. 'Oh, you again. I might have known it. What is it now?'

Phoebe issued the usual warnings then put a plastic bag containing a grubby handkerchief in front of him. 'Is that your handkerchief, sir?'

He didn't look. 'No.'

Phoebe shook the plastic bag so he could get a view. 'Please look.'

Freedom gave it a cursory look, and then shrugged. 'It's a handkerchief, if you think it is mine, then prove it. Much good may it do you, because I don't know what all this is about.'

'We may be able to prove you have others like it.'

'Well, good luck to you.'

'And if I tell you that it was wrapped round a gun that killed a woman and almost killed a man?'

'I don't know what you are talking about.'

'And you never went to the Abbey Road Gun Club to ask about shooting?'

'No, I did not, and if you are going on like this, I want my solicitor.'

Phoebe paused. 'We could stop, sir, while you call for him.'

'No, he works in London and he costs a bloody fortune just to write a letter. No, thank you.' He turned on Coffin. 'Why don't you say something? Instead of sitting there looking like the judge and the jury all in one.'

'What I want to say is: Will you be willing, in the interest of establishing your innocence, to meet a man who says he knows you and with whom you discussed guns.'

George Freedom threw up his hands. 'You're mad, the pair of you. Bring in your chap, but I warn you he is lying.'

Coffin gave Phoebe a nod.

'Sending her, are you? She goes trotting off, your pony, obedient to master.'

'Just checking,' said Coffin mildly. 'Something we have to do.'

'Don't tell me the boss man always conducts the checks himself? Seems a bit personal to me. You are exposing yourself, you know. Publicity, people asking questions. Wouldn't like it to get in the papers, would you?'

'I don't think the chief inspector will be long. In fact, I believe I can hear her now.'

'Chief Inspector, eh? I do get the high-rankers, don't I? Or is she your girlfriend?'

Phoebe was moving down the corridor with Bill Eager. He was talking with animation. 'Am I glad to see you, I was stuck in that room wondering what was going to happen. And why. I hope you don't mind me saying that I don't understand what I'm doing here.' He strode along beside her, anxious to oblige. She could sense his anxiety.

'Just want you to tell Mr Freedom you remember him coming into the Gun Club.'

'I remember all right.' Interestingly, Phoebe felt that his anxiety had not diminished.

The two went into the room, Phoebe first, ushering Bill Eager after her.

George Freedom looked at both of them but showed no special interest, other than saying: 'Now what's he here for?'

'Well, Mr Freedom, we thought Bill might be able to convince you that you wanted to join the Gun Club.'

She turned to Bill Eager and held out her hand. 'Your turn, Bill, go ahead. Refresh his memory.'

Bill stared at George Freedom and then he stared at John Coffin and back to Phoebe. 'What's the game? That's not Mr Freedom.'

George Freedom leaned back, clapped his hands and began to laugh. 'Well done, well done. Couldn't have done better myself if I had written the text.'

Bill Eager was puzzled. 'What's going on?'

John Coffin and Phoebe Astley withdrew to talk things over. 'It's fallen apart,' said Coffin, he was angry. 'Get hold of Tim Radley.'

Radley, his conscience which usually slept easily, was awake and irritating him so that he went on duty determined to do a good job.

He was at once sent out in a patrol car to drive down to the docks where it was expected that a cargo of dodgy beef was being loaded. Rotterdam was the port destined to receive the beef carcases. Operation BEEFSTEAK, it was called, and had been running for a week with no notable success.

'They know they are being watched,' said Radley to the two detectives who appeared quietly from a side alley.

A shrug. 'Probably sold the stuff over here, you might be eating it tonight.'

The patrol car circled the dock area, pretending just to be on a routine job, then drove off. Reporting no sign of anything.

This was the sixth day of the watch. Radley had been part of the team once before, and was uneasily aware that he knew where some of the beef might be resting in frozen peace.

'Can't blame chaps,' he thought.

He did not think he himself had eaten any dicey beefsteaks. He was careful where he ate.

They were considering dropping in for a quick cup of coffee in the Stormy Weather eaterie where both men were known when a call over the radio told DC Radley that he was wanted in DCI Astley's office.

'What have you been up to, you naughty boy?' said his driver as he swung the wheel and reversed away from Drossers Market. 'Nothing more than usual, I daresay. Perhaps she's going to ask you for a date.'

Radley, who was equipped with special sensitive sex antennae, which had already told him that DCI Astley did indeed find him attractive, blushed.

He was deposited outside Headquarters and the driver promised to wait if he wasn't too long . . . 'seeing that you could call it an official fuck.'

'Shut up, and watch your tongue,' said Radley as he disappeared.

The driver blew him a kiss before backing the car into some shade.

Radley felt like a dog that might be going to get a whipping or might be offered a hot meal, it all depended. When he met Phoebe on the corridor outside the incident room, he knew the dish was cold and empty.

'The Chief Commander wants you.' She led the way briskly back down the corridor to the interview rooms. She threw open the door. In the room, the Chief Commander and George Freedom sat on either side of the table. Radley gave them both a quick look. He was still puzzled, unsure why he had been brought here.

In the corner of the room was Bill Eager, looking depressed. He managed to give Radley a tired smile.

'Good morning, sir,' Radley managed to Coffin.

'Good morning. Now say hello to Mr Freedom.'

Radley stared. 'Eh?'

'Greet Mr Freedom, greet Mr Freedom,' said Coffin.

Radley looked for help to Phoebe Astley. 'I would if I could, ma'am,' he said, thankful to be able to speak at all. 'Shall I go round and call on him at home. Is he at home?'

'He's here,' said John Coffin, pointing to the man at the table with him. 'Here.'

Radley knew now he was mad. 'That's not my Mr Freedom,' he said.

Is this a farce, or is this a farce? Play it for laughs.

'Not unless he's had a face change, sir.' Be hung for a sheep as a lamb. 'Lost six inches from his legs and put it on round his bottom.'

Coffin went back to his own office, having exchanged a few words with Phoebe. 'Well, I don't think that lad will climb to the top of his career ladder, if indeed he stays on it –' hint of a threat there – 'but he certainly made his point.'

'So we have someone using Freedom's name, pretending to be the man.' Phoebe was thinking aloud. 'So is he someone who knows George Freedom?'

'That would help us find him, but possibly not. He knows who George Freedom is, but so do a lot of people.'

'He knew who didn't know Freedom,' pointed out Phoebe. 'He knew that Radley did not know him, except by name, and neither did Eager. We know he was taller and thinner than Freedom.' Eager and Radley had together provided a description of a man nearly six feet tall, thin, with a lined face. Spectacles, and dark hair.

An image flashed through his mind of the man running away from Albie's room at the hospital. A tall, thin man in a black hat . . .

'One thing we can be sure of,' said Coffin. 'He went to all that trouble, acting a part, to get a gun, then he did the shooting all right. We have to find him.'

'I reckon he did know Freedom and didn't like him.'

'Who does?' said Coffin.

'Think it could be a woman? One who didn't like Freedom. And . . .' She had been going to say, and has a grudge against you, but prudence suggested she keep quiet.

Coffin knew what she was going to say. Anna, he thought, my God, not Anna. She was tall for a woman and might now have a lined face.

It was more than ever necessary to find the missing torso and head to the limbs left outside the house in Barrow Street.

'Phoebe, collect all the new info that I don't know, anything extra about the two shootings and the cat and the limbs. Get them to me by this evening, I will take them home with the rest of the files to study tonight. I may pick something up that I have missed.'

At the end of the day, George Freedom went back to his flat in the building now called The Argosy in Rickards Passage where he was alone, where he knew the number to call to see the right sort of girl was sent.

Bill Eager went back to his set of rooms above the Gun Club, from which his wife had long since moved out.

Tim Radley repaired to his Victorian dwelling where he was alone, the cat being out ratting and not expected back till dawn.

Phoebe Astley was also alone, but she had dinner with DS Tony Davley in a Chinese restaurant across the river from the Second City and then went to see a film. Crime was not mentioned. Nor was sex, love or hate.

Coffin did not walk home, as so often, to give the dog a walk, or he might have been aware of a tall, thin, dark-haired figure following him at a distance.

The figure's motives were not friendly, vicious rather, but the figure knew that this was just a time for looking. The spectre (which Coffin might have thought it was) turned away before St Luke's, a thought surfacing.

Inside every fat creature is that thin one trying to get out. This was something the figure knew at close hand, and how dangerous it could be.

The unknowing Coffin was in the official car in which he sat in the back and documents in thick folders were piled in beside him and on top of which sat Gus so he could look out of the window, bow his head, and wag his tail, pretending to be the Queen.

But he was thinking about the strange tall figure. He ought to have discussed the puzzle of that figure at more length with Phoebe. If he could bring himself to talk about it to her she would probably be helpful.

Sergeant Grimm was still on his travels. Home soon, though.

14

Coffin and the royal beast entered the tower of St Luke's together. It was calm and quiet. Security was still about but being tactful.

He stood at the bottom of the stairs listening for any sound of Stella, but all was still. She was not a noisy person but somehow you always knew when she was there. Or he did.

Once again, he thought that it was empty without her. Protective urges, and more urges than that, ran through him. He stood there in the hall, bags dumped about him, dog sitting on the stair looking at him, and thought about her.

Then he heard a car draw up, the door slam and Stella talking and laughing. She was alive, bless her.

She threw open the door and dropped her own deposit of bags on the floor to line up with his.

'That was Vi bringing me back,' she said.

'Good.' He had no idea who Vi was but if she brought Stella home to him then she had a place in his own private pantheon of gods worth bothering over.

Stella studied the bags on the floor. 'You've brought work back and so have I . . . discussing two new productions . . . Robbie is coming in with me. But we can work together and listen to music and have a glass of wine. After we've eaten.'

A vague look came into her face. 'Except, I don't know what we've got to eat.'

'A woman's work is never done,' said Coffin. 'Fear not, I ordered a meal from Max, cold, and it should be in the fridge now. And something nice for Gus.'

Gus wagged his tail. He was good on signals, this one said: Food soon, please.

'Max delivered it himself.'

'You let him have a key? After you know . . .'

'I trust Max, but no, the security guard let him in.' Otherwise the alarm system would have sprung into instant and noisy action. 'I gave him the keys and he returned them. You have to trust your own men.'

Then he remembered one or two of his own men whom he did not trust and wished he had been less vehement.

The food produced by Max was good and the wine even better. 'You've been extravagant,' said Stella as she spooned up the syllabub.

'Comfort food.'

'That's what you wanted?'

'It's been a bad day. Can't pin anything on Freedom. Doesn't look as if it was he who went to the Gun Club, just someone acting as him. Interesting in itself, but I'm not sure what it tells us.'

'An actor?'

'Any candidates?'

Stella shook her head. 'If I think of any, then you will be the first to know.'

Stella made some coffee and cleared the dishes away. She could be very efficient domestically when she chose. Then both settled down with their papers.

Once more Coffin went through the list beginning with the limbs outside the Serena Seddon. There had been a handbag too. He sat back thinking, trying to remember if Anna had had a handbag like it.

Forensics had not been able to pick up anything from it, except to say that the bag was old, from the styling about ten to twelve years old, and that the newspaper cutting had no fingerprints on it.

No fingerprints on anything. They had taken prints from the hand but they were not on the record. Not a criminal, then.

Then there was the death of Etta; she had rung up to say she was frightened and she was leaving. Before she could do so, she was shot.

The women at the Serena Seddon had said that Etta was

192

mixing in bad company and had hinted a police officer's involvement. He thought he had a name there, or possibly two. Ryman-Lawson, who had got in with Mack Mercer and Tolly Lightgate. Tim Radley, friend of Ryman-Lawson, and Sergeant Grimm. If Etta knew that lot and the people they went with, then she was in bad company.

But had one of them killed her?

Next, Albie, who thought that he was the one that the shot was for, and Coffin thought that it was for him. Someone could have been waiting for him and mistaken Albie for him. They were much of a height.

Did he believe that? He shook his head.

One thing I do believe, he said to himself, is all that has happened is aimed at me.

Whoever is behind it wants me either out or dead. Perhaps it would be better to resign now, before gossip and public pressure force me out.

He looked at Stella sitting happily at work, and knew he did not want to leave the Second City.

She looked up. 'I love our tower, don't you?'

Coffin looked about him, there were times in his life when he had come close to hating the place, now it was, quite simply Home. His Home.

'Yes. You made it what it is, Stella. I couldn't have done it. And the theatre, all your work.'

'Your sister put money in,' she protested. 'I don't forget it.'

'You're a good investment,' said Coffin fondly. 'Letty knows where her money will earn for her. But it's all you. The Second City owes you a lot.'

'Hey, this is beginning to sound like an obituary.' Stella was laughing.

'I owe you a lot, Stella. Everything, really.'

'It works both ways.'

Coffin continued working after Stella had gone to bed. He read through the reports once.

A figure was beginning to walk out of the pages, building itself up out of details like that Green Man of the woods who was made up of branches and leaves and twigs.

First, a misty figure that might be real and might not, then becoming more solid, first arms, then legs as well. They could move fast, those legs. Drive a car. Strong hands that could aim a gun, seize a cat, then cut off its head.

Not a nice person at all.

At last a face began to take shape. A face known in Albie's prison.

Not the one he had expected.

It was dawn by the time he had finished, not eager to believe his own thoughts. 'Only half an answer,' he told himself. 'Why? Why did this person kill?'

He was not the only person to have a disturbed night. In one of the empty factories behind Drossers Market and only a few hundred yards from Chopping Tree Lane on the one hand and The Argosy block of expensive flats in Rickards Passage, a business meeting was going on.

This factory, formerly the home of a freezer firm which had tried to undercut foreign markets and failed, was not as empty as it looked. Nor was it without an owner, but the owner preferred his outfit to be anonymous. He specialized in moving on fast. Which indeed was a trait built up and inherited over the centuries, since before Sam Pepys's time and after, among some of the traders and businessmen of Drossers Market.

Two men were sitting round a rough table, one on each side, both were wearing thick overcoats since the establishment was cold. Freezing cold. A light was suspended from the ceiling and several white cabinets lined the walls and stood in rows around the table.

Commercial-size freezers, all plugged in and working, which would have been a surprise to the Second City Electrical Power Company, who believed the place to be empty and disconnected from the mains with no meters working. In fact, it had been tapping in illegally for some months. Ever since the present occupant had moved in. Illegally and rent free too.

'Of course, this is good Scotch beef, Hamish?'

'The best from Fife, Ed,' Hamish assured him. He poured

Ed a large whisky and himself another large one – he was already into his third, and the whisky was one product of Scotland that he did not muck about with. Why improve the best?

In fact, his beef had never seen Scotland, its provenance was obscure, except that it came from cows, or beef cattle that should have been slaughtered as a protection to the public against disease.

Hamish knew this, as did his buyer.

'Hamish, Hamish, my dear chap, that's far too much whisky. You'll have me drunk.'

Fancy that, Hamish thought, as if I didn't mean to. He took another nip himself. It was precious cold in here.

'Not a bad time to do business,' he said. 'The middle of the night is so quiet.' Not that it was ever truly quiet in the Second City. 'Got the van nicely parked, have you?'

'Just down the road and I can drive in, load up and be off.'

'Of course you can.' Hamish himself had suggested the right place to park and then ease into the warehouse and back out for a quick exit. The police were pretty decent round here near Drossers Market, he had good relations with at least three of them, but you had to go along with foibles like not putting yourself where you could be caught.

Darren patted his pocket. 'Let's get down to business. My bird expects me back. If I'm not back in two hours, ring the police.' He grinned, showing tobacco-stained teeth. 'Joke.'

It was not a joke, but his primitive security – I have someone who will tell the police if I don't make it back.

Lovely boy, thought Hamish, he hadn't done business with Darren before and they might never meet again, but for the moment they had bonded.

Beef and money did the bonding.

'You'll be back with Lorraine,' he said, smiling. 'Come and look at the goods . . .'

They went along the row of cabinets, all full of neatly jointed beef. It looked like beef anyway. Darren prodded the odd joint as they passed.

It looked all right to him, and he already had a buyer lined up.

'We'll have to load it ourselves but I have a mate coming in.'

The truth was that Hamish, to use his trade name which was not one his mother would have recognized, although he liked beef cooked, could not stand the sight of blood.

The business side was soon done, and the money handed over. A satisfactory sum. He felt inspired to do some more business with this nice chap.

'I've got some lamb just come in. Are you interested?'

Darren expressed keen interest, and patted his pocket again. 'Knew to come with some spare cash. Show me what's on offer.'

Hamish threw open a freezer full of legs of lamb. Darren bent over to examine what was there while Hamish moved on to the next cabinet.

Darren heard a strange noise from Hamish and then a crash. He looked round to see Hamish slumped on the floor. Then he took a look in the cabinet.

'My my,' and he took out his mobile.

DC Geoff Little and WDC Eleanor Brand were the first lucky arrivals after the squad car had radioed in to get to the Felix Freezers.

They knew at once what they had got there. 'This is too big for us,' said Eleanor, reaching for her mobile.

The news sped up the chain of command fast, and reached Coffin as he was drinking some coffee before having a shower. He had taken Gus for an early-morning walk and felt ready for action.

Perhaps he hadn't expected it quite so fast.

'We have the torso, sir.' Phoebe Astley tried not to sound triumphant. 'There's no doubt it's the right one, arms and legs gone, but the pathologist is on his way.'

'Who else have you told?'

'Chief Superintendent Young, sir, he's on his way too and I am just about to leave.'

'I'm coming.'

'Are you sure, sir?' She nearly said, There's no need, but prudence held her back.

'Tell me where.'

Back of Drossers Lane, just off Chopping Tree Lane, easy to find, the old warehouse with the word Felix Freezers painted on it. But she would send a car.

'We've had worries about the place and the Health and Food people passed on their suspicions. It was one of our men who phoned us. He was pretending to be a buyer . . . there's more, sir.'

'Tell me when I get there.'

He took Stella a cup of coffee, and put it on her bedside table. She opened her eyes. 'You're going out?'

'Yes, I know it's early.' He kissed her cheek. 'The body has been found . . . the torso, I mean.'

'And the head?'

'I don't know.' For the first time, he realized that Phoebe had not said whether the head was there with the body or not. 'No, I think it isn't.'

Stella sat up to drink her coffee. 'That's odd, isn't it?'

'Everything about this case' – if it was one case and not a trio of cases – 'is odd.'

Phoebe Astley, together with Archie Young, was waiting for him outside Felix Freezers.

The police surgeon had been and gone, certifying that the woman was dead, not a difficult diagnosis since she was frozen and headless.

'I'm glad,' said Coffin at once.

'Not all good news, no head, so identity is still tricky.' Archie Young was frowning. 'We've had our eye on Hamish Scott for some time, hence the fact we had our man in there . . . He was the one who telephoned in. Hamish fainted. I don't think he's our killer, seems as shocked as anyone.'

They were walking forward into the big room lined with freezers. Hamish was sitting on a chair, his face white. Darren was talking to a uniformed constable and laughing as he did so. Hamish looked at his betrayer morosely. 'Heartless git.'

'Something else you won't be pleased about, sir,' said Phoebe. 'We've had a quick look at some papers here and it looks as though some police names come into it.'

'How many?' said Coffin in a sharp voice.

'Three . . . Radley, Ron Ryman-Lawson and Grimm.' Phoebe was not pleased herself to issue that roll call. 'All from Cutts Street.'

Bloody Cutts Street, always a trouble, and one he thought had cleaned up. 'Right, well, lay into them hard. They are suspended from now.'

He could see Phoebe had more to say. 'It looks, sir, as if the man Dave who works for you is in with Scott too. We will have to get him in for questioning.'

'Oh God,' said Coffin, thinking of Stella. 'Let him do the dusting first.'

The body was still in the freezer, rigid, and discoloured. Blue and red blotches disfigured it here and there. There was no head. It was the body of a mature woman, heavy breasted and with well-rounded hips. In life, although not looking fat, she would not have seemed slender either. He tried to think of this as a body he might have fondled, kissed and entered, but there was nothing.

As Coffin looked down, trying to remember Anna, he admitted that you can remember a face but you cannot remember a body.

Or he could not.

He turned away. 'At least we will now know how she died.'

'Of course, we will have to wait for her to thaw out,' said the police surgeon.

Coarse brute, thought Coffin. He heard Phoebe draw her breath and respected her for it. 'She's not a leg of lamb, but a human being,' he told the doctor coldly. 'Get on with whatever has to be done, but leave her a bit of dignity, please.' The word please had the crack of a whip in it.

He turned away. 'What are you going to do about Hamish Scott and the rest?'

Chief Superintendent Young looked at Phoebe, who spoke for them both. 'Take them in and question them. Suspend Radley and Ryman-Lawson and the same for Grimm? He's on sick leave at the moment.'

Coffin looked bleak. 'You know what they said of the early

Bow Street Runners? Private speculators in crime. Things don't change.'

He was driven back to St Luke's where Stella had got up and was taking a shower, he could hear the rush of water.

He considered telling her about Dave, the house cleaner, and decided to leave it for the moment.

Gus met him at the foot of the stairs, looking up at him hopefully.

'Right,' he said to Gus. He needed time to think. 'Walkies, Gus.'

Gus never minded where he took his walk, every street corner was as interesting to him as the most beautiful wooded stretch of country. He was prepared to pace slowly beside his thoughtful master while Coffin tried to decide what to do.

He was pretty sure he knew who the killer of Etta was and the same person had also tried to kill Albie. He now agreed with Albie that he had been the prime target.

Oh yes, this killer wanted Albie out of the way, but that did not answer all the questions in his mind. It was the Chief Commander the killer wanted: to smear and bring into public contempt. Death for him might or might not come later.

He was hated.

There was the uncomfortable feeling that this pot of hate had been stewing on the heat for a long while, and had now boiled over.

He kicked a piece of paper on the pavement, it rose up and floated away, followed by Gus. The wind was getting stronger.

He and the dog walked on, Gus just alive and happy, Coffin deep in thought. Where did Anna come in all this? Or was it fantasy, just his imagination? It was a fine day, with blue skies but not warm. He walked faster.

Gus did not bother to keep up with him, he knew from long experience that Coffin would turn, see where he was, then wait for him. He strolled over to a lamppost that needed careful examination for what messages it carried of earlier passers-by. A dog had to know the neighbours. One smell suggested a complete incomer, and on an interesting diet too. He considered, no not something he would fancy on the whole.

Coffin marched on. Phoebe Astley had done well on this case. Kept her head when others had lost theirs.

Like the poor victim.

Without turning round, he yelled: 'Gus.' Then he walked on, confident Gus would catch up. By this time, he was near the tube station, and there was Mimsie Marker handing out the newspapers to her regulars, to read as they travelled to the City or the other way towards the estuary of the Thames.

Mimsie served a customer, sold him some cigarettes and told him that although it was against her own commercial interests, he should give up smoking.

Coffin strolled across. 'If he gives up cigs, you will only sell him some vastly expensive chocolates, I've never known you a loser. You're the richest woman in town. We all know that.'

Mimsie grinned. 'I wanted to work though, Mr Coffin, sir.'

'Don't overdo the humble peasant act, Mimsie. We come out of the same basket, remember . . . two old cockneys, hardly any one left but you and me.'

'It was about that poor young girl that was shot dead . . .'

'Go on.' He was alert now. 'Did you know her?'

'No, but I had seen her around. And when she was killed and the ambulance collected her, I happened to be there.'

I bet, thought Coffin. Just happened.

'And I saw her shoes, pretty little shoes, she had nice feet, I thought the shoes might be Italian, they're the best at the moment, aren't they? But there was a bit of a stain on one of them, as though something greasy had dropped on it. Pale shoes do mark so, don't they?'

Get on with it, Mimsie, he wanted to say, but was too wise to do so. Interrupt Mimsie telling a tale at your peril.

'Well, I remembered those shoes and remembered where I'd seen them, and when I heard that you were finding it difficult to pin down where the girl had been, I thought I ought to say: the Stormy Weather café.'

She produced the name triumphantly. 'And she was there with that police feller, I don't know his name.'

'Try, Mimsie.'

She gave him a sideways look. 'Death, would it be?'

Coffin nodded. 'Could be, could be. Thanks, Mimsie.'

'Think nothing of it.' Then she smiled. 'There's that dog of yours, back there, sitting under that tree. I reckon you'll have to go back and get him.'

'How is Alice?' he asked Mary Arden on the telephone. 'Robbie hasn't taken her to the country yet?'

'No, he wanted to, but the doctor at the hospital wanted a last check on Alice. I was glad to keep her here, she helps me and we all like her. I think she's happy doing something.'

'Is she fit enough to go for a walk?'

'Yes, I think so,' said Mary cautiously. 'If she wanted to.'

'Of course, it goes without saying. But it would help clear up her story. You can come if you like.'

'No,' said Mary. She hesitated. 'It wouldn't be easy for me to come. Nor Evelyn. I trust you.'

'Thank you.'

'But Alice must say.'

He turned back into the kitchen at St Luke's where Stella was drinking coffee. She shook her head. 'I hope you know what you're doing.'

Then Mary spoke: 'Alice says, Yes. Will you come to collect her? And will you bring the dog? I think she'd like it.'

Stella shrugged, but went to fasten the leash on Gus's collar. 'I want to be sure he comes back with you.'

Alice was waiting for him in the hall at the house in Barrow Street, she was wearing pale-blue jeans and a blue silk shirt. She was pale but quite astonishingly pretty.

Gus took to her at once, wagged his tail and prepared to lead the walk.

Alice smiled but said nothing. But the smile said: I want to come.

They set off, with Gus in front.

'This is good of you, Alice.'

Alice bent her head shyly.

'I think it might help me solve something that worries me. You too, perhaps.'

Alice gave him a blue stare, not unfriendly but sharper than he had expected.

'I think you truly want me to know where you were when your stepfather took you away and –'

Alice bent her head again.

'And hid you, Alice. But you won't tell me. He threatened you if you did talk, that's right, isn't it?'

They had got as far as the tube station and Mimsie Marker's stall which she had closed temporarily while she went for lunch. Papers were laid out and buyers trusted to put their money in a tin. Most did.

Coffin went on: 'Let your feet do the talking.'

He studied Alice's face, to his relief, she was laughing. She could see the joke. They've underestimated you, girl, he decided.

He led her through the back streets towards Drossers Lane where the market would be in full swing. After a point, when the noise of the market came their way, while not appearing to do so, he let her point the way. He held back, gently following her, trying to read her face. At the same time, she had her hand on his arm.

Hard to be sure who was pushing and who was pulling.

Pepys Street, Armour Road, Villiers Close . . . a modern in-filling, that one. The noise of the market getting louder all the time. Was someone shouting: prime legs of lamb at bargain prices? Buy now.

And go to prison later. But no, not prison, hospital possibly if you were unlucky. Very unlucky you might move further down the chain and die.

Samuel Street, another modern in-filling, and next to it Chopping Tree Lane.

No push, little pull, with Gus leading down Chopping Tree Lane.

If you looked down Chopping Tree Lane you could see just the facade of roof and walls that Alice had described as those she had seen from the room she had lived in. Been imprisoned in? Could you call it that?

Coffin thought he could do.

He looked at Alice's face, waiting. She turned to him and nodded.

'Let's go down Chopping Tree Lane, don't worry, just a few yards.'

Gus liked this path and was very willing to stop halfway down, investigating a most interesting smell on a side wall while Coffin looked up at the back of the houses and shops which fronted on Drossers Lane.

One set of windows seemed likely but there was no recognition on Alice's face; after all, she had been inside looking out, not outside looking in.

But she had something she wanted to say and she said it in that sweet, gentle voice that was so simple too: 'The woman there, she was kind to me.'

He patted her shoulder. 'Good girl, you've done well. I'm taking you back now.'

He found a cab just by the tube station (Mimsie was still absent, obviously enjoying a long lunch) and took Alice back to Barrow Street.

He was walking Gus back to St Luke's Tower when the mobile in his pocket rang.

'Hello,' said Phoebe, as he tried to get the phone in a good position to hear her. 'A bit of news . . . the pathologist's first quick look at the torso says she died a natural death . . . Heart.'

'Is that so?' said Coffin thoughtfully.

'Of course, there could always be a bullet in the head. Only we don't have that yet.'

'Any more good news?'

He heard the sigh. 'Yes, sir. As well as the meat business which was probably small beer, it seems as if drugs and porn come into the picture.'

He was quiet.

'Did you hear that, sir?'

'I heard. Listen: I am going to Drossers Market. Probably going to drop in at the Stormy Weather eating place.

Give me time to get there and order some food, then join me there.'

He pushed Gus through the door of his tower home with a pat and a word of praise. 'Good boy.'

After all, you couldn't take a dog on this particular errand.

15

Drossers Lane Market in mid-morning was full of its usual rumbustious life. Even the surface business on stalls and open shop fronts (the centuries had passed unnoticed in the market, Coffin felt) looked illicit so that you could only guess what went on inside and in the dark.

Coffin was known and a stillness and hush passed over the stalls as he walked on. He felt observed, watched but safe. Drossers Market was a danger area even for the police who went through in patrol cars or in pairs, but he doubted if he would be challenged.

He considered buying an ice-cream off the stall selling 'Frozen Whoppers' but walked on, although he liked ice-cream and had happy memories as an East End kid eating frozen water on a stick from an Italian who sold ice-cream from a barrow outside Greenwich Park. The bugs and antibodies thus created had seen him through many healthy years.

He looked at the Burger Stall – 'Hot Whoppers' – and wondered what relation it had to the beef stored in the FELIX FREEZERS outfit.

His feet halted outside Stormy Weather, whose windows were clouded with steam while from whose doors floated a smell of good coffee.

He walked in to see that the place was crowded, but there were a couple of places at the bar, and that Mimsie Marker had a table to herself in one corner. Of course, turn Mimsie away if you dare, she probably owned the ground freehold of where you were living.

He looked at the property holder and waved; he got a wave back.

'Wonder why I thought you'd be in?' Mimsie finished a mouthful of chips quickly to get the words out.

'And I wonder why I thought you would be in here?'

'Best place to eat. Good and cheap. Very cheap.'

'I suppose you call it subsidized food,' said Coffin, thinking of a possible connection with illicit beef and even more illicit drugs.

'You might be right,' observed Mimsie placidly. 'I'm the ground landlord and their lease is coming to an end. I like to check up.'

'You are right to watch your investment,' said Coffin. 'Several happenings have suggested it might be a good idea for me to look in.'

'At least one quite personal.' Mimsie had finished her chips.

He was taken aback. 'You keep your ear close to the ground.' Mimsie did not deny it; she had been around a long time and knew everything. People told her things. 'Thanks for the tip about the shoes. One of my reasons for coming now.'

'The food is good now they've got the new cook, Jo was standing in when the old one went off, but she wasn't that good.' She looked towards the bar. 'Don't see Jo, expect she's having a rest. A woman the size she is needs to get off her feet.'

'Thanks, Mimsie.' Coffin moved away to the bar. 'I'll get some coffee. I might come back.'

'Call me if you need me.'

He felt she meant the offer. He knew Mimsie, he knew it meant that she had thought things over and was taking a line. She was by no means always a supporter of the police, quite the reverse sometimes, although always personally friendly to Coffin.

By now she had heard, he was sure, from her own sources, that several police officers were under questioning, and she had made a deduction about the killing of Etta, the shooting of Albie (unpredictably, for such a lawless lady, a favourite with her) and the limbs in Barrow Street. It might even be that it was the killing of the cat that had tipped her over to one side: she was a notable animal lover. She was also believed to have a mink coat, if not two, hanging in her cupboard. But that was Mimsie: many-sided.

At the counter the new cook was making a sandwich for a stallholder to take away. He was issuing orders about what he wanted and what he did not want between the bread and butter: ham, a slice of cheddar, no mustard but sweet pickle, tomato optional.

When it was his turn, Coffin asked for coffee but no milk. The coffee came out of a big pot on the stove behind the counter but was none the worse for that.

A woman came out through the door in the wall. She was the fattest woman he had ever seen. Legs, arms, body, were gross. The face was imbedded in fat.

He looked at the face, and from the depths of the flesh, the eyes looked back.

He knew that face. 'Anna?' Not dead, not chopped up into bits. 'Anna, it's you.'

She came right up to him so that he could smell her.

'You've been here all the time?'

'Yes, just growing the flesh to hide in.'

He thought she had succeeded.

'You had no chance of recognizing the lovely, slim Anna, did you? Not just food, you know. I didn't eat my way to greatness . . . heart did it. Swelled my body like a steroid balloon. So I thought your heart could suffer a bit.'

Coffin was silent.

'You've had troubles, haven't you? Read it in the papers.'

'You could say that . . . I think you knew the girl Etta, Mimsie said she thought she had seen her here.'

Anna . . . Jo, was she now, looked across the room to where Mimsie Marker sat. 'She always knows everything.'

'And I think you had Alice staying here.'

Anna blinked. 'I can't have children, you know. Hormones all wrong. Yes, I took her in. Freedom dumped her here. I've known him a long while, he's been kind in his way. I owe him.' She hesitated. 'He knew I had a strong feeling for a baby. He could trust me.'

'Alice said you were kind to her.'

'Poor little beast. I'd have kept the baby if it had come to term ... popped out like a pea from a pod, it did. You ever seen a baby born like that? Don't bother, you wouldn't believe it.'

'And you buried it.'

'Said a prayer. If I'd told the father, that pig, or Dave, he'd have said, Just burn it.'

This is *Grand Guignol* all right, thought Coffin, as this washed over him. Soft talk but he could hear and Mimsie could watch. She could probably lip read.

'That was good,' he said simply, trying to get his bearings.

'No, I'm not good. You got it right when you turned me away. I wasn't good then, and I've got worse.' She put her head on one side. 'You don't believe me? Let me introduce you to Win, she used to cook for us.'

She led him round the back.

'She's here?' He looked around. 'Is she comfortable?'

Anna laughed. 'Suits her. She can't walk, you see?'

'Is she crippled?'

'Oh yes, she's crippled. Very crippled.'

He began to have a sense of the macabre dialogue in which he was taking part.

Anna threw open the freezer cabinet. Looking up at him, eyes closed, features blue and pinched, was a head.

'She dropped dead in my kitchen.'

Coffin said nothing, he had nothing to say.

'She donated her limbs to a good cause ... the good of getting at you and your lovely wife who was the love of your life. You shouldn't have said that.'

Dave appeared through the further door. He stood looking at Coffin, then he walked forward with a flourish: he was an actor and he was on stage, centre stage. He put his arm protectively around Anna.

'No, you shouldn't. Pushed her over the edge.'

Coffin shook his head. That was done by the tablets and the sniffing and the drinking. You don't get like that on cups of tea.

'She was young and you made her feel like dirt. She never got over that. I was just getting her right when you did it to her again.' He paused. 'So she sent you the messages.'

'And you did the rest? Why?'

Dave reared up like a hero from a Greek tragedy: he shouted, beginning low and rising to an ear-cracking bellow: 'She is my wife.'

'I don't believe it was all lover's passion. You had another interest at your killings.' Coffin was willing to take them both on. 'I want you to know that I saw early this morning when I was going through all the reports that I could see you were the one who had the chance to kill Etta . . . you picked up her message on the answerphone in the refuge and realized she was going to tell what she knew about you and Grimm and the others. There was a report of a white van near the car park where she was killed. Forensics will be checking that van. You aimed to kill Albie Touchey because he had been told you were in the drugs game and were willing to kill. Once again, you heard his recorded message. You knew he was on the way.'

In his mind, he had the picture of Dave, the actor, acting George Freedom and getting into the Gun Club. He looked at Anna and remembered what Stella had said about the large woman in the library who had jogged her arm so she dropped the books and forgot her handbag, which Anna must have picked up. Dave got the keys copied and took the bag back.

He hadn't needed to break into the St Luke's Tower. He had the keys and he had a gun. Or had had the gun. The police had it now.

In spite of himself and his confidence in his power to look after himself, he felt a shiver run through him.

'I wanted you,' said Dave, as if he read Coffin's mind.

'I was certainly to be a victim but you wanted to bring me down first. But the cat . . . why the cat? That was you, I saw that once I read all the reports. You had the cat's head hidden in your cleaner's bag and you broke the window – outwards . . . A real act, just as you acted George Freedom in the Gun Club . . . tall and thin, that was you. You're not a bad actor.'

'A bloody good actor when I get the parts.'

Anna said: 'I did the cat. I did all the choppings. I with my little axe. I knew it would make you sick.' Anna went on: 'Most of all I wanted you sick and hating yourself. To know that feeling and know that I had given it to you and the love of your life. How is she, the loved Stella?'

I can't accept the blame for all of it, Coffin thought, but might have to take some. It will all depend on what Stella says.

Then he thought: Damn it, I'm getting as mad as they are.

I am not guilty.

He was relieved when that figure of sanity, Phoebe Astley, walked in with Mimsie behind her.

'I knew how it would be,' Mimsie was saying in a loud voice. 'Nasty, I could just smell nastiness. Not just mad: evil.' And fixing Coffin with her strongest glare and giving him an extra blast of sound: 'And don't believe all that man there says. It's money with him all the time. Whatever he's done there be money for him somewhere.'

Coffin was late home that night, there was so much to tidy up, interviews to be given for television, the radio, and the newspapers. No hope of keeping things quiet with Mimsie on the spot.

He had also had to talk to the men and women in the incident room to congratulate them on the result, and thank them for their hard work.

He had taken the precaution of telephoning Stella at the theatre and telling her everything. Or almost everything. He kept quiet about the sickening fear that Anna and Dave had created in him, as if they would chop him up and eat him if they could.

Stella, when he got home, was at her best, loving and gentle and quiet. If it was a performance, at least it was tailored to her audience.

He came in, sank down on the sofa, let Gus massage his feet and Stella his ego. She let him talk, repeating himself a bit, and then came in with a tray of hot food and cold wine. This time she had done the cooking herself, a baked salmon with a lemon sauce, one of the dishes she was good at. There was hot crisp bread with it too.

'Not the time to have a cold meal, you need the warmth.'

He tried to say something, to complete his confession, but she held up her hand:

'Sometimes I feel much more worldly than you, my love. The way to deal with this is to treat it like a play. Some good parts, some a shambles . . . you know what the shambles are?' He nodded silently. 'The killing ground, where the animals are slaughtered. We've had that, the show is over.

'Draw the curtain down.'

Sergeant Grimm arrived late that night at Waterloo Station from the shuttle. He crossed the platform to catch the tube out to the Second City.

Lucky fella, I am, he told himself as he waited for the train. Money in that lovely bank in Geneva, and that bloody Etta off my back. It was money well spent getting her dealt with. The train was arriving. Wonder if he had any luck with Albie? Good to have him out of the way too. It had been part of the contract.